NIGHT EYES

Claire Stibbe

United States of America

NIGHT EYES

Acknowledgements

My thanks to New Mexico for providing the inspiration for the Detective Temeke series. To my mother for giving me a safe and loving home, and to my father who gave me his love of language and books.

Special thanks to all the police officers and detectives I have worked with, especially for their dedication and sacrifice, and for the Albuquerque Citizen Police Academy. For the invaluable services of Twisted Ink Publishing, The 13th Sign and An Tig Beag Press. A huge thank you to Kingdom Writing Solutions and editor Jeff Gardiner for molding the clay into something worth reading.

As always, I owe the greatest thanks possible to my husband, Jeff, for his love and support and to my son, Jamie, for his encouragement and humor.

Claire Stibbe
Albuquerque, New Mexico
March 2016

Other Books by Claire Stibbe

The Detective Temeke Series
The 9th Hour
Past Rites

Historical Fiction
Chasing Pharaohs
The Fowler's Snare

ONE

He struggled alone in that deep, dark place, head tilted back as far as it would go. Water plugged his ears and the sharp pain between his ribs reminded him to take small breaths to preserve what little oxygen he had left.

It was some kind of urban runoff—a sewer that had become filled with sea water from one of the worst storms he had ever seen.

All because he'd kissed the girl.

He drew a bite of oxygen into his lungs and sunk slowly to the bottom. He tried to see something in those murky waters, pushed off again, broke through the surface and gasped for air. No way out. Not that he could see.

During Basic Underwater Demolition Training, the instructors wouldn't allow a twenty-one-year-old SEAL to die in a watery grave, not with their shark eyes. The next phase was drown-proofing, and that meant bobbing and swimming and somersaults, hands tied behind your back. Lucky his hands weren't tied, nor were his feet.

Where am I?

They had been on the beach that morning, shivering in the darkness and covered in mud. Surf torture. He couldn't see the ocean behind him, but he could hear the waves. It took hundreds of push-ups to get warm, body sagging in the front leaning rest, waiting for permission to recover.

He remembered the instructor; a cold hulk of a man who did the PT with them, voice piercing through the early dawn. "Run with your thighs. Keep your arms loose. And breathe!" If they looked sleepy, they did it all over again.

He kept up with the pack, never looked back, didn't even blink when one of his team 'rang the bell'. He wouldn't quit. He'd never see her again if he did.

And here he was in a storm drain, a torrent of sea water gushing in through a cement pipe and large enough to stand in. Screaming to get out, screaming to be free and every part of him craved air. *Where were the rest of his class*?

They were gone, that's what. Him against the instructor. Him against that terrible accusation. He hated everything. Everyone. It started when he saw the girl, frail like a little brown bird. He knew she wanted him, eyes following his every move. If felt good. It felt wrong. And he had fought it with every muscle in his head.

Now that same head felt tender on the left side and he thought he could smell blood; thought he could hear shouting. Another test perhaps, where the instructors watched from an observation chamber? Goosebumps pricked his flesh and his mind began to focus on his heart rate and the sudden peace he felt.

Be calm. Block the negative. Slow each breath, control the rhythm.

He had done more push-ups than he could count, as well as sit-ups, chin-ups and runs. Tried to get into shape, tried to be like the best of them. A friend persuaded him to take the PST, pushed him to swim five hundred yards in eight-and-a-half minutes. Called him Dingo. Because he could run.

It seemed so long ago when he swam in that wide ocean, waves breaking about his face and blurring his vision. A large bird flew overhead, a winged shadow in a dark sky. It blocked out the sun for a time; a climbing speck breasting the morning wind.

He had a fast crawl stroke, faster than the rest of them until he felt the vicious stab of cramp in his right calf. Kick-and-breathe… kick-and-breathe. He switched to sidestroke, but had no technique whatsoever, except the will to finish as fast as he could. And he did finish. Eight minutes and twenty-seven seconds with three seconds to spare.

He barely remembered six pull-ups from a dead hang. He did eleven. Some did twelve. Trained to ensure that all muscles had adequate strength, a split body routine, no muscle left out. He should have been proud of himself.

His inner voice told him to give up and to look forward to a steaming cup of coffee. What it didn't tell him was that he would drink it in front of his teammates, watch them persevere, watch them become heroes. If he didn't survive the trials to go on to BUD/S, he would never become a SEAL; an unstoppable force, an elite group that the United States of America sends to do the impossible during times of war.

He gripped even harder then, got past the chaffing of sand on raw skin, the burning of salt water, the lack of sleep. He always looked past the fierce blue eyes of his instructor, through them, around them, anywhere but straight at them.

If only he hadn't seen the girl in the surf that Friday night all alone, cheeks spattered with tears. Looked like she'd been slapped around a bit. Looked like she wanted some comfort. He did a lot more than comfort her. Rolled in the sand for a while, held her close, and loved her until the morning.

June… the year 2000, he thought. Blood poured down his face and the slit above his eye yawned wider than a crater. He'd need stitches when he got out. If he got out.

Something different. His feet touched bottom and he felt the final catch in his breath.

Hell Week. That was the last thing he remembered.

TWO

Adam peered through the windshield of his scoutmaster's car as they approached the house. A bitter January wind butted the trees and snaked in through a slit in his window. Street lamps stood like sentries and staggered every fifty feet. He knew it was fifty. His dad had told him a hundred times.

He noticed the truck parked about twenty yards from the front gate. Every twelve-year-old's dream and black if he could bet on it. It wasn't a security car. Looked more like a Silverado with a bull bar on the front fender.

He pulled a Bible tract and a pen out of his pocket. His dad told him to write down license plates, especially if there were any unfamiliar cars in the neighborhood.

"See that truck," Adam said, craning his neck around as they passed it. "Z71, black rims, even got blacked out bowties."

"God only knows how you see all that stuff," Wendover said, leaning out to dial the access code of the front gate. "You could be a ferret."

"Dad says I could be a pilot."

They swept into a circular driveway covered in a light coating of snow and floodlit by solar lights. A single lantern, which hung over wrought iron front doors, squeaked in the wind and the constant rumble of cars could be heard from Coors Boulevard.

"OK Adam?" Wendover said as the car grunted to a

halt.

"Yes, sir. What time is it?"

"Ten thirty."

Half an hour late, Adam thought. His dad would be mad. Probably make him rake leaves tomorrow and time him with a stopwatch.

"Thanks for the ride." Adam hauled his backpack from the rear seat and stepped out into the cool night air.

Goosebumps sprang along his arms and spine, and he felt jumpy. Dropping his pack by the front door, he blew warm air on his hands and watched Wendover pull away. The back tires sprayed up a jet of water from a nearby puddle, brake lights blinking until they were gone altogether. Squinting through a cloud of exhaust, he walked down the driveway to the front gate, listening to the rhythmic hum as it closed.

One last look.

The truck was still there, parked beneath a sycamore. It had a nice lift on it, made it look bigger than it was, and there were a few scrapes along the front right fender. Must have belonged to one of the staff.

He jogged back to the house, unlocked the door and dropped the backpack between a chair and a mahogany chest. The hallway was lit by a single beam escaping through the half-open living room door; the only light on downstairs. Flames crackled and popped in the fireplace and he could smell the fresh scent of cedar.

A swishing sound made him pause, which stopped him from closing the front door. It had to be the sliding patio doors at the back of the house; might have been dad letting the dog in. And then he heard a voice in the living room, accusing and loud.

"Remember me?"

"How did you get in?" His father's voice sounded tense and something told Adam to be quiet, something he couldn't define.

He could hear leaves skittering on the driveway behind him. Ahead, came a sliding sound and then a click. His feet whispered across the hardwood floor until he reached the table in the center of the hallway. He slipped under it, crouching behind the pedestal. Looking at a slit of living room beyond the partially open doors, he could see his dad sitting on the couch, eyes peering over the rim of a newspaper at someone Adam couldn't see.

He had been handsome once, or so Adam's mother said, and now the signs of old age showed on those graying temples. His eyes seemed to narrow at something on the far side of the room and then they widened. He nodded, folded that newspaper and set it on the cushion beside him.

"Bet you thought you'd never see me again," the voice persisted. "Bet you *hoped* you'd never see me again."

His father made an attempt at the man's name, finger pointing limply in the air.

"Surely, you haven't forgotten. Look at you. Mayor of Albuquerque. Done well for yourself."

"Why don't you sit down."

"That wouldn't be smart." The man moved forward, just enough so Adam could see him. Hair tied up in a man-bun, jaw tight and hard, and a gun in his hand. "You remember how it was?"

His father's forehead was locked in a frown and one finger ran along the edge of his chin.

"We can talk about it if you like."

"It's too late for that." The man wore a leather holster wrapped around one thigh and his jeans were faded and ripped. "Didn't even answer my letters."

"I never got your letters."

"No. Of course you didn't. But you know don't you? You've always known."

"Known what?"

"What's mine's mine. And I can prove it. There's not a hair on a man's head that doesn't tell a story." The man placed a document on the coffee table, fingers swiveling it towards the Mayor. "Sign it. Then we'll have all the proof we need."

Adam recoiled and took a lungful of breath. Those same hands were covered in black leather gloves, like the gloves a robber would wear. Every instinct told him to stay still, to shrink into the shadows like a rat. If he was smart, he could crawl backwards into the kitchen and call the police.

Don't make him mad, Dad. Don't make him mad.

A cold draft distracted him. He glanced back through the open front door, at the dark driveway beyond and the open gate. A thick flurry of snow settled on the ground with a whispered hush and he could see the trees; some hidden behind the deepening shift of darkness and some rustling in an occasional breeze. He could run for it.

Murphy began to growl, low at first and then he must have opened his mouth because it was always louder when he opened his mouth. He had probably been lying on a brown beanie bag under the kitchen counter, only now his claws clacked across the tile floor before bursting into the living room, snarling all the way. Like the household cavalry charging to a Labrador's bark.

The man turned towards the sound, eyebrows arched, gun leveled, and he staggered backwards as the dog barreled into his thigh. Two shots echoed around the room and the sound of shattering glass. The old dog, faster than a torpedo, made a wide loop, shot back through the hallway and out through the front door.

Adam began to pant, heartbeat thrashing in his ears. He closed his eyes then, snapping them open at the sound of a moan. His father lay on the floor, cheek pressed against the carpet. Pale eyes flickered for a moment, grazing along the floor before fixing themselves on the hall table. He was mouthing something, lips curling over bloody teeth, barely a whimper over the snapping flames in the grate.

The man steadied his gun, cleared the slide and thumbed the safety. He snatched two tie wraps from his pocket and tied the Mayor's hands behind his back. All the while he muttered and cursed, stooped to pick up two shell casings that had bounced across the carpet, one under the table, the other as far as the grate. He rammed them in his jeans pocket, grabbed the document and threw it in the fire.

Adam felt the blood drain from his face. He struggled to breathe, to move, to do anything. All he could do was back away on all fours until he cleared the kitchen door. Easing the cell phone out of his pocket, he tapped 911.

The hallway was visible through the gap in the frame and he could see the curled arm of the banister until the lights went out.

"Police," he whispered into the mouthpiece. "There's a man… in my house… with a gun."

The beam of a flashlight made him hit the END button. It came from the living room sweeping from side to side and curling towards the back of the hallway. The air around him became suddenly heavy and he was conscious of the quiver of a full bladder.

Someone must have gone for help. Someone must have seen or heard something, surely?

There were no sirens coming along the back lanes and no dogs barking. Not even Murphy, an ex-military working dog, a combat-tracker. Adam felt abandoned, cheated. The dog should never have left him.

A hand snatched his phone and covered his mouth, nearly taking his breath away. He kicked and wriggled as hard as he could, but his mouth was covered in duct tape. He was lifted off the ground and forced towards the front door. Outside he could feel the air moving, then felt the pressure in his lungs. His feet never hit the ground, carried over the snowy driveway towards the front gate. Then he remembered something his father once said. *If you have to leave home without telling anyone, if you're taken by force, leave evidence.*

The scout troop was a church troop and his pockets were often filled with Bible tracts. Tonight he only had a few. Probably ten scruffy pieces of paper, last he looked. His hands weren't bound so he slipped two fingers into his pocket, scrunched one into a ball, and watched it flutter away on a puff of wind. He had no idea what it said. No idea if the police would ever find it.

What if the man saw it? Adam didn't want the barrel of a gun pressed against his head and filthy words spitting in his face. He didn't want his hands tied either.

On towards the wall to a place where a hole gaped between the hedge and the gate post. He hadn't noticed it before. Twigs snapped and then a ripping sound as he was wrenched through.

The truck smelled of new leather; the driver's window open a crack, let in a cold draft of air. The man pushed him over into the passenger seat from the driver's side and locked the doors.

"Stay down!" he shouted, snapping on the seat belt.

There was something in his voice that sounded pained, like he'd sat on something sharp. Then he slammed the car door and ripped off the duct tape. Adam yelped. It hurt like hell.

The truck lurched down the road, engine rumbling and growling onto Riverfront Drive. In those few precious moments while his pulse throbbed and blood streamed through each limb, he remembered writing down the truck's license plate on the back of a piece of paper. Only like an idiot, he'd left it in Wendover's car. His mom would be home soon. She would know what to do.

He could see car lights on Coors through a thick veil of snow, see someone getting out of a car at the gas station. So close, but too far away to hear him. They were almost at the intersection before the man slammed on the brake. "Ho-lee crap!"

He let out a string of cuss words, something about a cyclist and a barking dog, and then he picked up speed after that.

Adam still felt the prickle of fear as he slumped in that seat, felt his throat go dry. "My dad… is he dead?"

The man lit a cigarette, took a deep breath and let out a jet of smoke. His head seemed to rock from side to side and he was grinning like a clown at the fair.

THREE

At the end of her shift, Detective Malin Santiago changed into jogging clothes and ran two blocks along the street to a leafy track behind Corrales Cafe. She was thirty-five but with a youthful glow attributed to Hispanic roots, she could easily pass for twenty-five.

As she ran through the parking lot, through seams of amber light cast by the restaurant windows, all she could hear was the steady crunch of her running shoes on snow.

Eleven-thirty on a Sunday night and a thin mist meandered listlessly between the trees, three strands of it like thick-bellied serpents floating on air and close enough to touch.

She thought about the Ringmaster, a name the press had given to the killer of eleven young boys missing since 2001. Boys ranging from six years old to thirteen, all snatched from a skateboarding ramp where teenagers gathered after school to blow off steam. It was thought the killer had lured them into his car with a promise of a ride home and a bottle of alcohol.

They were found tied to trees and arranged in a circle two hundred miles away in Gila National Forest. The bodies bore evidence of high levels of drugs and alcohol in the blood system, rendering them insensate before being killed.

The trail had gone cold after 2011. A dead end. No

evidence. Nada.

Then a phone call came in a week ago, a deep voice that sounded genuine. "There's a boy," it said, "or what's left of him… tied to a tree… must have been there for years."

They found Evan Trader, the last victim in a circle of trees, wrists and ankles bound. Dr. Vasillion had reported extensive blunt force trauma to the head and death by asphyxiation, probably within five to six hours of the kidnap. Twelve years old. Missing for two years. They cut him away from a pale-coated aspen still pink with dried blood. Just like the trees she saw now. It made her sick if she thought about it, played tricks on her mind as if she could see it happening in real time.

She could hear the rhythm of each breath and the distant sound of friendly chatter from the street. After twenty minutes the track became a concrete roadway, winding behind a strip mall into a parking lot.

She stopped to catch her breath, looking up at steely clouds in a dark sky.

The snow came down hard now and she could hear cars racing through slush. There were two servers sitting at a table in the café kicking back at the end of their shift. She could see them through the window, kissing, laughing, touching.

It had been three long months since she last saw Sergeant Hollister in New Jersey, the one man she could really call a boyfriend. Three long weeks since she saw him on Heartfree.com, the only dating website worth joining. He invited her to chat, reminded her of the good times, even said he'd keep in touch.

She hadn't dared talk to him again, not after making such a fool of herself. Begging was a fool's game. You never tell someone you love them online. Never… never… never. And the same fool couldn't wait another three long weeks for a reply.

She'd sent a photo this time. A selfie leaning against a tree, hair mussed by the wind and eyes staring off into the distance. An Hispanic model with perfect skin and a few touchups here and there. If he asked, she would tell him it had been taken by Detective Temeke down by the Bosque five weeks ago. Let Hollister figure out why they had been there in the first place.

What's the point?

Hollister made himself available with a bunch of other single men desperately seeking who knows who. There was no avatar. He was too smart for that. And she wondered if he would ever reply.

She glanced at her watch, aware of her wheezing breaths and the sound of a throbbing heartbeat.

There was a scuffling sound a few yards to her left. Something ran along the top of the wall behind the houses. Instinct told her to look back along that track, through a milky haze where a shape darted into the shadows and out of sight.

She was too close to the road to be gripped in some paralytic terror only to find a coyote, the most skillful of impostors, prowling among the trees. She stood there on the sidewalk wondering why the creature was comfortable in such a populated part of town. It must have been attracted to all the rotting food in the dumpsters.

A silver-yellow moon illuminated the way back to her apartment and the rich scent of cedar wafted towards her in the windless air. She bolted through the parking lot and across the road to Calle Cuervo, spine sheathed in a film of sweat.

She took the steps to her second floor apartment, two at a time, and unlocked the front door with one flick of her key. Not much of a run, but at least her heart was pumping now.

Breathless, she stared at the laptop on the kitchen

table and grazed the mouse with her middle finger. Typing in her username and password, she saw a single message in her inbox.

Wingman: Love the photo.

Wait... that was it? She felt the slow, steady thud of her heart, felt her fingers tapping the keys.

Malin: Good to talk to you.

She waited for a moment, heard the clock ticking on the mantelshelf and the loud breath of the heater. The screen glared back at her for nearly a minute. Three dots and a bubble. He was typing.

Wingman: I've been waiting for you.

Malin blew out a loud sigh and sat back in her chair. She wanted to know what he'd been doing. Instead, she typed just three words. Where are you?

Wingman: I could be outside your front door.

Malin listened to the leaves outside as they skittered down the stairwell and the high-pitched moan of the wind. He wasn't the dark shape behind the café. She'd be in his arms in a heartbeat if he was, asking him if he missed her, wanted her. Did he?

Malin: Do you miss me?

She winced after she pressed SEND. A fool never learns. A fool knows if a man doesn't call, doesn't send flowers, doesn't say those three glorious words, it's because he doesn't want to.

She stared at that screen, thoughts fading in and out, knowing the excitement they once had was all but gone. He made her wait. Always made her wait. Three minutes this time as she made a cup of tea and sat in front of the computer mashing that bag with a teaspoon until it was a heap of leaves and soggy paper. The cloud popped up again and the same little dots flickered back and forth.

Wingman: Know what I think? You shouldn't have said goodbye.

So that was it. He didn't like the night they'd spent

together, the night where she slept in his bed without taking off her clothes. He hadn't exactly been the model of good manners, picking at her bra with his fingernails, grunting like a pig in a pen. It scared her, that's what. Malin bashed out a message and hit ENTER.

Malin: You're full of it.

He wasted no time, the dots virtually vibrated now.

Wingman: That's my Malin. That's my girl. Plenty more bullets in your chamber. So… been jogging?

She was about to type something when he beat her to it.

Wingman: Lost any weight?

Malin scratched her chin. There wasn't a squelch of fat around her stomach and thighs. All hard and mainly muscle. Fifteen pounds. I look like Barbie.

Wingman: You'll always be my Barbie.

All of a sudden she wished she hadn't said *Barbie*. There were loads of bottle-blondes in the Camden pubs all looking for good night out, all happy to give themselves away without a wedding. ADA Valerie Weeks for one, or the twenty-two year old from the liquor store on Madison Street.

Malin wrote: Thought you didn't like blondes. He didn't like assistant district attorneys either. More blinking dots.

Wingman: A guy can change his mind can't he? Now, now. No need to be jealous.

She gulped in air, as if she had been winded in the stomach. He was playing her and if she wasn't careful she would plummet down a mine shaft and never get out.

Malin: Who said anything about being jealous? Two minutes passed this time, not that she was counting. Are you still there?

Wingman: I'm always here.

Part of her wanted to ask him if he thought of her during his downtime. She stared at that screen, took a sip of tea and peeled a stray leaf from her lip. Why talk to a man who had broken her heart, dumped her and run off with a blonde.

Wingman: Any good cases?

Unreal. All he wanted to do was talk about work. She wanted to tell him to mind his own business, but settled on: Same old.

Wingman: If you need any help just let me know. I'm always here.

So you've already said, she whispered between gritted teeth. The conversation was going nowhere. Feel like using the phone?

Wingman: Better this way. More private.

She imagined a blonde in his apartment fumbling with the zipper on a tight blue dress, felt the familiar prickle of jealousy and began to chew herself out.

Malin: We could text?

Wingman: So many questions. So little time.

She wanted to tell him to stop messing about, to be serious. Instead she settled on: Why can't we talk on the phone?

Wingman: It's too late for that.

Too late for what? Three little dots blinked, only this time Wingman faded to a blur and signed off. Not even a goodbye. Probably still mad, that's what. Mad that she had once been an escort on a well-known website in her younger years to pay off a student loan; mad she wasn't cheap and slutty like he'd hoped.

She knew a thing or two about computers, knew her way around the chat rooms, the dating sites. So what was he doing on there anyway? Surveillance? All that talking on the computer made her body feel cold.

The phone rattled on the table beside her and scooted to the floor. She stared at it for a moment and decided to let it go to voicemail. Five seconds later, it rang again. She had an uneasy, nagging feeling and this time she picked it up.

"Might want to get down here, Marl," Detective Temeke said. "Twelve-year-old boy's gone missing and his dad's taken a bullet. The Mayor's residence. Big yellow house on Riverfront Drive. Can't bloody miss it."

FOUR

Detective Temeke wiped a hand over his bald head and took a deep breath. He checked his watch against the mantel clock. Eleven thirty-six. He took one last look around the Mayor's living room, smelling the tart scent of cedar in the hearth and imagining flames leaping up a long throated chimney. There was only a faint glow in the ashes now.

Deep-buttoned couches smelled of expensive leather and there was a hint of furniture polish in the air. White shelves lined with books, dark gray walls, hardwood floors, Persian carpets you could sink your toes in. The room was large enough to hangar a Zeppelin.

A shattered window revealed a small hole in the mid right-hand section and the outside security cameras had been covered in duct tape; while blinded by the look of it. A thorough job, not an inside job if his gut was working right.

He had worked for long enough in criminal investigations to realize several things. First, there was never a *usual* suspect, and second, keep working your witnesses. Mayor Bill Oliver was a private man who preferred to spend his evenings alone in his study. And tonight was no exception. There were no witnesses.

Instead, Temeke stared at a recent picture on the grand piano: Oliver's son, green eyes under a fringe of artfully messed hair, sallow skin and a cheeky face.

Twelve years old, about five feet tall, and he had hung up on the police less than an hour ago.

Temeke stood at the edge of the room and nodded at a field investigator by the piano. "Hand me that photo, will you?"

He also requested a picture of Adam's mother. He would need both where he was going.

"No forced entry," the field investigator confirmed. "Except a length of rope over the back wall. Looks like he came in through the back door."

"Why do you say *he*? Could have been *her*, could have been *them*."

"Only one set of footprints in the driveway, another set in the rose bed, sir. Lug design, probably a hunting boot. Size eleven, same size as mine. Found a few threads near the gate post where someone had hacked a hole in the hedge. Pale fibers, lining of a ski jacket possibly. We didn't find anything else so we figured he was alone."

Tall, thought Temeke, glancing at the field investigator. He was at least six feet. "Where's this rose bed then?"

"Near the patio doors. And watch your feet. It's all taped off over there."

Temeke followed the line of the patio door to the couch with his eyes. It was possible the intruder had been watching the Mayor for some time before he made contact with him.

A female investigator wearing gloves and booties knelt over a blood stain on the carpet, following a spatter of blood from the couch to the base of the coffee table with a latex covered finger. Blonde curls spilled out of a badly tied bun and the cloying perfume she wore made his eyes burn. Pauline Bailey had been out on a date.

"Anything unusual," he said, taking care to stay in the doorway and noticing a younger woman with her.

"See these blood smears?" she said. "Some are arced across the carpet when the Mayor slid forward. He was shot at close range." She seemed to watch his gaze as they veered towards her companion. "That's Lily. She's interning with us for six weeks."

Temeke nodded at the redhead, thin as a stick and strangely beautiful. She gave him a brief smile.

"Where are the staff offices?"

"On the south side. Through the kitchen."

"Thanks, Pauline," he said.

Temeke saw her eyes flick towards Captain Fowler as he swaggered in through the front door. If style could blow in off the streets, this was it. An edgy buzz-cut and a square jaw, and narrow brown eyes that squinted even in the dark.

Pauline's cheeks were flushed right down to the open buttons on that tight white blouse. Temeke suddenly remembered the pressing reason why Fowler needed to make good, needed to claw his way back into Hackett's good books. A new promotion – Watch Commander – one step below Hackett if he played his cards right. Only, he'd missed some crucial evidence on the last case because his attention had been sabotaged by a tight white blouse.

"According to the Press Secretary, Adam was due home at ten o'clock," Fowler said. "His scoutmaster said it was about ten thirty when they got back. Since he made the call to the police around ten forty-five, we assume he was snatched soon after he arrived."

Temeke knew it was an exclusive neighborhood, houses sitting on four acre lots, personalized gate posts and miniature fir trees winking with seasonal lights. He wondered what the neighbors saw. "Anyone see anything?"

"The nearest neighbor was walking his dog. Claimed he saw a truck streaking up the road going faster than the speed limit. So he wondered what all the commotion was about. Didn't get a license number. Too dark. A Mr. Sandoval… *Eli* Sandoval. Been fishing with the Mayor a few times."

"Who found the Mayor?"

"His wife. She got back from work just before eleven. Found him lying on the floor, wrists tied behind his back. Had a deflective wound to his right hand and another above his right ear. Knocked him unconscious. She also said the front door was open and the dog had run off."

"I know how he feels. Where is Madam Mayor?"

"At the hospital with her husband when I saw her. Told me to call her Raine." Fowler said, spelling it out.

How Fowler had the knack of putting women at ease, squirming headlong into first name terms, Temeke would never know. "Are we tapping cell phones, landlines?" he said, pointing at two phones on a desk in the corner.

Fowler let out an enormous sigh. "Obviously."

"When she called 911, which phone did she use?"

"The landline."

"Anyone instructed her on how to talk to the kidnappers?" He saw Fowler nod. "Lucky our man was a lousy shot."

"We can't assume he was a lousy shot."

"Suicide attempt was it?" Temeke jutted his chin at the shattered window, finger prodding the air. "Bleeding impossible to shoot yourself unconscious and then tie yourself up. Anything taken?"

"She said nothing was taken." Fowler's eyes were suddenly locked down Pauline's blouse, an irresistible target. "All yours."

"Before you bugger off home, can you tell me if you found any shell casings?"

"Nothing."

"Something must have gone through that window. Probably the same thing that hit the Mayor."

Fowler rolled his eyes and raked a hand through his hair. He turned his head to a clinking sound from the officers in the kitchen. "Keep the noise down in there!" He turned back to Temeke. "I radioed Santiago. Told her to drive over to see Adam's scoutmaster before she got here. She called back, said the kid saw a black Z71 he hadn't seen before. Took down the registration and wrote it on the back of a Bible tract. Lucky the kid left it in Wendover's car. Oh, and we found truck marks down the street, heavy load tire."

"Who's it registered to?"

"A Mr. Silus Marner of 2331 Lantern Yard."

"I think you'll find there's no such address," Temeke muttered. "Silas Marner is a weaver and a miser. In a book that is." He noted Fowler's cheeks getting redder by the minute. "Judging by the mess in this room the Mayor and our Mr. Marner must have had a barney."

"A what?" Fowler said, turning an ear as if he hadn't heard properly.

"An argument." Temeke knew the boys still got a kick out of his English accent. They also got a kick out of his Ethiopian heritage, skin darker than a cinder path.

"Where's Adam's room?"

"Upstairs. Third on the left."

Temeke took a deep breath and glanced at an investigator peering into an open laptop. "What's he doing?"

"Looking through the Mayor's calendar. Three staff members are on vacation and five left the house on Saturday night somewhere between five and six o'clock. Protocol demands no staff members are allowed back on the property after then. Sunday's a family day. Only today they had a birthday party for the Press Secretary."

"How many staff were on duty?"

"The cook, the gardener and the Press Secretary," Fowler said, counting them off on his fingers. "And get this. The gardener was shooting up in the shed."

"Maybe he's a diabetic."

Fowler seemed to be preoccupied with the glitter of his cuff links in the light. "We found a few needles in that garden shed and there were more in the outside trash. It's a freaking dope house."

"Nice place." Temeke noted the open stonework on the pillars and the vaulted ceilings. There was a pile of transparent evidence bags on a card table, neatly staggered and labeled. He noticed a charred sheet of paper in one pack with the words *...mitted* and beneath it *....itioner* typed at the bottom right-hand edge. They had been snatched from the fire too late to make any sense of it. "So this is how the toffs live."

"Built in 2000. Just over twelve years old."

"Adam an only child?"

"Yep."

Temeke felt a lump in his throat. He'd never had children, couldn't begin to fathom the grief of losing an only child to a kidnapper.

"Kid's been in scouts for two years, has good eyesight. Apparently, he can pick out a hair on a dinner plate in the dark."

Temeke grinned. "It would be useful if it was true. What's he like?"

"His mom said he's smart. Good grades. Lives and breathes the Anasazi. Has a picture of a chief on his wall. Tarahuma?"

Temeke shook his head. Never heard of him. But he knew about the Anasazi, prehistoric Native Americans who once lived in northwestern New Mexico. "Anything else?"

"Likes to memorize Bible study verse."

"Religious then?"

"It's scouts isn't it?"

"Happy? Popular at school?"

"Very."

Temeke came to the point. "This is a tight little neighborhood. Someone else must have seen that truck."

"Man on a bike coming out of the Chevron gas station nearly got run over by a truck. He wasn't able to identify the make, but he thought it was black. Said the driver headed south along Coors with a large dog in hot pursuit."

"Any identifying features?"

"Labrador, I think."

"Not the bloody dog. The man!" Temeke resisted the urge to sigh. "You say they were headed north?"

"As far as we know. APB issued at eleven forty."

"Pity it wasn't sooner. But with you leading, kid's bound to show up in an hour or two."

Temeke walked out into the hall and noticed a library opposite, kitchen directly behind. He started up the sweeping staircase and when he reached the top all he could think of was time. The sooner they found Adam the greater chance there was of finding him alive.

Adam's bedroom faced south, two windows dressed with blue and white curtains and a life-size airplane propeller propped in one corner. Dark wood furniture; blue quilt decorated with spitfires; chest of drawers full of the usual things a young boy wore. A watercolor painted by a local artist hung above the bed; a man dressed in rabbit fur and feathers, carrying a spear. He had root-like tendrils emanating from his feet and a stylized eagle in the background.

A display shelf ran above two windows just below the crown molding, wide enough to hold model airplanes – spitfires mostly and a German Fokker. A desk stood in the corner where there had once been a computer, already taken as evidence.

As Temeke headed back downstairs, he saw a backpack on the floor by a chair. Unzipping the upper compartment, he found two bright orange scout shirts neatly rolled to the size of a burrito. One had definitely been worn by the smell of it. Grabbing an evidence bag from a pile on the hall table, he slipped the shirt inside and tucked it under one arm.

Swinging to his left he briefly peered into the kitchen, saw a team of officers huddled in the corner whispering. The only thing he could see that would have caused a clinking sound was a china dog bowl, water seeping towards beanie bag as if someone had recently kicked it.

He walked out into the street and looked for a black Explorer. The blinding glare of the headlights told him Malin had just arrived, tires not quite managing to avoid the largest puddle in the driveway which showered Hackett in a muddy spray. Temeke couldn't resist a chuckle and then a quick cough as Hackett caught his eye. The poor old bugger was wet through from the waist down.

A sheet of yellow paper scuttled across the tarmac, wedging itself in the car radiator. It fluttered about for a bit like an injured bird as if waiting for someone to free it.

FIVE

Adam stared at a coil of smoke that hovered over the dash and then fixed his eyes on the man behind the wheel. Wavy hair, a straight nose, eyes that smiled.

"Do you have a nickname in scouts?" the man asked.

"No."

"I bet you do. Bet it's a good one."

Adam wasn't going to tell him. It was like a trump card you played at the end of a game.

"Know what I think? I think you don't trust me."

Damn right, Adam thought. What was there to trust? He had the inexplicable sense the man studied him like an unusual insect and it stirred a wild fear inside, the kind where you wake from a nightmare all wrapped up in sheets. "Where are we going?"

"Where no one will find us."

The man drove one-handed, right hand resting on his thigh where that cigarette smoked for all it was worth. His eyes seemed to shift across Adam's face and then back at the windshield. "So you're a scout. Think you can be brave for a few hours?"

Adam nodded and kept his eyes on the road. If it was only for a few hours, he could handle almost anything. The digital clock read eleven fifty-nine and they were driving east on Paseo Del Norte. Every time they went under a street lamp, he could see the paint on the door frame. Black and shiny, and the cab stank of smoke.

Adam was certain he had missed an important detail. His mom was a doctor at Rust hospital and she rarely got home before eleven. He tried to hold fast to an image of her and suddenly felt like having a good cry.

Crying's good, so his mom said. It lets out all the sadness and makes way for a chuckle or two. It was true. After a good cry came laughter, only Adam didn't feel much like laughing. He could still hear gunshots and smell the stench of firecrackers under his nose.

"You shot my dad."

"It was an accident. Gun went off because of the dog."

"He's trained to attack."

"So I noticed."

"We should stop. Go back—"

"No going back. Never good to go back."

The man crushed the cigarette in the ashtray and reached into the glove compartment. He snatched a yellow container and popped the lid, palming two large pills into his mouth before flushing them down in a single swallow.

"Name's Ramsey," he said, sliding a map off the top of the dash and resting it in his lap.

Adam already hated him. He wanted to put up a wall between them thick enough to protect himself, thick enough to hide behind. And he wanted his cellphone back.

The cellphone. It had a tracker. Adam bit his lip, fingers balled together in his lap. If his mom remembered… if only she remembered.

Ramsey's eyes kept flicking from the rearview mirror to the clock and then down at the map. His finger seemed to trace I-25 all the way to a patch of dark green where the word Gila National Forest was poised on the arc of his fingernail.

It's too far away, Adam thought, suddenly wishing

they could stop, hoping he could make a dash for it. "Mr. Ramsey? I need to pee."

"There's a truck stop in about four miles. We'll stop there."

Adam studied Ramsey out of the corner of his eye. A shadow of stubble rested on his upper lip and chin, and his cheeks were high and round. It made him look a bit girly, only he was probably mean enough to eat a plate of food and watch *Bones* at the same time.

The truck stop had no bathrooms, no stores, just a weigh-station off the side of the highway and two tall street lamps. He saw a large Peterbilt parked beside a clump of trees, too far away to shout at.

Ramsey walked around the front of the truck and opened the passenger door. "See this?" he said, jutting his chin at the gun in his hand. "You run, I shoot."

Adam swallowed and nodded. He jumped down onto a cracked pavement where grass burst through a pothole and the headlights cast a beam along the road. He could see well enough, but if he walked towards the hood where two halogen lamps gave off an eerie yellow glow, the trucker might see him too.

He could make out a few portables in the distance and a car lot of rusted out parts. He didn't dare run. Didn't dare look behind him at the man with the gun. All he could do was water a small piñon tree because his bladder was complaining.

Before Adam zipped up his pants, he had an idea. A Bible tract in his pocket talked about a big forest and if he could get to it without making Ramsey all jumpy and suspicious it might help the police find him.

Keeping his head down and angling his body slightly towards the headlights, he pulled out a handful of tracts. He found the one he wanted and balling it up in a fist, made a big deal out of his zipper before letting the tract drop between his fingers. The tiny ball of paper drifted between tall blades of grass, dashing about in the wind like a frantic grasshopper. It was a chance in a million. But a chance all the same.

When Adam turned, he saw Ramsey leaning against the fender. The gun made him start. Dangling first against Ramsey's leg, then the muzzle came up a couple of times to make a point.

"Get in! We're not stopping again."

Adam barely nodded. He struggled to breathe, to think, to do anything but let Ramsey know he was scared of that gun. He hoisted himself into the passenger seat as Ramsey slammed the door, walked around the front of the truck, aiming the gun right at him.

"Better get some sleep," Ramsey said as he climbed in, switched on the heater and scooted that gun under the driver's seat.

I won't sleep, Adam thought. *I can't. I'll watch every car that goes past and memorize the make and model.* He felt his tongue poke through his top teeth in concentration taking care to preserve all the energy he had. Listening to the hum of the engine, he could see little out of the window except rolling hills and the tops of piñon trees – a roughly hewn landscape where dinosaurs once roamed. He wanted to shut out the sound of gunshots, and all he could see were his father's eyes flickering as he lay there on the floor.

Adam knew his dad had seen him, knew he was frightened. Tried to warn him, tried to tell him to run away while he still had the chance. Adam worried that thought, even to the part where he saw Ramsey grabbing his dad's wrists and tying them behind his back.

Adam shifted uneasily beneath the seat belt, feeling dazed by the day's events. Squinting under the fluorescent glare of an oncoming car, he lifted his chin slightly. All he could see was sagebrush streaking past the side window and miles of rugged wasteland you wouldn't want to get lost in. Signs to Los Lunas and Belen took them through meadows and flat-topped mesas, and a filigree of clouds spread out before the moon in the shape of a lazy dog. A spine of rock hovered in the distance under a thick blanket of stars... that's when his eyes became heavy.

It seemed like a few minutes before the truck jolted and woke him up, hotter than a furnace, heat blasting from the vents. The clock on the dash said twelve twenty-six.

"Dark isn't it?" Ramsey said.

The voice pulled Adam up short. The type of voice that gets deep inside and stays there. He was suddenly afraid of it. His scoutmaster had always told him to watch for marking points and as far as he could see they were still headed south on I-25.

Adam glanced at Ramsey. His arms were cabled with muscle beneath a black tee shirt and his fingers tapped out a rhythm on the steering wheel. "Where are we?" he asked.

Ramsey must have known the answer. He just wasn't talking.

SIX

Temeke forced a smile at a few familiar officers in the driveway. Typical Duke City PD all looking at him with conspiratorial glances and whispering things they thought he couldn't hear. Probably licking their lips wondering what was in that brown bag under his arm. Not a flaming chicken sandwich that's for sure.

"…wouldn't be tolerated downtown," said a piggy-eyed Lieutenant. "How he made rank I'll never know. Must be handing out promotions for stupidity these days."

Pulling a packet of cigarettes from a top pocket, Temeke lit one up and took two long drags to get his mind working. Smoke oozed from his nostrils and he fanned it away with one hand.

The department had accepted him under protest and ever since his brother-in-law, Lt. Alvarez, wound up in hospital from a gunshot wound, Temeke had been fighting his own wars since then. Hackett was a crawly bastard, who'd told Temeke he was the department's most recently commended detective. Commended? My ass. More like *criticized, belittled, hated*.

Talking of hated: his wife had left him before Christmas. Serena couldn't stand the loneliness, the fights, and the long hours wondering if he would ever come home. So he'd locked himself in a room in Motel 6 one night with a bottle of whiskey and a bag of sleeping pills. It could have been viewed as a suicide attempt; he viewed it as a booze-up followed by a good night's sleep for once. Trouble was, a pastor patrolling the upper gallery saw fit to knock on his door and hand him a Bible tract. He said it would help. He said it would heal.

Load of guff, of course. The big geezer in the sky was supposed to make everything better. Only it wasn't better. It was never better.

The wind churned up a bit as he walked over to the Explorer. Detective Malin Santiago scratched a few notes in a spiral notebook, dark eyes sparkled beneath arched eyebrows and teeth flashed behind a sensuous mouth.

"Glad you decided to show up. It's Monday morning," he said, checking his watch. Twelve thirty-six. "Next time answer the bloody phone. I called three times."

"Correction," she said. "You called twice."

"Should have seen that swimming pool of a puddle when you pulled in. Gave the Unit Commander a right old soaking."

Malin slapped a hand in front of her mouth, eyes wider than cups. She looked as guilty as a priest with a copy of *Playboy* in his hymnbook.

"You talked to Wendover?" He saw her nod. "So what have we got?"

"He said the boy's got merit badges in navigation, fitness and scout spirit. Got good night eyes. That's his troop nickname. Oh, and this," Malin said, holding up an evidence bag with a slip of yellow paper about six inches long and one inch wide. On one side was a Bible verse and on the other a series of numbers. "License comes up under a—"

"False name, false address." Temeke blew out his cheeks and sighed. He handed Malin the brown paper bag hoping she wouldn't look inside. "And unless the sky's raining Bible tracts, I saw another one of those a minute ago."

He pinched out his cigarette and tucked the remainder back in his shirt pocket. Walking to the front of the car, he peered into the radiator. Nothing there. He looked up and down the street, hadn't considered the wind.

A honeysuckle bush hung over a wall, spent shoots pruned to encourage new blooms in spring. In the fulcrum of two branches he thought he saw a hint of yellow and reaching into the vine, he snatched it. It was identical to the other, only this one didn't have a car license number on the back.

Then the king, with the queen sitting beside him, asked me, "How long will your journey take, and when will you get back?" Neh 2:6.

The word *journey* send a cold shiver down Temeke's back. "What do you make of this?" he said, slipping into the passenger seat.

Malin turned the dome light on, angled the paper to one side, read it and handed it back. "It's from the book of Nehemiah. He was a cupbearer to the king. There's no relevance."

"Doesn't have to be. I think Adam dropped this one on purpose. It's a bit Hansel and Gretel, but I'm thinking he might drop a few more."

Malin ran the edge of her notepad along her bottom lip and smothered a yawn. "Bit far-fetched isn't it?"

"That I found it or the kid left it?"

"Both."

"What other merit badges does our second class scout have?"

"Apart from a Baptist Church emblem, he has orienteering and hiking. Not very helpful if he's locked up in a basement."

"He's on the road," Temeke said, dropping the tract in the evidence bag. "Whoever took him registered the truck in a false name. A big truck. The type you take up a mountain."

"There're over eighty mountain ranges in New Mexico," Malin muttered. "Looks like our only witness has been kidnapped."

"What's his scoutmaster like?"

"Charles Wendover. Ex-marine. Fifty-six, fit and sharp."

"An ex-marine knows a thing or two about survival. How resilient is a twelve year-old?"

"Depends on the kidnapper."

"This kidnapper shot the Mayor. Means he might not give a toss about the boy."

Malin tucked a loose strand of black hair behind one ear and dropped her notepad between the handbrake and the consol. "He'll call us to make an exchange. Money for the boy. That's how it works."

"He'll negotiate before he asks for money. Working us up, that's what he's doing. And he'll draw it out as long as he can."

Malin looked down at the brown paper bag on the consol. "What's that?"

"You don't miss a trick, do you, Marl? One of Adam's tee shirts. It's been worn."

"You know you shouldn't cross that line."

Temeke knew Malin wouldn't say anything. She was his partner. "Fowler said the old dog's gone missing. *Adam's* dog. Might want to find that dog. Ex-military so they say."

"So, what did we miss?"

"Opportunity. And timing. This guy waited until Adam came home. He only had twenty minutes to get him out of the house before his mother arrived. I would say that was excellent timing."

Malin shuddered. "Someone just walked over my grave."

"Feel like going for a drive?"

"It's past midnight. Feel like going home to bed. It's time Hackett got you a driver."

"Know anyone? No, I didn't think so. Step on the gas."

Malin chuckled, turned the key in the ignition and let the car idle for a while. Without looking out of the window she muttered the word *Hackett* and nodded politely at the approaching Commander with a cell phone pressed to his ear.

A stocky man in his fifties, hands in pockets and a scowl, leaned in through the driver's window and peered over his half-moon glasses. "I think I've come up with something. How would a *raise* work for both of you?"

"That would be nice, sir," Temeke said. "How much were you thinking?"

"Not that kind of raise, you moron. The type where you *raise* your freeloading butts off those nice warm seats and go after your witnesses. We don't want a bunch of boy scouts and an ex-marine putting us to shame now, do we?"

"No, sir," they said in unison.

"Two things. Adam's phone's on teen-safe tracker. Shows the general area of Main Street and I-25, Los Lunas. They're headed south. And another thing, a trucker just called. He was just settling down in a rest stop on I-25. Gave the nearest cross street as State Road 317 out by Isleta. He saw a black pickup about ten yards behind his rig. Couldn't be sure, but he said there was a man leaning against the truck watching a boy taking a leak. Says he thinks the man had a gun. Made him feel uncomfortable enough to call 911. Says he'll wait for you if you hurry."

"We were planning on going that way, sir," Temeke

said. It was a lie but it was worth provoking the boss.

"You were?"

"A vague scent, sir. Can't explain it. Can't defend it."

"Well, get on with it then. Oh, and by the way, I'll be holding a press conference tomorrow morning bright and early. Make sure you keep me posted."

Malin was already cruising out of the driveway before Temeke could respond, tires screeching as they veered onto Coors. "Why didn't you show him that Bible tract?" she asked.

"Because we don't want anyone knowing about our little paper trail. And we don't want the press having a field day over it either."

They slowed at the hill before the Chevron gas station where an old black dog sat on a grass verge, sweeping the ground with his tail. A name tag dangled from the collar, metal and shaped like a bone.

"If that's who I think it is," Temeke said, "it's our lucky day."

SEVEN

Adam kept his eyes on the road as they drove past signs to Truth Or Consequences and Hatch, turning right on NM-26 towards Deming. He must have slept for three hours before he awoke, because the next thing he saw were ghostly white aspens on either side of a bumpy track.

The truck lurched from side to side and he struggled to stop from gasping, body racked with fear. There was just the growl of the engine over his harried thoughts. He wanted to pluck a few hairs from his head and leave them behind the seat. The police would know he had been in the truck if he left a few hairs lying around. That's how they found kids. By their hairs.

"I'm hungry," he said. He couldn't see Ramsey's eyes too well but he knew they'd be watching every move.

"What kind of hungry is that now? The kind where I open the door and you streak off through the woods and I shoot you in the back? Or the type of hungry where you keep quiet until we get there?"

"The second," Adam said, wondering if streaking through the woods wasn't a bad idea. He was fast on his pins and if he weaved through the trees like they did in the movies, he'd dodge a bullet or two. He had his scout uniform on and a compass in his pocket. He'd get further than a mile that's for sure.

"Hard to find your way out here," Ramsey whispered, "just in case you were wondering."

"I wasn't."

Ramsey made a snort of laughter as he reached under the seat, pulled the gun onto his lap. Adam gave it a long, hard stare, knew he couldn't get to it quick enough without a punch in the face and he felt sick and nervous like he was going to throw up. Ramsey swallowed too many pills, too much drink, and his brain boiled with crazy things.

He brought the truck to a halt and powered down the window. Took Adam's cell phone from his pocket and threw it out into the night. "Got a tracker on there, right?"

"I... I don't know." Adam shook his head. Heard the grunt of a laugh anyway.

"Not taking any chances."

Adam held in a gulp for as long as he could. Throwing that phone away was as bad as someone crushing it with a heel. It was a gray Samsung with a dark blue screen, one he'd saved all his pocket money for. Now he wondered if the police would ever find him.

Visions of his dad swiped in and out of his mind and a voice that always told him what to do. *If you are kidnapped, son, talk to them. Find out what you can. Because when you're found... and you will be found... anything you can tell the police may save another child's life.*

"Do you live up here?"

"No."

"Oh," Adam whispered, noting how thin and stern Ramsey's face had become. Talking about home might make him mad, bitter perhaps. He was probably homeless.

"Do you have a dad?"

Ramsey took his time to answer. "I did. He was a

bastard."

"My dad's always been with us. Except when he went to Afghanistan. Something to do with caves and destroying weapons. He was gone for more than six months and my mom cried every night."

Ramsey gave one of those frowns like he disagreed with what he was hearing. "Every night?"

"Well, no, I was the one who cried actually."

Ramsey nodded then reached over the dash for a box of cigarettes, flipping the lid with one hand. "Want one?"

"No, thank you." Adam heard the click of the lighter, watched Ramsey take a deep breath and exhale a cloud of smoke.

"You do drink, don't you?"

Adam had never heard anything so stupid. "Of course I drink."

"There's a bottle of wine behind my seat. Might shut that big mouth of yours."

Adam hated wine. He'd tried it once at his grandma's funeral and it had come up quicker than it had gone down. The pastor pulled him to one side, told him drinking was for fools. *Do not look at wine . . . it sparkles in the cup . . . goes down smoothly. . . bites like a serpent . . . stings like an adder.*

"Did you know you can get adders and serpents in your belly if you drink," Adam said.

Ramsey scowled at him with an upturned lip. "Who told you that?"

"Pastor Razz. And mom's a doctor. She had to take out someone's intestines once. They were covered in green slime and worms. Big ones."

Adam noted how quiet Ramsey became after that. It served him right. He shouldn't have been drinking that stuff in the first place. The worms weren't a lie, not really. Just a warning. And then he thought of his dad.

"My dad's not dead is he?"

"Who?"

"My dad."

"He's a hard man. No, *hard* doesn't do him justice. He's worse than hard. Cruel."

Adam shook his head. "My dad's not cruel. He wouldn't hurt anyone."

"Gentle as a pussycat, isn't that right, Adam? Curious expression. Because cats aren't gentle. Ever seen one catch a mouse? They prolong the agony for as long as possible." Ramsey grinned between puffs. "Natural enemies can never be friends."

Adam swallowed and felt his gut churn. He could hear his scoutmaster's voice over the thumping of his heart. *Kidnappers lie. They say your parents are dead, don't love you any more, sold you into slavery. Don't believe a word.*

Adam wondered where they were. Saw a sign to NM-15 and another to Lake Roberts.

It was another half hour before Ramsey coughed and ground the remains of another cigarette in the ashtray. It was hardly smoked. "Get me a beer."

Adam reached behind the driver's seat and flicked open the cooler. There were six green cans lying on a bed of ice, most of which had gone to slush. He handed one to Ramsey, heard him twist off the tag with a loud hiss, saw him grip the can between his thighs.

Adam glanced through the wing mirror. He saw a cloud of sand in their wake and ahead the road stretched out like a silver snake, curling ever upwards into the dark gray dawn. Somehow he felt more comfortable, more hopeful. The police were on their way, he kept promising himself, and they would find him within the hour.

The road narrowed and twisted sharply to the left and there, on a massive shelf of green grass, was a wooden chalet with a gently sloping roof and wide overhanging eaves. A large picture window reflected the mountain range to the west and a ripple of clouds hung gray and ghostlike on the glass.

Despite Adam's change of mood there was an air of grimness about the place. Ramsey had promised to shoot him if he ran away and he'd already killed his dad.

Killing was one of the big ten. It meant only one thing, Adam thought. Ramsey would get a holy thunderbolt straight between the eyes and then he'd be squealing like a baby. Adam wondered if that might be worth looking forward to. Blood everywhere. A big gooey mess.

He found himself standing before two wooden doors listening to the click of a key in the lock. Lights suddenly illuminated a large living area with vaulted ceilings and wood stove at one end. A marble counter wrapped around the kitchen and there were bar stools high enough for a giant.

"Better get some rest," Ramsey murmured.

"How long are we staying here?"

"As long as it takes."

"I need to call my mom. She'll worry, you see."

"You like history, don't you? Like to know about the Anasazi." Ramsey took a deep breath like he'd just come up for air. "We're going to the caves. So you'll see it firsthand."

His voice was distant, less gruff, and there was a change in his face, a fresh light that hadn't been there before. Adam felt the frown between his eyes and nodded. The only place he ever wanted to go was the national monuments. To the pit houses and the cave dwellings. To see Tarahuma for himself. Today, all that seemed wrong.

The first bedroom they came to had two wrought iron trundle beds and a small shuttered window in a stone wall. Large windows faced over the driveway draped in curtains you could see through and the rods were thicker than a man's arm.

He sensed Ramsey staring at him, looking at his hair, his face and then his mouth. It wasn't a creepy look. More curious, like he was sizing him up or something.

"You'll be safe here," he said. "Safer than in the woods."

Adam sat on the bed as the door closed behind him, key clunking in the lock. He could see the chalk-white road they had taken through the large windows, twisting down between the trees and out of sight. There were no other houses. No signs of life.

He cried a bit then as he fumbled with the compass in his pocket. Looking at where the direction of travel arrow intersected with the degree dial, he knew he was facing twenty-three degrees southwest.

Now what? He wiped one eye with the back of his hand. He was thirsty and the water in the bathroom faucet tasted salty and bitter. It was yellow too. There was a map on the wall in a small white frame. It showed Lake Roberts and NM-35 to the east. If he could get to that highway, he could certainly hitch a ride home.

The big windows were double-paned and locked, but the small shuttered window was easy to open. He looked out over a sloping roof, hoping he was thin enough to crawl through, hoping he could hide in places a man could not go.

Open the window, Adam. It's so stuffy. His mom's voice echoed in his mind. She always said that in the mornings when she came in to open his curtains. *There now, good fresh air. Can't you smell it?* Trouble was, Ramsey would be able to smell it too. Adam snapped it shut and winced at the noise.

Wendover always told the scouts to live without worry, without fear, to be grateful for all blessings both good and bad. This was one of those *bad* blessings and he was frightened all right.

I want my Eagle, he thought, eyes tearing up again. *Please give me another chance. It wasn't me who sprinkled Dr. Windbreaker's Farting Powder in Wendover's tea, God. Honest. It was Kevin. He's always doing stuff like that.*

It was no use. God wasn't answering. That heavenly switchboard was all clogged up with incoming calls and the angels were shorthanded as it was. God was likely busy elsewhere. Maybe he was angry with Adam and had decided to let him stew in his own juice. Or maybe… just maybe, he wanted Adam to use his head. He was a scout after all.

Adam heard the rattle of the key in the door, stuffed the compass under the pillow and sat down on the bed. Ramsey placed a bowl of soup on the bedside table. There was a thick slice of brown bread half submerged and leaning against the rim like an old weathered tombstone.

Ramsey crouched and gripped that pistol of his. "Gotta make a few phone calls. You'll be OK up here."

"Mr. Ramsey?" Adam swallowed hard, anything to keep him in the room. "My mom's called the police. They know where I am."

"All good mothers call the police."

Adam clenched his fists, felt the muscles tighten in his thighs. He hoped Ramsey couldn't see what he saw. Little bits of paper floating in the wind. Yellow bits of paper with words, God-given words that would help the police find him.

Ramsey stood now, gun pointing down at the floor. He was like a black shadow in front of the window, looking as if he had suddenly thought of something. "Empty your pockets," he said.

It was the slow wide smile that made Adam do it. He

swallowed first, tongue searching for every last bit of spit. When his pockets were empty and those precious tracts lay on the quilt, he heard Ramsey grunt.

"Where's the compass?"

Adam didn't want to lie otherwise the launcher on God's thunderbolt would only change direction. He slipped his hand under the pillow, pulled out the compass and laid it in Ramsey's open hand.

Ramsey read a few of those tracts, studied the compass and tossed it back to Adam. "You'll need this. But you won't need these."

The papers were balled up in a large fist, tossed down the toilet and flushed away. The sound of water churning down the pipes made Adam whimper. Not loud enough to be heard.

"Wasn't supposed to happen this way." Ramsey wiped his mouth repeatedly as he walked back towards the window. "You weren't supposed to see... any of it. Weren't supposed to know."

Adam was starting to feel faint, making his mouth dry and his stomach heave. He looked towards the open door; could have made a dash for it if he wasn't shaking so hard. Couldn't stop looking at those eyes. Ramsey disgusted him, making him feel weird and drawn in at the same time.

"There have been bad men near here, boy-killers, you know. I'll protect you."

Ramsey could easily be the boy killer, the one on the news. He had the same squinty eyes and a chin full of hair like the composite sketch of the Ringmaster. There was something skittish about him all the same, something not quite right.

It gave Adam an idea. "Do you want me to fetch your pills?" he offered.

"Ah, smart that," Ramsey said, smiling and rubbing a scar on his left temple. "You go down to the truck and drive off into the sunset. I'm not that stupid."

"I can't drive, Mr. Ramsey. I don't have a license."

Ramsey's head began to twitch and he dropped the smile. "No, but you can run."

EIGHT

Murphy craned his head between the front seats, snout only inches from Temeke's nose. He panted for a time, tongue lolling through a pink set of gums. When he closed his mouth, he let out a pleading whine.

"This is it," Temeke said, pointing at a rest stop, trees aglow under two streetlamps. "Leave the headlights on."

Malin turned into the narrow road and parked about fifteen feet behind the Peterbilt. A man jumped down from the cab, gray hair in a ponytail and a tattoo on the arm he waved.

"Before you show him this photograph," Temeke said, sliding it out of his jacket pocket, "find out if he remembers what Adam was wearing."

Temeke took the tee shirt from the brown bag and let the dog take a good long sniff. Murphy nudged his way onto the front seat and launched a solid ninety pound mass into the dirt. He tore off behind a portable storage building before breaking into a cornfield.

Temeke watched corn tassels bobbing to and fro as Murphy ran beneath them flattening the grass and chuffing. And then he came back, circling an area a few feet from where Temeke stood, nose stuck down a crevice where the tarmac met the trunk of a small piñon tree. The dog whined and then barked.

Temeke pulled out his flashlight and trained the beam at the base of the tree. He crouched, let his fingers brush over bark and grass, feeling nothing but dog drool. Wind whispered through the corn stalks, a hollow sound that reminded him of a seashell against his ear, and there was something in the dog's persistent grunting that gave him hope.

The wind tugged gently at the collar of his ski jacket as he scanned the ground, back and forth, back and forth. There had to be something. No matter how small. He wondered if it was a trick of the light or wishful thinking when he saw a small yellow ball nesting between two blades of grass. He pulled on a pair of black leather gloves, snatching the paper before the dog did, warding off the leap with his forearm. It was a Bible tract all right, verse printed in black ink but he couldn't make head nor tail of it. He looked at his watch and then at the horizon. Four more hours before daybreak.

He glanced up the road at Malin still talking to the driver of the Peterbilt, arms crossed, jaw set just enough to get the man's attention. Coaxing the dog into the back seat of the car, he couldn't help thinking of the Monday morning news; the hype; the drama.

Troops of grieving boy scouts trample the Bosque for any sign of Adam Oliver...

Malin jogged back. "Mr. Delaney thinks he saw them well over forty-five minutes ago," she said, climbing back into the front seat. "He watched the kid through his wing mirror, saw him in the beam of the headlights. Said he was standing somewhere around that tree. He was wearing a scout uniform. It's him alright."

"And the man he was with?"

"Tall, six foot, he said, well-built, shoulder-length hair. Had something in his right hand, held it down along the length of his thigh like he was hiding it. Could have been a gun, could have been two fingers. It wasn't until the man motioned with it a couple of times Mr. Delany assumed it was a handgun. He confirmed the truck was a black Chevy Silverado Z71. Used to have one himself."

Temeke wondered how the trucker could have seen the gun unless the man turned sideways to the fender and flapped the damn thing about.

The cell phone buzzed in his pocket. It was Hackett again. Adam's phone had been traced to a cell tower in Belen. Seemed like every unit on I-25 had been alerted. Fortunately, the press still thought the official search was on Riverfront Drive and the surrounding area because some daft old git tipped off Jennifer Danes at the *Journal*. She had too much in the way of guts and stamina, thrived in twenty degree weather and loved talking to worst of them. She was probably standing in front of a camera crew right now waiting for a hostage situation to break.

Only he's not there, Temeke thought. Not if the poor kid's headed south on I-25 towards Socorro. Hackett had likely kept that away from the press.

He looked down at the tract in his hand and read it aloud this time. "*So also the tongue is a small part of the body, and yet it boasts of great things. See how great a forest is set aflame by such a small fire! James 3:5.* Where was the most recent forest fire?"

"Carson National Forest," Malin said. "One of their rangers claimed the fire was the largest in history. He said they lost over one hundred and twenty square miles of forestland."

"There's your boasting tongue. It was Gila that won the gold. Two hundred and sixty-five square miles burned to the ground. All black and scorched and full of dead animals… all because some idiot lit a cigarette and hurled a lighted match out of his bloody tent!"

"Better call Hackett," she said.

"And tell him what? To toss a bleeding coin? Just head for Gila, will you?"

It was another twenty minutes before they reached

Los Lunas, tripped the siren in heavy traffic and shot out the other side. Temeke heard the chirping of his phone. "Temeke," he snapped.

It was Hackett again. Temeke sat up a little straighter.

"Want the good news first or the bad?"

"Good."

"Our man just called Madam Mayor. Seems he wants to make an exchange."

Temeke gave Malin a sideways nod. "How much?"

"Three hundred grand, half in hundreds, half in smaller denominations and none of it must be sequenced. Had to wake up Oily Streuli and ask him to open the vault. Making copies now. It could take a few hours."

"You got an address?"

"3265 Forest Road, Gila National Forest. Kidnapper says he wants the bag dropped in the driveway at five thirty in the morning. No police or he'll shoot the boy."

Lucky they were going the right way, Temeke thought. It would be a right sod if they had to head back through all that traffic. "So, who does the house belong to?"

"Sandoval Properties. A two week rental in the name of—"

"Don't tell me. A Mr. S. Marner." Temeke sensed a disabling feeling of dread. This was the work of someone highly organized, someone who knew a thing or two about keeping a low profile. And how many times had a kidnapper failed to keep his promise? "Who's doing the drop?"

"DCPD Air 1. Make sure you're in the vicinity before they get there. I'm right behind with the follow team."

Temeke knew kidnappers got skittish when they heard helicopters, especially the smart ones that knew about the infra-red heat detectors and snipers leaning out over the skids. He just hoped this one had the sense to wait until he got the money before topping the kid.

"And the bad news?"

"Media's got hold of it. They think it's the Ringmaster. Hundreds of them are demanding a story or they go on the air and make one up. I've asked Sarge to call all media reps, get their ID and ask to speak to the Editors in Chief. If they run the story they'll be risking Adam's life."

Temeke heard the click of Hackett's phone as the line went dead. "I'll kill the bastard who told the press. I'll kill the press too."

The car sped towards signs to Socorro before Malin said anything. "Hopefully, Adam won't run out in the woods and get hypothermia and exhaustion."

Temeke knew what she was really thinking. The woods were littered with hungry wildlife and a killer they had never managed to catch, and any chance of finding the boy seemed to flit away. "Of course he won't run out in the woods. He's a bloody scout for crying out loud."

NINE

The sharp screech of an eagle pierced the silence and jolted Adam awake. He lifted his head from the pillow and squinted at a shaft of moonlight through a man-sized window. It was still night, gray clouds rolling in from the west. He hadn't slept for long. Ten, fifteen minutes tops.

Through a veil of tears, his mind wandered to the last few hours, diving further into a tunnel of fear. Things Ramsey said. Things he did. So many memories seemed to spool around Adam's head and he couldn't rid himself of the image of his father lying on the floor.

Adam wiped his eyes, chest tightening with each sob. He was hungry again, but not hungry enough to shout for the killer downstairs, one that would reel him in like a fish on a pole and then gut him down the middle.

Lifting his legs over the side of the bed, he struggled to stand, felt nauseous, with tongue sticking to the roof of his mouth. He had to pee.

The en suite bathroom was small and dark with a shower that stank of mold. He sat on the toilet for a time, staring at his face in a mirror that hung over the sink. He looked different. Hair all mussed and creeping over one eye. There was an odd pallor to his skin like he'd aged a few years in a couple of hours and his eyes were shiny with fresh tears. He didn't dare flush the toilet. Didn't want Ramsey knowing his personal business.

There was a musical box on the chest of drawers, key projecting from a blue painted case. Gold stars were etched around the edge and there was a figure of a man in the moon on the lid. Adam walked over and stared at it for a moment, turned the key a few times and heard it sputter into life. A well-known melody he couldn't place lasted for about seven seconds before running out of steam.

He had no idea why he did it. He was just lonely that was all. When he reached inside his pocket, fingers fumbling for those little slips of paper, he felt nothing but the lining of his pants against the warmth of his body. Beads of sweat trickled down the sides of his face and he brushed them away with both hands. It was his one and only chance to get out. Ramsey was downstairs with a gun in his hand, likely circling the living room and deciding how much longer he could wait.

Adam couldn't wait.

He opened the small casement window and was met with a shiver of cold air and the smell of pine trees. Taking off his belt, he wound it into a ball and tucked it in his top pocket. Easing himself out onto the ledge, he pushed forward a foot at a time. The tiles felt cold beneath his hands and some began to move.

Dropping onto the ridge of the gabled roof, he slid down a narrow valley to the eaves. He knew the gutter wouldn't hold his weight and shuffling forward on his butt, he peered over the edge. Taking a deep breath, he laced his hands behind his head and jumped onto the grass below. There was a dull thud as his feet took the impact and he rolled forward on the ground, arms breaking his fall.

He lay stunned for a few seconds, legs tingling as if they would suddenly snap. Three tiles rained down onto the grass beside him; first a dull thud and then an echoing shatter. He struggled to stand as the noise diminished, limping for the edge of the trees. It would be too obvious to take the track back down to the service road where the trees stood further apart and left no hiding place. So he chose instead to head for the woods.

It was the sound of a loud groan that made him freeze. Peering around the east side of the house, he saw a blaze of light from the back porch. It was the musculature of a man's back he saw, muscles contracting with every move. Ramsey was sitting on a tree stump lifting weights. Only he paused when he heard that sound, face turned slightly to one side.

It was now or never. Burrowing under the canopy of fir branches ahead, Adam hurdled over a low fence of railroad ties and down the slope into the darkness. Each breath burning in his lungs, he set off towards a pathway half-buried under a pile of pine needles. He didn't look back, didn't want to know if Ramsey had seen him. All he could hear was the crunch of detritus under his feet and as long as he could still hear it, he knew he was alone.

He picked up speed under dense branches that appeared black in the meager light and headed southwest, keeping the dirt track to his right. A rabbit startled him as it bounded across his path, darting between a skirt of gnarly brown branches and dead leaves. Adam paused, held his breath and listened.

Only the whisper of a breeze through the fir trees and the screech of an eagle. The air was pungent with the scent of sap and piney woods and in the distance, he could just make out a large lake shimmering black like a puddle of oil.

Scanning the underbrush, his eyes became accustomed to the gloom. He pelted down the slope towards a stream, crossing over a group of flat rocks to the other side. Continuing up the opposite slope at a steady jog, he headed towards a knot of box elders and sagebrush, realizing he had no container for water or iodine crystals to purify it. He wouldn't last long out in the woods without a drink and the next water source was likely to be the lake he had seen well over a mile away.

It was here the predators came; wolf, bear and mountain lion. None of them scared him, not like Ramsey did. It was another rabbit that made him jump, scampering over a tree root, pausing for a moment to sniff the scent off a bleak wind. Something had disturbed it, something bigger. The air was chilled as the night wore on, made him shiver, made his teeth chatter. Lucky the moon was hanging just above the treetops, full enough to provide light. He found the hills and valleys a struggle, footfalls punctuated with labored breaths.

And then he froze, hand pressed against his chest. He could hear panting and branches snapping back in the wake of a runner. A flash of movement to his right. Ramsey was fast, angling sideways to gain purchase on the slope, arms out by his sides. His mouth was set in a clenched grin, breath misting beneath his nose.

Adam dropped to a crouch, blending with a stand of young Douglas-firs. He watched the dark figure some fifteen feet ahead, pausing suddenly as if getting his bearings. One hand seemed to hover over his belt, the other hung in the air, fingers spread. He was gauging the wind. It was something big-eared bats did when they spread their wings, as sensitive as a human fingertip.

Ramsey began to head east and then quite suddenly north as if he traveled an arc around Adam, plotting his course with the accuracy of a sniffer-dog. He stopped once or twice, glancing up at a small helicopter humming in the sky, lights flickering in the darkness. Then he disappeared around the base of a large boulder.

Adam tried to think. He could turn back and run towards the house. It was the last thing Ramsey would expect. He could even try driving that big old truck. It wouldn't matter if he didn't have a license. The police were looking for him anyway.

The more he thought about it the more he liked it. Teeth rattling, he took a mental inventory of his surroundings—the slope back up to the lodge behind him and the service road beyond. It wasn't like he was equipped with a thermal blanket and a few energy bars to go hiking off into the unknown, and there wasn't enough light to get safely down to the lake.

Turning back towards the slope, he pushed on through the trees, boots clawing at dead leaves. Branches sprang back into his face, cutting across his cheeks as he blinked the tears away. Sometimes he ran, sometimes he stopped to listen. He was ten minutes away from the lodge, ten minutes away from safety.

Shadows were creeping at the base of the trees and an owl hooted nearby. Just as he came to a standstill behind a shaggy spruce, his foot caught on a root and he came down with a thump, sliding half-way beneath its spiny skirt. He was rewarded with the bitter smell of dead leaves and the echo of breaking twigs. He tried to crawl closer to the tree trunk, but the root had somehow caught on the rubber sole of his boot and the only way he could free it was to crawl back out.

He heard footfalls beating up the slope. There was no way he could move, not with Ramsey standing a few feet away, eyes darting back and forth like a school of fish. He must have sensed something, heard something. If Adam let out that big breath he was holding, Ramsey would hear that too.

"I'm the falcon, you're the prey," the harsh voice crooned. "Wouldn't want anyone to come between us now would you?"

Ramsey's head turned first to the right and then to the left. "If you don't come out soon, you'll smell gunshot. You're upwind of it. And it'll blow right in your face."

Adam refrained from letting out a whimper of pain. He knew Ramsey couldn't see him. It was just a lame trick.

"You want to go home, right. Or maybe you've changed your mind. Me, I'd bet my ass on it."

Of course Adam wanted to go home, but thinking about it didn't bother him as much as the pain that shot up and down his shins and the spiny bed beneath his elbows.

Just as the wind wheezed its way between the trees and a steel-gray cloud covered the moon, he let out that breath. It went dark then and there was an ashen hue in the shadows as if he had suddenly found himself in a winter wonderland. He had to move, he couldn't feel his leg.

A second gust brushed the ground, whipping shards of bark and pine needles, and filling the air with a thin brown dust. Adam saw his chance. He inched forward on his elbows and it was then he heard the scrape of leather on wood and a loud pop as his foot slipped free.

Ramsey crouched.

Adam froze.

He imagined eyes that stared bone deep, gazing over his right shoulder to the trees beyond. Then they twitched to the left, stayed there for a time before sweeping again to the right.

Adam's dad had once told him how Shadow Wolf officers could see in the dark, not with infra-red lenses, but with their own eyes. They could even sniff out a black beetle in a storm drain. They were that smart.

"I hope you have a Bowie on you, little scout! Because you're sure going to need it."

Adam almost jumped at the sound of that voice. *What use is a knife against a gun?* he thought, avoiding eye contact in case Ramsey felt it and came tumbling in beneath that tree. The voice had an odd pitch to it similar to the one his dad used when they played hide-and-go-seek. The one where he had no idea where Adam was.

"Must be frightening to be lost out in the wilderness with a cold-blooded killer. But killers can be kind, little scout. They can be cruel. Which one am I?"

Adam could taste pine dust in the back of his throat and if he didn't find water soon, he'd be coughing his guts up before long. There was nothing to do but watch those roving eyes, just enough to take in every grain of detail in their periphery.

"I know what your nickname is. Night Eyes. That's what they call you."

Adam almost jumped when he heard the name, stared at the ground on which Ramsey crouched, saw the bluish tinge on each stem of grass. And then something dawned on him.

Ramsey could make out a shape against a gunmetal sky and a silver-gray moon. But he couldn't see anything against the darkness of the tree trunk. He couldn't see anything among the leaves. He couldn't see Adam at all.

TEN

It was four fifty-three when Malin switched off the headlights as they coasted along the latter end of Forest Road. Colonies of aspens bordered the track, pale as Grecian pillars and coated with warty bumps. Her eyes seemed to flick this way and that, looking for a place to park.

"There," Temeke said, spotting a small clearing about fifteen feet from a house nestled between a gravel driveway and a row of pines. His belly was complaining again and as far as he recalled, a can of refried beans was the last meal he'd had.

3265 was the last house on the right, sitting on ten acres of prime land. The front looked out on an open mesa of boulder and brush, and the back faced a stand of trees. Huge wood-framed windows and a pitched roof that slanted down towards a chimney, the house likely sat on twelve acres of private land with a barn about twenty feet away.

Temeke estimated about forty-five hundred square feet and at least a thousand of that included the wraparound deck. Like the other four, it overlooked a small lake. Unlike the other four, there were no lights on inside.

He half expected to see the barrel of a shot gun breaking through the trees, although he would have had a face full of metal to prove it. Nothing moved except a slight bend in a nearby branch to indicate a stiff wind and there was an essence about the place; a feeling of déjà vu.

Malin reversed a few feet up that bumpy track which petered out before a large white boulder. She radioed Hackett, told him they were in position, and then turned to Temeke with a scowl. "Don't think he's run off, changed his mind?"

"He's not going anywhere. Not without the money."

Temeke wasn't sure about the money, wasn't sure about the motive. He waited until four fifty-six, hoping the other cars would soon be in position with a few snipers lying about in the brush.

Malin pushed the dog's nose back into the car as she got out, eyes scanning the skies and ponytail bobbing against a dark sweater. She reached into the back seat for a ballistic vest and a thick woolen scarf. "Air's thin up here," she said.

"Probably about eight thousand feet."

"We could take the dog, you know."

"Nah. He'd need an oxygen mask."

"I'm serious. He could find Adam."

"Not until we've had a good look around. Don't want the bugger running off after a squirrel."

Temeke shrugged on a ski jacket over his vest, heard Malin mutter something about thunder.

"It's the chopper," he said, handing her some latex gloves.

He checked his gun and racked the slide. Keeping to the tree line, they sprinted towards the house, stopping occasionally to listen to the wind.

"You take the front," he said, pointing to where the deck jutted over a steep slope. "I'll cover the back."

He ducked beneath a low-hanging branch, snow trickling down his wrist, and he was conscious of the silence.

Something crunched underfoot and made him stop, made him crouch right there in the darkness and run his hands through the grass. He recognized the feel of it, a scattering of tile and some type of roofing felt, and he looked up at a small casement window that swung on a latch.

He had a flash in his mind of when he was young, when his dad came home from Vietnam. Said he captured a Viet Cong activist near Da Nang Airbase during a search and clear operation. Paid for it with half his arm. It was Kukri knife, he said. When he came home there were good times and there were bad. It was the drinking Temeke couldn't stand – the quarrels, the beatings. That was before his old man tied a rope around the mullion bar of an upper storey window and hanged himself.

Bloody miracle with only one hand, Temeke thought.

He never breathed a word of it at school, never wanted to damage his father's reputation. If indeed his poor old man had ever been to Vietnam in the first place. War destroyed people. They never came back the same.

He looked up at that roof, sensed the residue of what might have been... where Adam might have been. A warning shot fired in his head, that age-old trickle of dread. What if Adam had been in that upstairs room, crawled out of the window and broke his neck? There'd be a body around here somewhere or a freshly dug grave, which in a few days would smell like a year-old carton of milk.

Creeping on the balls of his feet, he listened to every sound. He was at the back of the house now, halfway up the steps to the porch and positioned to cut off the kidnapper's retreat.

A lantern cast an eerie beam on a set of dumbbells on the deck, neatly stacked and ranging from five to twenty-five pounds. It was the two twenty pounders that bothered him, lying at the base of a tree stump someone was using as a seat.

He held his breath, shifting from one foot to the other, back pressed against the wall. There were four wooden chairs facing that breathtaking view and the patio doors behind them were open a crack. A reading lamp inside cast a blush over a black leather chair and there were no sounds, nothing that would suggest a presence. Just the inherent feeling they were too sodding late.

Temeke heard the distant beat of rotors somewhere to the south. It was loud enough to scare an owl. The sky was a gray canopy overhead where dawn would soon shimmer on the horizon in streaks of rusty red. That big old New Mexican sun would beat down on the forest floor in a couple of hours, waking chipmunks and all kinds of chuckling things.

Malin came around the side of the house, weapon drawn, eyes flicking towards the patio door. Temeke knew it wasn't like her to waste time so they were both inside before you could count to three. The living room gave off a faint odor of cigarette smoke mingled with alcohol and musty carpets. Temeke felt right at home.

A picture window gazed out at towering trees and above them a gallery ran beneath a timbered ceiling. On the kitchen counter was a fire extinguisher and a pad of college ruled paper.

Temeke put a hand against the coffee pot. It was still warm. The remains of a chicken sandwich sat in a nest of aluminum foil and three empty beer cans had been pitched onto the lid of a trash can. There was a book propped up beside the toaster that caught his eye. *Armed & Inglorious* by Bo Kinsella.

Temeke repeated the name in his head. If he wasn't mistaken, Kinsella was a *New York Times* bestselling author and a sniper instructor. A dangerous book in the wrong hands.

He nodded at Malin and gestured towards the stairs. Edging forward, he hoped his movements weren't betrayed by a creak or two. There was a bedroom to the right, clean except for an uneaten bowl of soup on the bedside table. The quilt was tousled, pillow dented and Temeke smoothed a hand against the sheet. Cold.

The bathroom was clear except for a few strips of paper on the floor under the toilet. Temeke turned them over in his hand. Bible verse. He couldn't afford to get his hopes up, couldn't assume Adam had left them on purpose. Not all of them at the same time.

The urine was fresh, the only solid proof and it was dark orange and concentrated.

A cold draft came in through a small casement window and Temeke looked out onto the pitched roof. A patch of underlay peeked out from a crooked tile, suggesting someone might have shinned their way towards the gutter before dropping to the grass below. It would explain the broken tiles underfoot.

Each slow breath told Temeke to be vigilant but his senses said something else. He checked the remaining rooms and found them to be empty. There was not a heartbeat left in that house.

Malin stood on the landing, hand raised to distill his alarm. She signaled all clear and they holstered their guns and headed back downstairs.

"These must have fallen out of his pocket," Temeke said, handing her the Bible tracts. "Climbed out the bedroom window by the look of it. Must be scared bloody stiff."

"No sign of the kidnapper. No clothes. Nothing."

"He won't miss the drop. All those nice crisp bank notes. No, he's out there. Somewhere."

He gazed towards the picture window seeing the shadow of a cloud racing before the moon. The musty smell of rain and the loud rumble of the helicopter overhead. It was five thirty precisely.

"They're here," Malin whispered.

"Just when the boy decides to do a sodding runner."

"You ok?" She frowned, gave him a sideways look.

"I'm pissed at that thing up there making a noise and churning up every bit of dust from here to Santa Fe. I hope he can run. Lord, I hope he can run."

Temeke heard scuffing on the front deck and snatched a glance at the sliding doors. A large bird exploded from the rail where a feeder hung, wings thudding against the wind. It took off when the trees began to bend in the downdraft of the helicopter.

Temeke headed for the front door and peered outside. Up there in the sky was a big gray belly and skids, and rotors that drowned out his thoughts. A duffel bag thudded to the ground about thirty feet from the cabin door, bouncing twice before rolling to a stop.

He heard an echo, then heard the changing pitch of the helicopter engine as it lifted, banking to the left and rotor blades clawing for the sky. It was the acrid oil and smoke that bothered him. He couldn't see what had caused it, not immediately.

The bag drove him outside and a shot from the woods. The helicopter seemed to buck like a horse with a throaty roar as bullets pinged off the tail boom and sparks lit up the sky. It was the one that ripped through fuel tank that brought it down, flames and shrapnel streaking through the trees. Like a great beast that had lost the battle to live, it lurched to one side, rotors pinned into the earth and squealing out a death rattle.

Instinct made Temeke reach for the fire extinguisher before running towards the wreckage. He was almost twenty feet away when he saw the flash, heard the explosion and his legs buckled at the tremor. The rain was coming down hard now, droplets patting the top of his bald head and trickling down his back. It was hot, too damned hot.

The helicopter lay in the brush on the opposite side of the track. Smoke trailed upwards into the sky and then the flames dimed to a ghostly amber.

It took him a few seconds to breathe again, heat searing his cheeks. He could hear Malin behind him, shouting for him to stay down.

He covered his face, lungs burning from the smoke, could barely see the blackened co-pilot through the shattered glass on the flight deck still belted to his seat. There was another officer on the ground tangled in a burning clump of box elder.

"Danny," he murmured.

It was Danny Michael wasn't it? Blond hair, stocky build, worked up at Twin Hawks regional airport. He'd met him over a month ago when they airlifted serial killer Ole Eriksen from the Tolby Ranch. Now he was motionless, face melting like a wax doll.

The tingling came first and then the pressure in his chest. Temeke tasted the acrid bile in the back of his throat before he vomited.

He hardly felt Malin's strong arms pulling him back into the trees away from the smoke, shouting things he couldn't hear.

He perched on the front bumper of the car trying to catch his breath and staring at a tangled frame of tail and struts. The debris had settled in a quarter-mile strip and sporadic fires flickered across the plain. He coughed again, tongue swollen and neck crawling with ash.

"Thank you," Temeke said between coughs. He couldn't stand. Couldn't feel his legs either. "Call Hackett, love. We're going after him."

"Yes, sir," Malin stuttered, fumbling for her radio.

Temeke heard her relay the terrible code for *officers down... all patrols respond*. He could hear her sobbing through one hand, the other pressing the radio to her chest. And then he remembered the drop.

"The bag," he wheezed. "Get the sodding bag!"

Hand over mouth, she shuffled forward a step or two.

"Anything?" Temeke said.

It was the words he was dreading, the words he knew she would say.

"It's gone."

ELEVEN

Something big fell out of the sky, and the explosion, when it came, brought Adam to his knees. He lay in a clump of wet leaves against the slope at the back of the house, watching a spire of gray smoke as it climbed above the trees. Then a whump of flames, sparks spitting onto the dead brown earth.

It was then he remembered the shot. A loud echo somewhere to the left of him where the wood glowed an angry red and something broke through the smoke on the crest of the hill. A face so pale against a tree, it was as if the man it belonged to had already died once and come back to life. His hands were wrapped around the polished stock of a rifle that glinted red in a flash of firelight. He cowered over that gun like he was coughing, or loading it, or something. And then he looked up at the flames and scuttled off sideways like a crab into the darkness.

It wasn't Ramsey. Too old for that.

Even though Adam's senses were jumbled, his gut reaction told him to stay down and watch, as he tried to steel himself to remember what was at stake. From where he was lying, he could see the back of the house. There should have been firefighters swarming towards it and police cars drifting in along that chalk white track. Nothing. Except the sound of a bellow. A war cry.

Adam stayed where he was, rain peppering his back,

cheek pressed against wet leaves. He couldn't think, couldn't move. It seemed like minutes before he crawled to the ridge of that slope and that was because he was cold. Peering over the summit, he squinted at a ball of fire in the scrubland several yards from the house, rotors poking out of the wreckage and the terrible smell of gas.

A flicker of movement to the left and a man powered through boulder and brush like a wild animal, limbs pumping with exceptional grace. He stooped and hooked something large over his shoulder before sprinting back the way he had come.

Ramsey.

Despite the risk Adam took, in keeping his head up, he knew he was safe in the darkness, clothes melding with the gray-green leaves. Even Ramsey stood like a frozen figurine about ten yards to his left, studying the fire through lifeless eyes.

Adam stretched out his legs, muscles trembling. If only trees didn't shed twigs and other noisy things he could have crept through the patio doors to the back of the house without being heard. He felt tired, unusually sleepy, as if all the energy had seeped from his body. *You're just hungry that's all. Should have eaten that bowl of soup. It wasn't poisoned. It wasn't drugged. It was good. Solid. Food.*

He thought he heard something then. Voices. Perhaps it was just the rain. He lifted himself a little higher, knees pressed into the ground. Measuring the distance between him and Ramsey, he reckoned he could make a run for it without being shot, reckoned he would be swallowed up in that smoky light. Just as he lifted one knee, he saw the sudden tilt of Ramsey's head.

He was hunkered down over there, elbows resting on his knees and mouth slightly open as if he was tasting the smoke. The eerie sound of flames crackled over the wind and a burning branch crashed onto the forest floor.

He turned at the sound, seeming to weigh it up in his mind before slipping back into the shadows.

Adam drew a deep breath. This was his chance. There was no sense in waiting. Not now that Ramsey was nowhere to be seen. Energized by hope, he took a running step, twigs snapping underfoot. He would have shouted loudly if it hadn't been for the foul taste of a rolled up bandana in his open mouth and the tight cinching behind his head. He didn't have to turn around. He knew who it was.

"Don't move!" Ramsey squeezed that gag for all it was worth and, gripping Adam by the shoulders, he swiveled him around. It was a raised finger that told Adam to be quiet, the other was clamped around his wrists.

Ramsey's hair was tied in short ponytail and his face was streaked with mud, eyes glaring in the rusty glow of the fire. The hump of a backpack peeked over one shoulder and a small axe hung from a shock cord.

"Someone out there," he said, looking over at the wreckage. "Sooner have the contraband on board that chopper than save the dumbass flying it. If you shout, he'll kill us."

Adam looked down at a gallon jug tied to the backpack bouncing against Ramsey's thigh. He could hear the slop of water in it and he swallowed.

"Moonshine," Ramsey said with a grin. "Want some?"

Adam shook his head, eyes falling to the ground. There was a duffel bag nestled against Ramsey's foot with a Police patch embroidered on the side.

"Things we might need," Ramsey said as if he could read his mind. "There's an old man in these woods. Tortures boys. It's a slow death."

For a long moment Adam stared into those narrow eyes and he began to feel queasy. Like the queasy he felt when he saw Ramsey for the first time. He felt the hand loosen at his wrists, saw it hover over the pistol in Ramsey's belt.

"He tied a kid up to a tree a few years ago. Cut him real deep. Left him for the wolves. Want to see what he did to him?"

Adam shook his head. He already imagined a skeleton in the woods with tattered clothing hanging off its bones and eye sockets picked clean by birds. He wanted to shout, to scream, anything to raise an alarm. He was muzzled like a dog and all he could do was struggle against strong arms, kicking and punching thin air until he was exhausted. The bandana pinched his lips and his jaw felt sore from all that clenching.

Ramsey began to cuss. Told him to stop whimpering. Took off that backpack and the coat he was wearing and wrenched Adam's hands through one sleeve and then the other. He pulled the zipper up to Adam's throat. It was warm in that coat even though it was two sizes too big.

"Be quiet. You can breathe can't you?" Ramsey looked dead serious when he said it. Looked like he was afraid of something. "You don't understand. If he finds you, he'll kill you. Probably eat you and all."

Adam took a deep breath and made his mind up to stay quiet. The forest began to seem smaller with trees bending in and out, and he tried to fend off a wave of nausea at the fetid stench of fumes and something sweet. If it wasn't for the cold, he knew he would have vomited.

Ramsey hauled the backpack on again over a thick sweater and picked up the gym bag. "Let's go."

Adam felt strong fingers around his arm, gripping, dragging, steering through the trees. He heard Ramsey's voice, thick and grating and warm against his ear.

"Don't look back."

TWELVE

Malin tried to look away; tried not to look at the charred remains of the officers. The mesa seemed alive with all that popping and sizzling and she could see the tremor of fuel in the air. It wasn't until now when she caught a sweet and putrid stench that she realized it had really happened. Covering her face with her scarf, she walked with Temeke towards the car. He put an arm around her, told her there was nothing they could do.

The dog was sitting on the front seat. It was the howling that got to Malin, that baleful sound like the animal could smell death. Like he knew exactly whose remains were in that thick clinging undergrowth. He whined when he saw her, and shook his big black head.

"Whatever you do, don't let him out," Temeke said.

"He's on a leash," Malin muttered. She didn't need to be told something as basic as that.

"When you radioed Hackett, what did you tell him?" Temeke bunched up Adam's tee shirt and pressed it under Murphy's nose.

"He asked if we had detained the suspect. I said no." Malin hated giving him the next piece of news. "He told us not to go after him. Told us to wait."

She heard Temeke give a long drawn out sigh and she knew how he felt. Every minute was too precious to waste on top of those they'd already lost.

"I can't stand around and watch this, Marl." Temeke

covered his nose. He didn't want to smell it either.

He turned on his radio. All they could hear was friendly static and then a few snarls from the chief.

"Seen them yet… crazy-ass fools. I told Temeke not to go after him. But no… He only had to flash his headlights and now he's dead. Do you know how much it costs to train a detective? Ninety-eight grand, so they tell me. All gone up in smoke. It's those damn Indians I'm telling you…"

The crackling cut out a string of cuss words and the radio terminated abruptly. There was nothing they could do but sit and wait, watch the flames and the sparks as they curled into the night sky.

Malin felt a surge of nausea, making her want to double over and puke right there and then. It was Temeke's shaking head that kept her standing, trying to keep her from falling apart. At strange times such as these, she studied those long limbs, the broad-shoulders and the dark skin. The impressive aquiline features made her wonder if he had a dash of German blood in his veins.

"He might even dedicate a park bench to me now that I'm gone." Temeke said, pressing a stick of gum on his tongue and chewing vigorously. "In memory of Detective David Temeke who hated the police department and everyone in it. You can already hear 'Taps' being played and my final dispatch."

Malin knew he was trying to humor her, to keep her mind off the dead officers. But it wasn't funny. The stench under her nose wouldn't go away and her hands were black from the dirt on her face. It must have been the same for him.

All of a sudden Temeke's striking face and prominent cheekbones were only inches from hers. He pressed a bottle of water in her hand, told her to drink up.

The barn was ablaze, flames licking the sky and leaning dangerously towards the house. The fuselage seemed no bigger than a school bus from where they stood, rotors and tail had broken away and there was nothing left but a blackened hull.

Murphy began to bark, ears pricked, claws clacking on the consol. Then he jumped off the passenger seat and barreled between them towards the trees. The leash snapped between her fingers and plowed through the undergrowth after him. She wasn't fast enough to grab it.

Temeke shouted at her to run. It was downhill all the way through the trees and soft springy earth. He was fast. Like a deer. It was hard to keep up, hard to take a breath. Harder still not to feel beaten before they'd even started.

She felt abandoned on a narrow path that led through a tunnel of trees, shimmering orange from the fire up there. After a few more yards downhill, a crisp wind struck her full in the face, bringing tears to her eyes. There was a ridge on the far side scattered with pale boulders and sparse scrub, and a stunted row of pine saplings in between.

Behind her, red sparks shuddered and died in the sky and in front were a cluster of furry-topped shrubs. She could hear things. An owl, a coyote, something burrowing under a pile of leaves. Adam was out there, lost, maybe injured in a fall. She sure hoped he was still alive. Hoped he was warm.

There was a clearing about ten feet to her right and a path that cut a way through it. Beyond that was utter darkness until a crisscross of beams lit up the forest floor about twenty feet to the north. It was probably the follow team, a contingent of rangers and county personnel armed with shotguns and semi-automatics, announcing their presence to every living creature in the forest. It was nearly five forty-five.

Leaning against a tree she doubled over to catch her breath, heard a flutter of wings and froze. There was something hovering over the tree tops. An eagle perhaps. And then it was gone. She had no idea what she was dealing with. A psycho run-away grimy like a street addict, or a smooth-talking con man in a freshly laundered shirt. She couldn't decide which was worse.

The rain stopped. Just a light pattering on the leaves and the howling of wind in her ears. She stood still and cocked her head this way and that. She could smell smoke and tree sap, and she heard the crackling of twigs behind her and the sound of a radio.

"Darker than the crypts of hell down here," Temeke said, holding up a leash with a sagging collar. "And there's not a pervert or a stiff in sight. Imagine what that's going to do to this month's crime figures."

"Where's Murphy?"

"Ran after a bleeding bird." There was a moment of silence before Temeke said anything else. "I'll be buggered if I'm going after him."

"Which way did he go?"

"North." Temeke let out a vapor of hot air as he climbed back up the slope. "He must have picked up a scent."

"Dogs aren't like homing pigeons, sir. It's not like he's going to come back and tell us where Adam is."

"No, but a man, a boy and a dog isn't a sight you'd easily forget." Temeke looked north along that path and gave a deep sigh. "Hackett wants us back at the house, remember? So not a word about the dog."

"But—"

"Not a word!"

That's when she heard that infernal squeal rising and falling in the distance, light bars flashing blue and red over a clump of sagebrush and the plaint of an ambulance siren. A drift of sand seemed to follow the cars like someone had blown dust off a pile of old books, and she watched a large black SUV nose its way up the dirt track and park a few feet in front of them.

Hackett was out first followed by Captain Fowler and Officer Jarvis. Fowler nodded briefly to Temeke and then peered at Malin. He sniggered behind a hand, mutter something about seeing better markings on a raccoon. She'd get him back later.

A few more heavies thudded across the plain, weaving in and out of the flaming brush and keeping to the perimeter. Some wore helmets and flak vests, and some were marksmen and dog handlers headed towards the trees.

Hackett pressed a scarf to his nose, eyes blinking furiously behind the half-moon glasses as they focused on Malin first and then Temeke.

"I was worried about you," Hackett said and he looked it. "Nasty business. Two good damn good pilots. See anything, hear anything?"

"Four shots coming from those trees," Temeke said. "Sounded like a bolt action, sir. Should be some spent cartridges around here somewhere."

Hackett glanced at the trees and narrowed his eyes. "Where's the bag?"

"At a guess, I would say it's with our kidnapper, sir." Temeke kept chewing on that gum. "Impossible to be precise about the circumstances. It was there one minute and gone the next."

"Where was it exactly?"

"Over there," said Malin, pointing at a position about fifteen feet from the trees. She was still grasping her chest. "In front of that sapling."

"Can we have some light over here," shouted Hackett, marching towards a broken twig which had turned black with ash. Five torch beams homed in on the area, exploring every blade of grass and then slithering up the trees, through the trees, beyond the trees.

"Is that wise, sir, signaling our intentions?" Temeke muttered, crossing his arms.

Hackett took no notice and answered a shout from the house. EMTs had arrived on the scene, picking their way through the glowing debris, and five Shadow Wolf officers, Navajo by the look of them – tough, persistent trackers who could go well into a week without failing. The tallest of the five ran towards Hackett and nodded. Introduced himself as Running Hawk.

"The missing subject is a twelve-year-old male." Hackett said, describing weight and height. "You're looking for a size nine track, Vans canvas lace-ups with a waffle outsole. His mom said he's heavier on the left side. Scout uniform, so he'll blend nicely with the trees…"

Temeke ushered Malin into the house and they were in the kitchen in less than a minute. A young field investigator sealed up a pile of evidence bags next to what appeared to be a urine sample. His badge revealed his name to be Matt Black. "Found that in the toilet," he said with a slight stutter, pointing a blue latex finger at the jar.

"Very good," said Hackett, hurrying in through the front door and stamping the snow off his feet. "Anything else?"

"There was this." Black pointed at what looked like a few taped off blood spatters on the carpet.

Temeke raised one hand. "I think you'll find that's a dab of Ketchup, son, on account of the chicken sandwich over there."

Fowler snorted. Jarvis cackled. Black cleared his throat and shuffled his feet. He placed the urine sample a few inches to the right of the evidence bags and then changed his mind and put it on the left. He spoke to

Hackett but didn't look at him.

"There was something else," he murmured.

Hackett's chin rolled forward straining to hear and he shushed Fowler to be quiet. "What is it?"

"We found a receipt in a trash can."

Hackett took the evidence bag and raised it above his nose as if examining a suspect dollar bill. The paper inside was yellowish and ragged at the edges. He read off the item number, the date and the location. "Looks like a steel camping axe with a fourteen inch handle."

"The Shadow Wolves will have plenty to track him with," Temeke chimed in, seeing a sea of frowns. "Whoever took Adam will be cutting a few branches down to make a campfire."

Hackett pointed at the rising sun through the kitchen window and said, "Just for your information, Governor Bendish called at the crack of dawn. Wanted to know how the search was going. Had to tell him there are two dead men under a pile of twisted metal and no sign of the Mayor's son. He's going to expect a report on the investigation later this morning."

"And the local rag?" Temeke asked.

"Another press conference tomorrow."

THIRTEEN

Adam's feet hardly touched the old footpath that descended down into the valley, shoes thumping against loose rock. They plunged deeper into the forest where fir saplings seemed to spring up from dense mounds of last year's leaves.

North, it seemed. Away from the lake and deeper in, where branches arched above them like the ribs of a cathedral ceiling. Within those natural aisles and pillars, he could almost imagine high towers and pit houses with the words *Tarahuma* engraved on the spandrel. If only he could summon the dreadful Chief with his long black hair and crown of goose feathers. They said he could kill with those sharp black eyes.

They stopped for a while and Adam felt Ramsey loosen the bandana behind his head and ease it out of his mouth. The water jug was only half-full and Adam paused before a gruff voice told him it wasn't moonshine. Just good old water.

"Where are we going?" Adam whimpered.

"Stay close," Ramsey said, pulling a windbreaker out of his backpack to keep the rain off, "because he's following us."

"Who?"

Ramsey pulled the bandana back in Adam's mouth, raised a finger and gave him a look. "Rogue ranger."

It seemed like hours before a thin shaft of sunlight

pierced a distant cloud and the rain became little more than a rhythmic patter. They stopped to pee among a cluster of saplings and it was brown and stung real bad. Adam was dehydrated all right. And hungry.

He fumbled in his pocket as they set off again, took the compass out. The housing had shattered and the bearing needles were nowhere to be found. It must have happened when he jumped off the roof. He began to drop bits on the path until there was nothing left of it.

He had no idea in which direction they were headed, nor how many hours they had walked through springy beds of pine needles and rust-colored dirt. Down one minute, up the next, and now walking along a ridge with a seventy foot drop on one side.

It stopped raining then, barely a patter against the padded jacket he wore, and his hands were warm in the sleeves.

He heard the rush of water as they came round the bend, felt the cold spray against his face, saw the head of a great waterfall in the last rays of a sinking sun.

"Just a little further," Ramsey said. And then, "There it is."

They camped that night on Devil's Elbow—a sharp bend on the crest of a ridge. Ramsey said there was no such place on the map, just a name the prospectors once called it.

"There's a hole someone blasted down there," Ramsey said, hauling out a green canvas tube from his backpack.

He took out a few sachets of hot chocolate and marshmallows, and he had a bag of vegetables too.

"There's pyrite and goethite in the tailings," he said. "We can take a look later if you like."

Ramsey would kill him down there against the shingle where roots grew from the ground like long spiny fingers. He'd shoot him between the eyes or ram his head against a boulder. One would be painful. The other quick.

Ramsey removed the bandana from Adam's mouth. "Make a sound and it goes back on," he whispered.

Adam wiped the spittle from his chin. "You're going to kill me, aren't you?"

Ramsey cocked his head and gave a bitter smile. "This isn't about killing—"

"What then?"

Ramsey opened and closed his mouth as if struggling to find the right words. "It's about a journey I took. About what I left behind."

"I want to go home."

"You will."

"When?"

Ramsey's face was blank under those muddy streaks, eyes glistening like he had pieces of grit in them. It made him look like a zebra, made him blend with the shadows.

"Things bad at home?" he said. "'Cause they can be, you know. Parents fighting over who knows what. A slap here, a tear there."

Adam almost nodded. He knew exactly how that felt. Like he'd wake up one day and find the house empty because of all that shrilling. But he caught himself before it was too late. Killers sometimes lured you into their confidence before they hacked you up and threw your bones into a shallow grave.

"How long are we going to stay here?"

"A few days. I'll teach you stuff. Teach you how to read the wind, how to track."

There was something in Ramsey's eyes that told him what he needed to know, oval with a few laugh lines in the corner. Reading people was something he was good at, especially when he had to choose a study partner at school.

Sometimes he was wrong. But not often.

Ramsey gave a deep sigh, gripped his chest with one hand. "My heart. Skips a beat now and then. Got a tear in it because it was broken once. I hope you never end up like me. A drifter, you know. I'll teach you to survive out here and we'll give ourselves names. They've got to be good names."

"What names?"

"Operation Gray Fox, that's who we are. I'll be Gray Fox. You'll be Night Eyes."

Adam liked the sound of two guys out in the woods with code names nobody had ever heard of. It was dangerous, he told himself. Only the big guys did this type of thing and he was hanging with one of them.

"How do you know my nickname?" he asked.

"Ah… let's say, you're very well known. Famous."

Adam liked the sound of that too. His scout group had been on the news twice that year for service projects. One was making bird feeders for a care home in Rio Rancho. Maybe they had singled him out. His bird feeder was at least two stories, a fieldstone design with a red front door.

Ramsey told Adam to stop daydreaming and pour water in a metal pot; told him to collect a pile of dry stickseed and bark; showed him how to use that axe, and how to clean it too.

Adam thought he seemed almost normal then, like Wendover at scouts.

He stared at the brown earthy clearing under the tallest trees he had ever seen. It was dry and out of the wind, and they could look down at the frothing waterfall and hear the rumble it made. There were pine needles and twigs and stripped bark to burn, and he collected a handful for the fire.

"You said there was an old man following us?" he asked, burdened by the thick jacket he was wearing. "Won't he see the flames?"

Ramsey slipped the knife from his thigh and crouched. He cleared away the pine needles with his hands and a section of topsoil. "Won't see flames. Won't see much smoke either. Not if we dig a hole."

"Does he really eat men? I mean, I thought cannibals lived in New Guinea."

"Some say the Anasazi were cannibals. Could be their descendants in these very woods."

Adam knew that wasn't true. The *ancient ones* were a desert culture, fishing and hunting small game and birds. They built sunken structures with rock and mansions in the cliffs. If he was lucky, he might even see the chief he made up in his head.

Tarahuma… hunter, gatherer, warrior.

"I think I saw him near the house," Adam said. "He was all thin and white. Had a rifle too."

"Skin gets like that when it's not washed. I already told you. He's a rogue ranger."

Ramsey was busy carving a hole about twelve inches in diameter going in deeper, going in wider. His face was stern, not a flicker of amusement on that tight-lipped mouth. He didn't mention the rifle either. Just made a vent about six inches to the left and connected it to the main hole.

"Tomorrow," Ramsey said, "we'll fill it in, leave a layer of pine needles on the top. Can't track us then. Tactical clean-up. Didn't they teach you that in scouts?"

Adam lifted his chin and stuck his chest out a bit. "They teach us how a compass works, how to orient a map."

"And you're trustworthy, loyal–"

"Helpful, friendly, courteous, kind, obedient, cheerful, thrifty, brave, clean and reverent," Adam chimed.

"Very good. You'll be doing the clean-up tomorrow."

A tarp went down and a tent went up in less than a

minute, a pop-up with enough room for two. Ramsey threw the duffel bag in with a couple of blankets and a blue leather-bound book.

After hacking a few small logs, he made a fire and burned it all down to a pile of red hot embers, balanced the pot on a wooden bridge, and left it to boil.

Adam looked up through the trees, too tall to catch fire and too tall to climb. He could hear the chatter of birds and the rustle of leaves. There was no way out now. Not unless he had a compass.

"How long will the water take?" Adam said, hands raised to the heat.

"Depends on the weather, the altitude."

It wasn't long before the water bubbled and Ramsey wadded up some dried leaves to grip the rim.

"My dad uses pliers when he doesn't have a pot holder," Adam said.

Ramsey lifted one eyebrow, looked like he was going to smile only he didn't. "Your dad's a smartass then."

Adam felt the tightness in his jaw. "He's a badass."

Ramsey bobbed his head, gave a half smile. Poured hot water in a couple of tin cups, filled them with a sachet each of hot chocolate and a marshmallow.

"There's tea bags in the pack. Coffee if you prefer. And if you think of running, I will find you." Then he stalked back into the shadows for more wood.

Adam wasn't going anywhere, not with that rogue ranger hiding in the woods. He kept looking behind him through the trees, kept wondering how fast an old man could run. If he had a limp like his grandpa once had it wouldn't be fast because old people had arthritis to slow them down.

It was only a few minutes and Ramsey was back again, stomping this time like he was fresh out of patience. He took a bag out of his pocket, poured something in his hand and began to chew it.

Adam lit a hurricane lamp which he hung inside the tent. It creaked a bit in the wind casting an eerie glow over the guttering embers. He coaxed what was left of the fire with a stick and wondered if the light would attract the rogue ranger.

"He won't come here," Ramsey said, spitting a brown ball of mucus from his mouth. "Fortunately, we lost him a few miles back."

"How do you know?"

"I just know."

And then Adam saw it again. A shimmer of a smile on those sallow cheeks, the dimple on his chin. He watched those fingers as they rolled a smoke. Watched the lips as they took a hit.

"It's for the pain," Ramsey said, tapping his chest with two fingers.

"Are you sick?"

"The pills take away the worst of it. Wouldn't want to be in hospital. Rather be free, rather be in the fresh air when I die."

Adam wondered how old he was if he was talking about dying. Asked him if he believed in God because the world was coming to an end.

Ramsey just shook his head, made a growling sound with his throat.

"There's going to be a battle," Adam said. "A big one. Bad people get trampled like grapes and there's lots of blood. Horses will be swimming in it all the way up to their bridles."

"Bunch of fairy tales."

"It's true. Mom says we need to watch for that prowling lion... not the mountain kind." Adam sipped that hot chocolate and wiped a coating of marshmallow from his lips.

"Better learn how to shoot and use a knife then," Ramsey muttered. "Better turn in before it rains."

That night they watched a fork of lightning on the horizon and a sheet of rain that hung under a cloud blowing across the valley. They huddled in their blankets to keep warm, eating dried crackers and beef jerky and a good cup of tea.

It was cozy in the tent with that hurricane lamp. Warm too. Adam lay on his back with his eyes half open, listening to the rattle of rain against the leaves. He didn't know why, but he wasn't scared any more.

"Hit the rack," Ramsey said, tilting that blue leather book towards the lamp.

"What are you reading?"

"Nothing."

"Doesn't look like nothing."

"Well, it is nothing. You wouldn't like it. Probably wouldn't understand it."

"I read *The Hobbit*."

"And that makes you smart?" Ramsey rolled on his side and put the book between them.

He looked up occasionally with those oval eyes and then he'd look back down, finger underlining each word. "Want me to read some?"

Adam didn't really care. But it was polite to nod.

Ramsey cleared his throat. It was a deep whispering voice when it came, kinder than before.

"She always liked it when I brushed her hair. It was thick and dark, and in the sunshine there was red in it. I remember a song once about a girl with nut brown hair. Can't remember who sang it. But she liked it. Sometimes hummed it when she thought I wasn't listening. We'd pick muscles off the sea bed when the tide was low, poke at the lobster pots and watch the sunset. We'd watch the boats and try to guess what type of sails they had. I don't know what part of her I loved the best. Her voice, her skin, her smile. Probably everything. I liked the way she looked at me. Made me feel special. Made me feel."

Adam liked the words, liked the soft resonance of Ramsey's voice. He could see a girl and a boy staring out to sea and he could see a fat-bellied ship with sails tightly trimmed and close to the wind. It put him to sleep.

FOURTEEN

Temeke fought to clear his head and smothered another yawn. Reluctantly, he hauled himself up from the nice warm bed and had a nose around. Sleeping in the cells was the only option when you're dead tired in the small hours and your house is cold and cheerless. And your sodding car won't start.

At least he had someone to talk to during the morning shifts when one of the admins woke him up with a cup of fresh coffee. It was Tuesday, and he could still smell the stench of slag and cinders under his nose no matter how many times he washed his face.

He padded up the stairs to his second floor office, carrying his shoes in one hand. Malin was listening to a recording of the kidnapper's voice and her eyebrows shot up when she saw him. "Do you ever answer your phone?"

"It's on silence, love. A bloke's got to get some sleep. Five hours I got this time. Bloody miracle."

"Officer Running Hawk called Hackett this morning since he couldn't get hold of you. Said they traced Adam's phone near the cabin. Not a scratch on it. Sent it to Flossy at Fingerprinting."

Temeke stood in front of the window, eyes following a droplet of rain on the glass. It was the view of the back parking lot that always fascinated him. Tattered gray trees dusted with snow and the distant hills of Santa Fe beyond—a view you couldn't see in the summer. And thirty black and white units arranged in tidy rows all except Hackett's. His was parked at an angle and taking up two spaces so it wouldn't get dinged.

The tape murmured on in the background and he hardly gave it another thought. The good news was Lieutenant Luis Alvarez was coming back to work in a week. Temeke couldn't wait to see his brother-in-law, couldn't wait to have a few pints at lunch. Might get a few nuggets of gossip out about his soon to be ex-wife. Serena was hiding again. And that's what bothered him.

"That voice," he began, turning his mind back to the tape, "doesn't sound threatening."

"Thick and gravelly," Malin said, tapping the screen of her phone.

He noticed her words tail off, eyes flicking to one side. "What?"

"The voice… it sounds familiar. Like the one on the Evan Trader tape. It's the same rhythm, the same pauses. I'll have it checked."

Malin was good with voices. About as good as he was with names. Temeke kept replaying the voice in his head, a voice that demanded three hundred grand in ransom. It was deep now she mentioned it.

Lost and found. He's with me. Three hundred grand in ransom, half in hundreds, half in small denominations. Better not be sequenced or the boy's dead.

It was Mrs. Oliver's response before the call ended that puzzled Temeke. *I understand…* It sounded too calm, resigned, and not the desperate pleading he expected. He thought Captain Fowler had instructed her on how to talk to the kidnapper, to get proof Adam was still alive.

There were photographs of Bill Oliver on Malin's desk. Hard but happy features and a deeply lined brow. It reminded Temeke of a wooden plaque he had at home where you could tell the age of the tree by counting the growth rings.

Malin looked pale. Or perhaps it was the light. He asked her why she was so glum, whether she'd finished typing the report. She said something about working late into the night, hadn't quite finished it yet. Said she was worried about Adam. Prayed for him too. But Temeke knew that wasn't all she was worried about, judging by the phone in her hand.

"What's up?" he said, turning to look at a face that was determined to remain passive.

"Hollister," she said, blowing out another sigh and dropping the phone face-down on her desk. "He keeps messaging me. Won't pick up the phone."

Temeke often wondered why Malin took him into her confidence, why she felt the need to tell him all the gory details. And why did his face always go rigid with fury at the mention of Hollister's name? She should have been writing that report instead of fawning over top brass. "On the computer?"

"Yes, on the computer."

"It's quiet when it's on the computer," he said. "No one can hear."

"It's not the first time."

"How many times?"

"Six, seven. I don't know. And he won't text."

"Maybe his old lady checks the phone. She wouldn't know where to look on the computer."

"He doesn't have an old lady." She gave him a tight-lipped look and crossed her arms. They didn't stay crossed for long. Couldn't drink that cappuccino with her arms crossed. "You think I could do better?" she said, slurping a mouthful of froth.

"There's always Jarvis," he generously offered. "He seems to spend a great deal of time loitering outside the women's toilets and I don't think he's after a safety pin."

"He's a pig!"

He stole a glance at her and reveled in her discomfort.

"Did you see the book?" he said, changing the subject and pouring a shot of coffee into a plastic cup. The lights flickered on and off as a bolt of lightning lit the skies and rain pounded on a darkened parking lot. He was glad he was inside. He hoped the villains were too. "The one on the kitchen counter in the cabin?"

Malin held her coffee in a death grip and gave him one of those of-course-I-did looks. She was too smart to have missed it.

"Let me ask you something," he said, knuckling one eye and yawning. "What type of man reads books on tactical warfare?"

"FBI, CIA, SAS, ATF… a hunter brushing up on his technique."

Temeke took a few sips of his coffee. It always tasted bitter like the last few dregs from a well-stewed pot. No wonder Malin got hers from the Double Barrel coffee shop on Coors, only hers came with a designer price tag. "Why Adam?"

"Why any kid? Sometimes it's random."

"This kid wasn't out walking in the woods, or jogging in a park. He was at home. Whoever took him knew his every move. He even bought a truck in a false name. Intent is what that is."

Malin stared down at her coffee, forehead a frown. "A disgruntled staff member who didn't get his bonus check. You want to hope he was wearing a mask."

"So Adam wouldn't be able to identify him? It's not that kind of kidnap, Marl."

"He'll kill him then, won't he?"

"He doesn't care about bloody masks. No, this one was well planned, probably planned for years. It's more than a truck bought in a false name, more than money."

Temeke took a cigarette out of his pocket and let it dangle between his lips in flagrant defiance of the 'no smoking' sign. "Aristotle once said 'We make war that we may live in peace.' Words like that should be written here above the front door."

"We've got enough graffiti on the front door," Hackett interrupted, craning his head in from the corridor. "Northwest Area Command is beginning to look like an apocalyptic ruin!"

"Any news, sir?" Temeke asked, shoving the cigarette in his top pocket and hoping for a few hits at break time. Hackett looked worried. Good. He'd give him something to be worried about.

"News? Oh, yeah, there's news. Two dead officers and helicopter peppered with shot made the front page in the *Journal*. Some idiot leaked it to the press before I did and now the public thinks it's a bomb. Fowler called in half an hour ago. Still no sign of Adam. Said the Field Investigator's report noted a big black dog lolloping about in the woods."

"I'd just like to make an observation, sir. Half the dogs in the police department are big and black."

Hackett sighed loudly and removed his jacket. His armpits were already dark with sweat. "Fowler said he found a set of tracks leading to a waterfall. That's before his flashlight ran out of batteries."

"A set, sir? It's important see. A set defines one person."

"He thinks they were human."

"Course that would be difficult to see without a flashlight and we don't want him falling down a hole like Alice in bloody Wonderland."

Hackett took off his glasses and began to polish

them. "You might also be interested to know he found a human jawbone. Fresh it was."

"Tell him to call me when he finds the rest."

"Very droll, Temeke," Hackett pressed on, readjusting his glasses and his smile. "Where Fowler's concerned, might be time you buried the hatchet."

"I'm not really sold on the idea, sir, not after he made a racist remark at the Christmas party. He wanted to shoot my brains out then. I expect you would have called that friendly fire."

"If you're referring to a certain disciplinary letter, I changed my mind. Fowler doesn't deserve suspension. He deserves a medal. I've already received his preliminary report from last night. Where's yours?"

"Why's Captain Fowler leading this case? What's he got that I haven't?"

"Tact, seniority, contacts. Hasn't rubbed up the District Attorney the wrong way or the Chief of Police."

"You've got an unnaturally soft spot for him, sir. Better watch that soft spot. Might go raw in a day or two."

The daft old bugger wasn't going to let it go, kept on with a drone of morale-boosting words that Fowler was forensics' favorite. Criminalistics' too. Fowler was a snappy dresser, had far too many shiny things on that polyester shirt. And who wears gold cufflinks with a uniform?

"Isn't he supposed to be studying crime reports in that nice plush office of his? You know, record-keeping, logs, budgets."

"I've asked him to supervise the investigation with the help of those Navajo boys."

"Shadow Wolf officers I think they're called, sir."

"I'm asking you to interview the witnesses. Is that understood?"

"Yes, sir." Temeke's cell phone gave a little cough

in his pocket and he checked the screen. Serena.

He would have taken it if Hackett hadn't been firing a salvo of insults from that overworked mouth of his. Something about the Impact Sergeant being off sick twice this month and how lucky it was he'd finally managed to drag his sorry ass in to work this morning.

"He can't keep dining out on the same excuse," Hackett whispered. "It was his daughter who was kidnapped, not him."

"How would you feel if your daughter had been molested by a man ten years her senior and just before Christmas? Lucky we caught the disgusting sod. Lucky we found her an all. Oh, I forgot. You had a minor for a girlfriend once. Seventeen wasn't she?"

That brought on a lip tremor and a flapping hand. "You dare tell a soul, Temeke. And you," he said, jutting his chin at Malin. "I promise you—"

"You'll melt my badge and pour liquid metal down my jocks. Got it, sir."

It was always the same warning, always the same secret, and the only sensational thing Temeke had on Hackett worth a promotion or two. Lucky Hackett's wife never found out about that little indiscretion.

The droning of Hackett's voice came on like a Japanese torture: *drip, drip, drip* in his ear. Hot, cheesy breath slithering its way into his Eustachian tube, coiling into the back of his brain and out the other side.

Temeke's mind wandered to Luis Alvarez, who had been in hospital from a gunshot wound to his head. Lucky for him, the damage was a torn up ear and now he looked like a scrawny dog from the pound. Temeke had gone to bring him home and ended up having a screaming row with Serena in the lobby, told her he wouldn't sign those damn divorce papers unless she killed him first. Even gave her his gun. It was all bollocks of course. He couldn't sign anything if he was dead.

Serena didn't know how badly things had been going; officers' complaints about his treatment of suspects, even a transgender male had sued for police brutality claiming Temeke had lifted his skirt. All right, maybe he had been a little overenthusiastic, but he had found a big pouch of crack underneath that skirt.

Hackett's snapping fingers brought him back to the present. "You'll be interviewing all staff members this week starting with the Mayor's wife. Sergeant Moran spoke to her on the phone, said she was all freaked out, wouldn't speak to Fowler. Said he was a jerk."

"Nice to see someone has taste."

"I would have agreed until I found out she wanted to talk to you." Hackett squeezed out a smile and lowered his voice. "Why do they always want to talk to you? And without an attorney? For crying out loud, you were practically fired from District 2."

Temeke didn't want to discuss his short tenure with the LVPD. There had been an unfortunate incident at Immaculate Conception College for girls, an exclusive private school for the filthy rich. One eleventh grader insisted she'd seen him naked outside the chapel one cold winter night. She later refuted her statement saying that it was dark and it could have been the ebony statue of Apollo in the water fountain.

"Let's make a start so I can get some sleep," Hackett said. "I've left a pack on your desk."

"Marlborough was it?"

"Obliged if you'd show her the contents." Hackett turned his head and narrowed his eyes through the gallery railings at the lobby below. "I'd get a move on if I were you."

FIFTEEN

The canvas was dry the next day, same as the tall brown pillars under which they lay. Disoriented at waking mid-morning and being in too much of a hurry to get moving, they ate nothing for breakfast and nothing for lunch, following the river downhill through the greater part of the afternoon.

Adam reckoned it was Tuesday. Had to keep count. Had to keep going.

Ramsey stopped for a moment, staring out over a grass plain where few trees grew. "Wind's in the east," he said, changing direction and stooping under a fringe of low hanging branches.

Beside a twist of piñon they found water trapped in two basins of age-old rock, bubbles rising as if from an underground spring. For a moment Adam thought it was the most beautiful thing he had ever seen, water trailing from a smaller basin into the larger and then out into a narrow stream.

Ramsey put the duffel bag against a tree and leaned the backpack over it. He pulled out three empty canteens and a bottle of iodine tablets from the back pack. "Fill these in the upper pool," he said.

Adam dipped a bottle into the cold water, watched it funnel towards the neck with a hoary glimmer. One tablet for each and it was half an hour before they could drink it.

"Take a swim if you like," Ramsey said behind him. He had the gun in his hand, and a fistful of bullets.

Adam shook his head. He wasn't going to get undressed in front of a stranger. Wasn't going to let the man see his—

"I won't look, if that's what you're worried about."

"I'm not worried," Adam muttered.

The water in the larger pool was clear. Not a flash of trout and there were pebbles in the bottom, blue and gray and black. His mother found a rock pool at a beach once. She removed her sundress and lay face-down in the water naked because she wanted to tan her back. She was funny like that.

Ramsey stripped off his clothes, draped his jeans over a boulder. He walked waist deep into the pool and lay back in it. "I can still see you," he said.

Adam knew he was lying. He was staring up at the trees now. There on his back. He wasn't even shivering, wasn't even blue, and that water must have been freezing. The gun was under those jeans, only a stone's throw a way. He could make a dash for it, grab it in one hand and point it. Only, it probably wasn't loaded and he'd look like a fool if he did.

Ramsey went under for a second, body a rippling shadow that moved so fast it reminded Adam of a torpedo pushing up to the surface, water dripping from its warhead. He tried not to look at a body speckled with gooseflesh and dark hair as Ramsey got out. Muscle on muscle, tightening with every movement. It took him a while to get dressed, to peel on those socks and jeans. And then he blew into his hands and rubbed them together. Adam could see he was cold, only a man like that would never admit it.

How many bullets had there been in Ramsey's hand? Four. Five. He remembered his dad saying his gun held six rounds. He had no idea how many this one had.

There was only one thing for it. Adam would do everything he was asked, do it with a smile on his face. Heck, they might even get along for a while. And then he'd run when Ramsey least expected it, when Ramsey had finished chewing that tobacco he had in his pocket. Because after a while it made him mellow.

Adam chewed on a few strips of jerky in silence, studied the man beside him out of the corner of his eye. Face aslant, ear catching every echo of birdsong. There were dark hairs on his chin and his eyes were slits beneath dark eyebrows. He reminded Adam of someone. He just couldn't think who.

There were no other sounds other than the shift of the wind and the groan of an ancient tree limb. Pale shafts of sunlight filtered through the leaves lighting up the forest slopes.

Ramsey stood and sniffed the cool mountain air. There was something out there, grunting and huffing and he raised his chin, eyes flicking to the right and working the wind. Adam saw what looked like a gray shape standing upright about ten yards away. It could have been a bear. It could have been a tree stump.

Ramsey barely moved his hand over the gun in his belt before something jerked to one side rattling through the trees and was lost. "Elk," he said, and then, "we were downwind and all."

Adam shook his head and whispered, "It's not elk. It's Tanoan and Keresan. They're the worst."

Ramsey gave a hard stare, forehead creasing into a frown. "Those are languages not tribes."

"They're braves."

Ramsey began chewing on something and then he grinned. "How about this. If we see a kiva or a pit-house you can have my compass. Replace the one you dropped back there."

Adam saw the twitch in Ramsey's eye, face clean

now and free of grime. Since the kidnap over fourteen hours ago he assumed Ramsey had coal black eyes but they were green. One was slower than the other, made him look dreamy and out of sorts. But he was none of those things if he knew where that broken compass was.

"Better hope the rogue ranger doesn't see it. We'll be easy to track if he does."

Adam swallowed and stared at the duffel bag Ramsey kept using as a pillow. "What's in there?"

"Money."

"Did you steal it?"

"No."

"What then?"

"Sometimes the police give handouts… they're fair like that."

"Like a bank?"

Ramsey half smiled and nodded at the same time. He sat on a boulder, shaving the end of a stick with his knife.

"What are you making?"

"A spear."

"What for?"

"Trout. There's wire in that side pocket," Ramsey said, pointing at the backpack. "You could make a noose if you like. Leave it in a rabbit run."

"How?"

Ramsey took two short stakes of wood and notched them. The longer stake he gave to Adam. "Make a loop with that wire about as big a man's fist. Then tie it to that stick."

Ramsey found a tree, one that had an old bird's nest lodged in one of the upper branches and bark peeling from the trunk like an old tattered coat. He drove the two shorter stakes vertically into the ground and tied the horizontal stake with the snare to an overhanging branch. Pulling it down he got the tension he needed, hooked it into the notches of the standing stakes and left it there.

"If you twist one of the notched stakes about 180 degrees the trap will work whichever way the rabbit goes through. And when he does, he'll be lifted off the ground and ready to skin."

Adam found himself grinning. "Cool," he said.

"You're going to like the taste of that rabbit." Ramsey rubbed his hands and strode off back to camp. "You're going to like the taste of squirrel too."

Adam followed him at a distance, hoping that rabbit would be snared in an hour or two. It was unlikely with all the rain and howling that was coming from the west.

"Just wolves," Ramsey murmured, seeing the look on his face.

"Are they big?"

"Big as dogs."

"They'll frighten the rabbits."

Ramsey shrugged. "With any luck they'll frighten one into that noose. Ever had rabbit stew?"

Adam made a face. His dad roasted one in the back yard when his mom was away. Made some mashed potatoes to go with it and then smeared the meat with cranberry jelly. It was disgusting.

"It's the difference between fresh rabbit and two-day-old rabbit," Ramsey said, reaching for his spear. "Same with squirrels. You can make a rich brown gravy with the drippings. If you can catch one that is."

"So one'll just happen along in a minute?"

"Maybe he will. Maybe he won't. Worrying never caught a rabbit."

Adam nodded. He wouldn't worry. He would just peek over there now and then. "Will you read that book again tonight?"

"If you like."

Then they went off to fish.

SIXTEEN

Temeke wasn't looking forward to meeting the old trout and he wasn't looking forward to telling her there was still no sign of her son. As he recalled, Mrs. Raine Oliver rarely went out in public and kept her family life private. According to her picture, she had shoulder length hair and a warm smile. A former ballet dancer born in Belgium with a striking resemblance to a well-known 1950's actress. She was a surgeon now.

Temeke showed the housekeeper his badge and glanced sideways at the taped-off living room as they entered the house. Walking into the library, he was suddenly aware his mouth was hanging open. This Mrs. Raine Oliver was no old trout, a petite brunette in her late thirties, her bust in the early forties. She was half the Mayor's age, sleek black pants and heels sharper than a bayonet.

Temeke squared his shoulders and held out a hand. "Detective Temeke and this is my partner, Malin Santiago," he said.

She ran two narrowed eyes down Temeke's shirt until they stopped at his belt. It was the gun that frightened her, or the badge, he couldn't decide which.

"Have you found him?" she said, gaze shifting from Temeke to Malin. There was the hint of a foreign accent and a puppy dog expression that seemed to turn on and off at the drop of a hat.

"No, ma'am, but—"

"You were only, what… half an hour behind them."

"More like a couple of hours, ma'am," Temeke said, sitting next to Malin on the couch. He tried to keep his voice just above a whisper. "We'll find him."

"What if you don't? What if you never find him?"

It was a good question, although Temeke was reluctant to voice it. He knew they would find Adam, he just didn't know what condition the boy would be in when they did. "The police are combing the area now."

"The area?" Raine tilted her head.

"The Bosque, the river, further if need be." He didn't want to tell her the kidnapper had a nice truck and might be headed for the Arizona border. He noted the tight nod and a pair of arched eyebrows that could only have been achieved with a stencil.

"I… I don't understand."

"We start the search at the house, ma'am, then spiral out," Malin said, making a circle with a finger. "Then we ask the neighbors since someone might have seen something. And then that circle gets a little wider."

Hopefully, not into outer space, Temeke thought, since they'd suffered a few budget cuts recently. "Your boy's smart. Got a good head on his shoulders."

"I need to get back to—"

"Your husband, I understand. And how is the Mayor?"

"Unconscious."

"He'll come round."

"Sometimes they don't, detective."

Temeke caught her frown and the silence after her words. "Let's talk about Sunday night. Let's talk about what you saw."

Raine gave a weak smile and looked up at the ceiling. "It was around eleven o'clock when I got home. There weren't any lights on… there's always a light on.

I left my coat on the chair, left my purse on the table. And then I heard something. A whimpering… I thought it was Murphy. Our dog. I thought he'd been shut in the kitchen." Raine began to breathe loudly through her nose. "I was scared… really scared. The sound was coming from the living room. I turned the light on… saw Bill on the floor. He was tied up and there was blood on the side of his face. I called 911 at around eleven ten… pressed my scarf to his ear. The ambulance came after that."

"How did you know it was eleven ten?" Malin asked.

"It was on the lock screen."

"Of your cell phone?" Malin caught the nod and continued. "Was there anything else that struck you as odd?"

"The front door. It was open. The dog was gone."

"He might have been in the back yard."

"No, he wouldn't have been in the back yard. Bill always brings him in at nine."

"Maybe he ran off to a neighbor's house."

"I think he ran after Adam," Raine said, staring hard at Malin. "They're close you see."

Temeke was glad to hear it. He placed one hand on the plain brown envelope Hackett had left. "Do you know anyone living in Forest Road?" he asked.

"Placitas?"

"No, the one in Catron County. Over by Gila River."

"I've never heard of it."

"You received a phone call from someone claiming to have taken your son." He watched her nod, watched her fingers as they curled over each knuckle. "We traced it to that address. Did you recognize the voice?"

Raine cleared her throat, eyes grazing past him to the door. "No… he just said Adam was with him."

"Did you believe him?"

"I had no reason not to."

"He could have been a crank caller. Could have been a neighbor."

"We don't speak to our neighbors. We don't even know them."

The comment was odd in light of a statement received from Eli Sandoval, a neighbor who regularly fished with the mayor. "Did you ask to speak to Adam?" Temeke saw the shake of her head, the downturned eyes. "To find out if he was still alive?"

"Do you know what it's like when the police take away your personal belongings? Look for fingerprints, tape off rooms so we can no longer use them. Do you know what it's like to stare out of your son's window and plead with God to find your child? Do you?"

"No, ma'am."

"I don't remember what I said, Detective. It was all a blur."

"I believe you said 'I understand.'" None of it was a blur to Temeke. He'd listened to the tape recording five times. "Just so you know, he's got the money. There was no exchange. That's why we don't have Adam, Mrs. Oliver."

He watched the blank stare, the sagging mouth and wondered what on earth she was thinking. Whether it crossed her mind that the kidnap could have been linked to the Ringmaster. It had certainly crossed his.

"You will find him?" she asked.

"The police are doing everything they can, ma'am. Did you also hear about the helicopter... the one that came down in Gila National Forest last night?" Temeke conjured an image of pilot Danny Michael peppered with shot and shrapnel as he studied that smooth brow. "It was on the six o'clock news this morning."

She returned Temeke's look with a scorcher of her own. "My husband was shot, detective. I was up all night at the hospital watching *him* not the TV!" Then came the puppy dog look. "They don't know if he'll live."

Temeke was silent for a while. There had been a choice. Stay by her husband's bedside in the hospital or stay at home waiting for the kidnapper to call. He would have chosen the latter.

He opened the envelope and pulled out a transparent evidence bag. Inside was a badly burned piece of paper, the corner of which was barely readable. He slid it across the table. "This was fished out of the fireplace. Seen it before?"

She squinted at first, eyes flicking from one side to the other as she read the few remaining words. Then she opened her mouth to say something and seemed to think better of it.

"No, I've never seen it before."

SEVENTEEN

In the morning the camp fire was flat on the ground and there was hardly any smell to it. The flames had long since died and all that was left was a patch of gray grass and fish bones.

The rabbit had been packed with onions to keep the flesh moist, so Ramsey said. A slow roast cooked on a spit until the outer flesh was the color of a baked red potato. It tasted like ham.

Ramsey was hunched over the fire, flicking through some photographs of a girl in a bikini. Snapped them back in his backpack when he saw Adam looking.

"What's that?" Adam said.

"Nothing."

"It's porn, isn't it?"

"No it isn't porn. You can see it's not porn."

"It was a girl with hardly anything on."

"I don't look at porn."

"I bet you did when you were my age."

Ramsey shook his head and something between sadness and fear crossed his face. He looked down then as if he was ashamed.

"Why do you keep looking at her?"

"She was special."

"Is she dead?"

"No, she'll never be dead. Always have a little of her in me and a little of me in her. That's how it is with love.

But you wouldn't know about that. You wouldn't know about girls."

"I know they're crazy. They don't say what they mean."

"It's a two-way street." Ramsey gave him that sideways smile. "Someone you like?"

Adam nodded. He liked Runa the girl from Bombay. He liked her long sleek hair and brown eyes. Trouble was, she was in seventh grade and smiled at him maybe once a year. What chance did a sixth grader have? Adam sensed those eyes digging deep into his head like Ramsey could see everything inside.

"Girls take most things a guy says and rotate it a hundred and eighty degrees," Ramsey said. "If you tell her you'll call her later, what exactly does *later* mean? Because to a girl it means that night or tomorrow. And you… you'll be thinking… eh, maybe after soccer practice or maybe next Tuesday. And she'll be checking her messages every ten minutes and if it's not your number on her caller ID, chances are she'll ignore you next time she sees you."

Adam scrunched up his face. "That's dumb."

"They operate on a first-come, first-served basis. If you tell them you're going to call on Tuesday and don't, and then she goes out on Friday and meets a new man… poof! You're history."

"Boys aren't like that are they?"

"Depends. I could say to a woman, 'I've heard a lot about you.' And what I actually mean is 'I've heard all your dirty little secrets and I'd like to include myself in a few.'"

Adam felt the chuckle deep in his belly and when it came up he doubled over like he'd never get up again. A hearty laugh through a wide open mouth.

Ramsey grinned and patted the air with his hand. "Better check your snare."

Adam had forgotten about the snare. The branch was bowed slightly and swinging dead center was a rabbit in a noose. He pumped the air with his fist. Unhooking it, he felt a stab of pity as it flopped to the ground. But Ramsey was right there beside him, picked up that rabbit and loped off towards the tent. "Fill in the fire. We're moving out," he said over one shoulder.

Adam set off at a jog just to catch up with him. "Is it the rogue ranger?"

Ramsey coughed up a wad of phlegm and thought better of spitting it out of his mouth. "He's tracking us."

"How do you know?"

"I just know."

Adam brightened. "Like I know about the Anasazi and the Mogollon."

"I guess."

"Can I ask you something?"

Ramsey nodded as he folded up the tent, knee anchoring it to the ground.

"Can I call my mom?"

Ramsey stared at him for time and then lifted his chin. "Did you hear what I said? Ranger's coming. And there's not enough bars out here to use a phone."

"But there might be... if we get to higher ground."

Ramsey blew air through his nostrils, one hand rubbing the back of his neck. "Let's wait until we get to the village."

"What village?"

"I would have driven there, would have turned off at 180. But I wanted to show you something. Something you'd always remember."

Adam began to mentally run everything through in his mind, his father's face, his father's blood. It was possible he wasn't dead and Ramsey was just plain lying. "When can I call her?"

Ramsey clenched his jaw and then rolled his bottom

lip beneath his front teeth. "Don't want that rogue ranger listening in. And he will. He'll even trace it to your mom and go after her. You don't want that do you?"

Adam shook his head. No, he didn't want that.

Ramsey shouldered up the backpack and blew in his cupped hands. "Ready to lead. Ready to follow. Never quit," he said, hooking the duffel over Adam's shoulders. "That's our new motto."

Adam repeated it. He felt important carrying that duffel bag, but felt a little uneasy too. He missed his mom, missed her voice. There was a strange whisper in the wind that afternoon and he stifled a sob, chest hurting a little more with each step.

He looked at Ramsey's back and the rabbit that dangled from his belt. He was taller than his dad, shoulders straight and level, and tanned skin that seemed to stretch over a stocky frame. He was an athlete. Had to be. The top half of his hair was tied up leaving the rest to fall down to his shoulder and there was a certain curve to his cheek as he turned occasionally to check Adam was there.

It was the mystery of it all that nipped at Adam's subconscious. He memorized the shape of Ramsey's upper lip, even the slightly crooked front tooth. The way he drank, ate, slept. All afternoon he thought about it until the sun went down. They were headed west.

God... it's me... Adam. I know you're up there with Dad watching, but please could you send a hundred police officers. Quietly though, because Ramsey's got a gun and he'll use it if he has to. I don't want Mom to worry. I don't want her to cry—

Ramsey stopped suddenly, held up his right hand and turned a half circle. He herded Adam alongside with one arm, eyes narrowed on something in the shadows.

"Stay behind me," he whispered.

Adam could barely swallow. He heard a twig snap,

heard the rustle of leaves. Smelled the smoke of a nearby campfire. He looked up the slope at a regiment of pine trees, brown and gnarly like an old man's whiskers. He saw a flash of light between them, a coyote running perhaps? Heart hammering, he thought he was going to choke.

He heard the pitter-patter of rain and deep pulses in his ears. Ramsey must have heard it too, eyes rolling back and forth with a wildness to them. Gun out in front, safety off.

Adam looked to the left and the right, didn't see Ramsey slip behind a cluster of chokeberry. It all happened so fast. He felt the arm across his chest, another across his mouth and he could smell the gagging stench of filth. Felt himself being dragged backwards and away from Ramsey. Couldn't scream, couldn't shout, just a whimpering that came from the back of his throat. On and on smashing through a dark puddle of water and up a steep bank.

He was yanked into the darkness and that's what terrified him. Damp soil and the scratch of spiny roots through his hair and cheeks.

Stop... please...

But the man wouldn't stop. Kept tugging at him, turning him around in circles, wrapping him in twine and then pushing him against something hard.

Adam couldn't feel his hands or his legs and he wanted to scream. But it was the scratching sound and the flare of a match that stopped him. A single flame illuminated the face of an old man whose chin was thatched with red whiskers, skin whiter than a dog's bone.

EIGHTEEN

The sky was beginning to darken and there were amber streaks above the Sandia Mountains. The crest was now covered in powdered snow and all Malin could think about was a boy out there in the wilderness with a collar turned up against the cold.

It had been another long day of phone calls, internet searches and interviews. She could have done with a rush of cold air, good clean air, especially with Temeke fogging up the office with a half-smoked cigarette he'd found under his chair. The office was almost empty except for four officers downstairs and the Impact Sergeant who had latterly gone out to get them a sandwich.

She watched the phone, wondered when forensics would confirm the voice on the Trader tape with the Oliver tape. Since they didn't have a suspect, they didn't need a court order. But the chief of the voiceprints unit in the forensics lab in Chicago was one of Malin's heroes. Audrey De Becker made you feel like you were in the presence of royalty. She had more than twenty-five years in forensic science, including the US Secret Service and the Internal Revenue Service. Malin wondered whether she should stand and salute when she took the call.

For the past four hours she had studied the Ringmaster murder books from cover to cover, tacked all those grisly photographs to the cork board and said nothing in between. And now Temeke was on the phone, saying one word over and over again.

"Yep… yep… yep…"

He finally put the phone down and pursed his lips.

"Talk to me," Malin said.

"That was Officer Running Hawk. Found a broken compass. Looks like our Adam's been leaving crumbs again."

"How long has it been there?"

"He reckoned three or four days. Said they found some flattened grass, possibly a tent. There was a forked branch low to the ground. Great for sitting in and doing your business. And they found that business hidden in a shallow hole. Two types."

"How can they tell?"

"Different color's what Running Hawk said. Two people. Two sets of footprints. One an adult: size eleven, lug sole. One a child: size nine, weight bearing on the left side. They were walking fast. He could tell by the stride length."

"And the dog?" She asked, knowing Temeke wouldn't have asked.

"He didn't mention any paw prints."

Malin wanted to pump the air, but it wasn't over yet. The news gave her a rush of hope, a feeling they were finally getting somewhere. "He might still be alive, sir."

"If he is, then something's changed." Temeke looked up at the map and frowned. Then looked at his watch. "Forensics should have called us an hour ago about that voice comparison."

Temeke's mouth was pursed around a cigarette and he was trying to balance on the two back legs of his chair, only the wheels prevented any acrobatics. "Better hope Adam's not popped to the eyeballs on drugs."

She had had many occasions to see what a real

detective looked like close up and this one, she thought, was solid, tough and sour, head tilted back and eyes closed for a moment.

"Mrs. Oliver," Temeke murmured. "It's something deep down inside, one of those distant voices you ignore and then wish you hadn't. Why do you think the kidnapper decided to pull off a ransom? And why did he make contact with the victim's father?"

Malin noted Temeke didn't refer to the kidnapper as the Ringmaster. "Because Adam's father is a prominent figure."

"It's not like there's blood and teeth all over the floor. He was a bloody bad shot."

"Well, there's two dead pilots and a missing boy." Malin flapped a hand to dispel the smoke. "You just don't like toffs. Isn't that what you call them?"

"Mrs. Oliver said when she called 911, she saw the time on her cell phone. Not the clock," Temeke muttered.

Any significance was lost on Malin. All she could think about was Mrs. Oliver in her scrubs in the operating theater on Sunday night. Never even knew her husband was bleeding on the floor at home and her own child was tied up in a truck with a madman and headed for who-knows-where. She tried not to think of Adam's face… his screams… Choked back a few tears, wasn't going to show herself up in front of Temeke.

"Remember the graffiti outside the Mayor's house?" he said, sighing deeply and flicking ash into an empty coffee cup.

Malin remembered the case. Three years ago, someone sprayed graffiti on the Mayor's limo, the pavement outside his front gate and then climbed over the wall and did the same thing on his front door. "Mark Hogan. Nutter. Hates Republicans. Doesn't have the brain capacity to pull off a kidnap like this."

"What about the time when Oliver traveled to D.C. in his private jet and they had that bomb scare. All flights were grounded."

"Douglas Cordova, former press secretary. Still inside."

"He might have a friend on the outside, Marl. Prisoners do, you know." Temeke screwed up his eyes and stared at his computer. "Mayor Oliver's got an impressive résumé. Even had an ex-wife."

"She died four years after they married," Malin said, staring at her own computer. "Breast cancer."

"Eagle Scout, Navy SEAL, Harvard. Seems our Mayor's done some great things. Homeless initiatives, higher graduation rates for high school students, economic opportunities. They've estimated savings in the millions. You only have to look at the I-25 project and the crime rate. And what's more, Albuquerque is the second highest area in terms of economic growth. He ought to be the best mayor we've ever had." Temeke went quiet and then, "There's some on the west wall now."

"Some what?"

"Graffiti. Happened last night. Says *'Murderers work here. Thanks to the effing DCPD.'* And beneath it, *'I'm still not loving the police'.* Do you think everyone hates us?"

"Some people don't trust cops."

"I don't trust cops." Temeke let out a big sigh. "Fergus the bleeding flasher. At least the dirty old bugger didn't trip the alarm at two in the morning. It happens when you pee against the glass."

Malin was glad Temeke had spent the night at home, glad he was showered and shaved and in a better mood than he had been in days. Glad his mind was ticking over every detail and every tiny speck of dust.

The wind dropped and everything was quiet. Even

the evening sky glowed a misty orange behind the building and there was that nagging feeling the office belonged entirely to them.

"Where's Hackett?" she said and then wished she hadn't.

"Kept up all last night listening to Fowler's squeaky voice. Apparently," Temeke said, taking the last hit from that tiny cigarette, "he was supposed to be combing the woods around 3265 Forest Road with a few of his old cronies when Agent Anderson found him behind a tree with Gloria Pacheco, you know, from special weapons. Anderson told the sod he was fiddling with evidence and wrote him up."

Malin waved the inappropriate comment away with one hand and still blew out a few short snorts. She needed the break just as much as he did. "How does Fowler know Hollister?"

"They're both captains, love."

What? Wait... did he say captain? How like Temeke to lob that little grenade. "Hollister's a captain now?"

"Got promoted three weeks ago."

"You never told me."

"You never asked." Temeke blew a large smoke ring towards the ceiling and dropped the cigarette in his coffee cup. He squinted at the thermostat. "Bloody budget cuts. Never mind me freezing my ass off over here. I need coffee."

"Sounds like you've had enough rocket fuel for one day."

The phone rattled on her desk. It was Flossy from Fingerprinting. The only prints on Adam's cell phone were his. Malin ended the call and groaned as she relayed the bad news to Temeke.

The honk of Sarge's car cut through the silence and Malin sauntered over to the window. The SUV nosed its way around the dumpster and came to a stop in its usual parking spot. The red brake lights glowed an angry red in the darkness before fading to black.

"He's here," she said.

Sergeant Moran took his time climbing those stairs, knocked on the door and gave Malin a steaming bag of hamburgers. He gave Temeke a curt nod as he stood in the doorway.

"You look happy, Sarge," Temeke said. "Has Fowler resigned?"

"No, it's better than that. Forensics just called about those voiceprints. There's a match."

NINETEEN

Adam tried to move his hands, but the bindings held fast and bit into his flesh. His feet were tied at the ankles and the best he could do was wriggle his toes. The air was thick with the stench of sweat and urine, and it made his stomach heave.

The old man sat cross-legged on the ground, sharpening a knife and muttering. Occasionally, he looked up at the opposite wall, a lattice of wooden strips, where two large meat hooks hung and where dark pools of animal blood had collected at the footing.

Adam saw the bones then, curved and ribbed like a spine and vertebrae stacked in a neat little pile. There was a large wooden mallet and a coil of rope with snaps and grabs, and a tattered shirt hanging on a hook with a red and white patch on the sleeve. *New Mexico Game Patrol,* it said, and underneath the word, *Ranger*.

Adam wanted to scream, wanted to shout. But it was those dark stains on the latticework, evidence of a bloody suffering that stopped his mouth. Four rifles were propped up in the corner, antique by the look of them and hopefully too old to fire. He couldn't see a thing through the wattle and wondered how dark it was outside. Whether the clouds had covered the moon, whether Ramsey would ever find him in the darkness. He wondered why the old man muttered, why he sharpened that knife. Why those arms of stringy muscle shook sometimes.

There was another scent, bitter and thick like the smoke from a campfire. Ramsey was bound to smell it and come running. Unless there were other rogue rangers out there skinning the big man this very minute.

Dread crept through Adam as he hung there, heart beating faster than usual, breaths ragged and quick. The old man must have heard all that anxious panting because he turned slightly, looked like he was half sick with pity. Then he puckered his face into the most serious of expressions as if Adam needed a different type of comforting he couldn't provide.

Somewhere beyond the daub and wattle that separated him from the outside world, Adam heard a shrill whistle. The old man heard it too, tensed and struggled to stand. His joints popped as he found his feet, back hunched a little towards the sound. He was wearing a long woolen coat, the type military men wore and his beard was tangled with leaves.

"Coyotes," he said, raising a hand that didn't appear to have a thumb. "They can smell yer blood."

He glanced one way and then another as if catching an unfamiliar scent. And then he shook his head as if he knew it was man-made. There was someone out there.

Adam let out a pent-up breath and then held in another. He'd use it soon to scream. But not yet. Not until the old man was far enough away to let that scream count.

The old man crept towards a burlap drape, knife out in front, trembling like a dowsing rod. He seemed to angle his ear to another sound, a click this time like the locking in of a magazine.

Adam took shallow rattled breaths, working himself to a scream. "Ram-sey!"

Something crashed through the wattle six feet from where the old man stood and bringing with it the sudden flush of moonlight.

"Get off my land before I hit yer!" the old man said, knife-hand extended like an eagle's claw. There was a trail of saliva on that big red beard and a cough wheezed through jagged teeth.

"Your land?" Ramsey's face was knotted with amusement as he stood next to Adam. He waved his gun to show the man what he was about, leveled it right at him. "Boy's mine."

"Gimme the boy. I'll pay you plentee."

"What with?" Ramsey said, squeezing the trigger. "It's not like you've got a clink of change in that old coat."

The man pointed his ear to the ground and shook his head as if something rattled around in there. "I'll give you fifty for 'm."

"He's not worth it. This one has fits."

Adam couldn't make head or tail of the conversation and he felt a mite queasy at being the object of a sale.

"Tie 'm up with yer belt. Won't bite yer then."

Adam sensed Ramsey's fury mounting, saw the twitch in his jaw and neck. The old man had no chance against a man all muscles and murder. He'd be dead if he came any closer.

But the old man's eyes were squinty and strange, and he took a few steps forward. "Won't shoot me. Got no balls, have yer?"

Ramsey raised one eyebrow, muzzle moving in now and aimed at the man's shoulder. He said nothing. Just stared and stood straight as a statue.

"Robbin' me blind at fifty. An' I got cold cash back there. Venison too."

"Back where?"

The man opened his eyes and in them was the mania of a rabid dog. He sprang for the gun, dug that knife good and deep into Ramsey's thigh. But Ramsey was too quick for him. A sudden *crack* and the man was thrown backwards onto the ground, one hand clutching a bloody shoulder.

Adam saw the tip of Ramsey's hunting knife as it sawed through the twine at his shoulder, each strand popping from his arms and legs.

"Run!" Ramsey yelled.

Adam didn't need to be told twice. Bolting down the slope, he came to a stop at the edge of a wide stream with flat rocks to walk on. He closed his ears to the screams. Left there with his own thoughts.

Ramsey was probably using that serrated hunting knife in his belt now, slashing, biting, ripping. Probably sawing the man's head off with a few hard tugs.

Hands pressed tighter against his ears, Adam watched bubbles as they rose to the surface from an underground spring, skating along the current and vanishing altogether. He began to cry, began to whimper. He didn't know what to do or where to go. He could run back the way he had come, he could even find the lodge. But the ginger man would only get him, pull his heart out of his rib cage with his bare hands. Adam wondered if he should run north towards the cliffs. It was in those precious moments that he hesitated.

Ramsey shuffled out through the leaves behind him, dark stains on his cheeks and forehead, gun in his belt.

"Here, take this" he said, handing Adam a rolled up raincoat. "Meat and money," was all he said.

Ramsey merely rubbed those stains off with the back of his hand, took out his binoculars to scan the country that lay to the north and a big moon that tracked the cliffs. His leg was bloody and so were his jeans.

"What happened?" Adam said.

Ramsey wouldn't say. Just kept repeating how sorry he was. How he thought the bastard lived in Albuquerque, not over here. How he should have known the madman would return to his old hunting ground just to gloat over his trophies.

Ramsey staggered and Adam walked along the edge of that stream until they found a boat. Ramsey put their pack in the stern and told Adam to jump in at the bow. He paddled out to the middle where the current was strong.

It was wide enough to be a river now with cliffs on either side. Sometimes curling north, sometimes curling west. Adam heard the chuckle of water under the bow, felt the breeze in his face. It was warmer in that boat and a whole lot comfier too and he let his face rest against the pack.

It was long into the night before Adam felt a hand on his shoulder and awoke to Ramsey's voice. They tied up the boat and made for a sandy bank, navigating across flat stones and boulders to the other side. Ramsey filled up the gallon jug and he gave that leg a good old rinsing. They were met by a north-facing cliff painted with hunchbacked figures playing flutes with a crown of feathers on their heads.

Adam stared at them for a time, heart soaring in his chest. They were ancient rock paintings.

"It's still a ways," Ramsey said. He pointed to where the cliff ended abruptly and curled down to a well-worn path. He handed Adam the gallon jug, gave him the first sip of water.

Adam followed Ramsey along a narrow strip of mud and wet grass, hugging the cliffs until the path turned gently into a small canyon. Above them was a steep mesa which reminded Adam of a stadium where the roof was no more than a jutting lip. It was blue and silver in the moonlight, wind rushing through the piñon and kicking up a moan here and there. He wasn't as scared as he was before, not with wilderness-man leading the way on that hobbling leg.

Ramsey paused at a fork in the path, taking the higher route, hand reaching down to haul Adam up the slopes. It was hard going in the dark with the packs on their backs and the climb was steeper than Adam realized, shoes tapping against loose rock for what seemed like hours.

Ramsey paused before a wooden ladder leading to a smooth ledge, finger jabbing the air in an upward motion.

"Get up there," he said, sweat dripping off his lip, "before the lightning comes."

TWENTY

Ramsey picked his way between two dwellings near the mouth of the cave, unhooked his backpack and let it slip to the ground. There was a circular pit with bricks to sit on and he took the rabbit from his belt and set it down beside him.

Adam's heart was fluttering worse than the night before Christmas. He wanted to thank Ramsey for saving him. Wanted to thank him for bringing him here. There were no words in his muddled head, even when he'd dropped the raincoat on the ground, shrugged off the duffel bag and fell into a deep sleep. He must have slept until the following afternoon because now the light was fading to a deep gray and rain was tapping on rock.

The last of the evening sun turned the cliffs a rosy red. There were white ribbons in the granite and black sooty stains that curled upwards as if the rock had once been scorched by an ancient fire.

Adam stood at the mouth of the cave, looking over at a stand of trees gripping to a sheer rock. He could hear the whispers of the Mogollon people in the stirring pines and he could see row-upon-row of stone ruins below, carved into the sides of the rock and open to the sky. He couldn't believe he was finally here.

It must have been Friday afternoon. The sun was already plunging towards the western horizon, barely a small dot though a gap in the clouds. As he stood there, a thought came over him. Ramsey wasn't about to kill him, because if he was he would have done it by now. Wouldn't have saved him from the rogue ranger, wouldn't have brought him here to the caves.

Ramsey said something, voice hollow and distant. Pointed to one side of the cave mouth which curved around a little, forming a short lookout ledge. "You can see the river and the pass from here."

Adam wasn't looking at the river or the pass. "These houses… they're old aren't they?"

"They quarried the stone, used mud and brought timber from the forest. You can see beam holes in the rock, volcanic tuft I think it is."

"Aren't you forgetting something?" Adam flapped his fingers in an upturned hand.

Ramsey grinned and took out his compass. "Remembered my promise, didn't you? Well, here it is."

Adam caught it in both hands, a military compass, khaki colored. The best he'd ever seen.

Ramsey pulled down his jeans. "I need to clean the wound." Blood trickled from a hole in his thigh and he poured water on it. It didn't make Adam sick like he thought it would, like the time when a scout leader got a rusty old nail in his foot. Looked like raw meat when he took that shoe off.

"First aid kit," Ramsey said, thumb pointing at the backpack. "Hand me the peroxide and keep the flashlight on it."

Adam found a white box and in it was a sixteen ounce bottle of peroxide and a hooked needle and thread. He watched Ramsey unscrew the lid with his teeth and let a few drops fall on his thigh. He sutured that wound like he'd done it a thousand times and then rummaged around for a tube of antiseptic cream and a bandage. He muttered a cuss word as he pulled his jeans back on.

"What does that word mean?" Adam asked.

"You don't want to know," Ramsey said. And then, "I'm sorry."

Better hope you're sorry, Adam thought. It sounded like a bad one and if he didn't like it then God certainly wouldn't.

"Know how to skin a rabbit?" Ramsey unsheathed the hunting knife and held it out hilt first.

Adam nodded. He wasn't sure he remembered all the steps but he wanted to give it a go. He stared at the tang of the blade and saw his face in the reflection. A small face, gray with dirt.

"We'll eat the venison first. Nice bit of backstrap," Ramsey said, unrolling the raincoat. He pocketed what money was in it and separated two portions of the cooked meat on the surface of a nearby brick. "Then we'll build a fire."

"Fires aren't allowed," Adam said. He turned off the flashlight and bit into his meat.

"A man's got to keep warm and so has a boy. It's darker than a man's armpit in here."

"I can see."

"Bet you couldn't thread a needle without a flashlight." Ramsey paused for a second or two. "I take that back. You probably could."

Adam tore at that venison in a few bites. It wasn't much. Just a few slices about half an inch thick and nicely browned. It got him thinking about that old man in the woods, eyes wide and pasty like he was already dead.

"Did you see any other rogue rangers back there?" Adam asked.

"Saw a dog. Heard it growling too."

"Coyote?"

"Maybe." Ramsey took the flashlight and trained it on the rabbit. "Slice a ring above the foot joint. Whatever you do, don't cut the flesh."

Adam took the rabbit, sliced a ring just where Ramsey pointed. He made another incision towards the backside cutting through the tail bone before peeling the hide off easy as a banana. He held it up for Ramsey to see and all he got was a tight nod.

He laid the rabbit on a rock and reached into the pit, letting the ash sift through his fingers. "Is this old?"

"The ash? Nah, someone's been here before us." Ramsey beckoned for the knife, wiped it on his jeans and then played it between his fingers. "There may be more of them. And if there are, they'll have heard the shot. Better get that rabbit cooked. We need kindling." Ramsey grabbed his axe and peered through the mouth of the cave at a lead-gray cloud as he zipped up his jacket. "I'll bring up the ladders when I'm done. Stay here. And don't follow me."

He was already bolting down that ladder like a wraith, gun in his belt. How he did it with a deep gash in his thigh, Adam would never know. But the man was fast, he'd give him that. He would be off for a while cutting tree branches and gathering twigs, and since there was nothing dry on the forest floor it was likely he'd be gone for some time.

When the wind sighed through the empty houses, Adam could almost hear the chatter of voices and the shrill laughter of children. He sensed the spirits of another time, heard what they heard and saw what they saw. When it was silent he was filled with an overwhelming sense of loss.

It was a national monument, with a visitors' center not far away and a warden to watch over the ruins. Unless there was a thunderstorm alert, there would be visitors along tomorrow. Or so he hoped.

He reached for the metal pot and brushed it against the ash in the fire pit to flatten out the surface. There was a musky scent in the air as the rain pattered against the rock and he tensed suddenly and listened to the rhythm. If he wasn't mistaken, he could hear a keening sound where a thousand eyes watched him from the slopes, reducing him to the jumpy reactions of a child—and he didn't like it.

Eager to see what it was, he made his way towards the ledge and squinted up at a dark sky where swollen clouds were twined with gray. He crept towards the ladder and looked down. There was no sign of Ramsey, not even in the long grass or behind the boulders at the base of the cliff.

The fine hairs on the back of his neck began to stir and he was rattled by the sense that something moved behind a wet veil of rain. At first, he backed away from that ledge and studied the wood and the trees beyond from a shadowy corner of the cave.

He could just make out the path that had led them to the canyon and the glint of sodden rock. It must be rogue rangers with pale faces and red beards, searching for boys to skin and roast over a fire. There was nowhere to hide in the cave and they would soon find him cowering behind a rock. Adam's heart continued to race at the thought of finding Ramsey. To warn him.

One . . . two . . . three.

His head was pounding as he turned around on that ledge and he found his feet on the rungs without recalling how they got there.

Now!

He inched down a little further this time, feet wet and slipping against the rungs. The sand and pebbles were soft underfoot from the rain and he scrabbled against a boulder, falling backwards on his butt. It hurt like hell, but he had to get up.

To his left and about a mile away was the river, the only escape from the horseshoe of cliffs. He had no idea of its name or even if it had one. Near the narrow opening there were boulders big enough to hide behind and if he was quick he could track out into the open without being seen.

He listened to the wind as it shrieked through the canyon knowing the very sound would mask his footsteps. Edging forward, there was nothing but stalks of grass and sandy pathways between the trees and he could smell the faint trace of sweat.

He wanted to conjure Tarahuma with his mighty spear, war cries rising out of the ancient stones. He was in the thunder and in the rain, he was in the *oshach* and the *tahwach*, the sun and the moon. He was in the thundering skies... everywhere and nowhere in the darkening land.

The rains came harder now, teaming down at a slant, large as pellets and hurting too. His hair was slick against his face and he was already soaked to the skin. He heard snapping twigs, heard pounding like someone was coming. Couldn't move, couldn't breathe, couldn't see much beyond the gray, except a shape shifting about like an uncertain dream, coming closer, faster.

"What the heck!" Ramsey shouted, reaching through a curtain of hail. His coat was wrapped around the kindling, one arm locked around that coat. "Get up there! Before the lightning comes."

They were back in the cave when the sky lit up, bright like a gash across the horizon. First white and then blue and then a ripple of thunder overhead. Adam knew it wouldn't last. Rain never did in New Mexico.

Ramsey was wet through and mad, and shouting over the pelting rain. He dropped the kindling beside the fire pit, a loud clack against stone. It made Adam flinch, teeth clattering in his mouth.

"You think you could just run away?"

"I wasn't—"

"Probably should have. Save me all this running

around! So where's your God now? See, when you screw up your eyes and take a good look, he's nowhere to be found. Trust me, I've already tried."

"I didn't—

"When I was your age, I thought I could conquer the world. But the world conquered me. That's how it is, son. Can't be too smart. Can't be too sure. It takes courage to be sure when you're staring down the barrel of a gun. If there are rangers out there, they'll smoke you in their boots."

"I wasn't running away!"

Ramsey's forehead puckered for a moment, head aslant, every muscle taut. He seemed to be in a trance, unable to shake off what Adam had just said.

"I was trying to warn you," Adam said. "There's someone out there. In the trees."

"You've got a wild imagination. There's no one out there… only me."

Adam could smell mud and sweat on Ramsey's skin. He was a great bulk of a man who probably couldn't move quite as fast as a twelve-year-old boy.

"I'm telling you. I saw something," Adam said. "Over there."

Ramsey went dead quiet then, clutched at his chest again. It was his breathing Adam could hear, short sharp bursts of it. Maybe he was having second thoughts. Maybe he was just plain scared.

TWENTY-ONE

It was two days later when they got the call. Officer Running Hawk had found tracks out by West Fork Gila River—one set larger than the other—and both had petered out at the water's edge. It was good news and another notch on Hackett's command.

They had also found a body, throat slashed and a gunshot wound to the left shoulder. The coroner took its time to get to Albuquerque. Six long hours, Temeke estimated, as he looked at his wrist watch.

If there was anything he hated more it was the office of the medical investigator. Aluminum everywhere and the unforgettable reek of decaying flesh and formaldehyde. It was lucky the extractor fan was working overtime.

Dr. Vasillion bent over an autopsy table, hand grasping a set of tweezers. He seemed to be mining something from inside the nose of the dead man whose head was blackened and blistered by fire. There were only a few strands of red hair on his chin and some on his chest.

"Morning, doc," Temeke said, giving a terse nod to the assistant, a plucky girl in a white coat wearing a roar of fruity perfume. She was tapping furiously on a laptop, fingernails a grisly shade of black.

"Morning, Temeke," Dr. Vasillion said, looking up suddenly and warming Malin with a come-hither smile.

"Nice to see you again, Malin."

"And you, Dr. Vasillion," Malin said.

"Call me, Joe."

"Joe," she said, clearly trying on the name for size. She began biting her bottom lip, eyes grazing over the tiled floor.

Blimey, Temeke thought. He never knew Malin was into watery blue eyes and tightly cinched aprons. The man had a certain sophisticated charm in that jaunty smile. He also had a soon-to-be ex-wife and a mistress on the boil.

"We've just had breakfast," Temeke confirmed. All he got was two tired eyes and a droopy smile. "Eggs Benedict wasn't it, Marl?'

"It was a sausage patty and it was gross."

"Well you won't mind losing it then," Temeke said, giving a tight smile. She already looked grayer than the aluminum sink she was leaning against. "And talking of losing things, I got your invitation, doc, only I lost it again under a pile of other rubbish you keep sending me. Remind me what it said."

Vasillion flashed a look at Malin and then down again at the table. "It said OMI will only see police officers and detectives with an appointment."

"We heard you got something new in stock and you know what they say, the early bird catches."

"Two pilots and this one," Vasillion said, hand stroking that one strand of red hair with a latex covered finger. It was an oddly affectionate gesture.

"Poor old sod," Temeke muttered. "He'll never see his state pension."

Vasillion nodded at his assistant and began his examination. "Physical markings, small tattoo on the inside of the right wrist. Eternity symbol by the look of it. Thumb missing on his right hand, a prior injury," he said, lifting the skin slightly near the buttock, "judging by skin grafts on the upper right thigh and back."

"According to Officer Running Hawk's report," Temeke interrupted, "he reckoned the old man got into an altercation with another hunter over a kill. He was shot only a few feet from his camp. There were blood stains on a tree, that kind of thing, and they found a knife, a Buck 110. Looks like he used it too. He was then dragged back to the fire and that's where his neck was slashed. Then Ginger was left face down to burn. What I want to know is how long he'd been dead?"

Vasillion shook his head. "Face down means the killer wanted his face obliterated. Extreme hatred. As for an altercation, doesn't sound like hunter etiquette to me. This wound isn't consistent with a folding knife."

"That's not all they carry," muttered Temeke.

"The field examiners found a bolt action rifle in a lean-to. 5-round magazine." Vasillion looked up at the ceiling for a moment. "P14, I think he said."

"Enfield?" Temeke asked, belly a churn of knots. Nobody had told him that crucial piece of news.

The doctor nodded. "I'd say he died anywhere between two and three o'clock on Wednesday afternoon."

He continued to prod and poke with painstaking scrutiny, nose almost touching the dead man's neck. "Second and third degree burns to left side of the face, neck and chest. Conjunctival hemorrhaging of the left eye." He then eased the mouth open, spatula clicking on the teeth. "Age sixty-five to seventy-five. Physical condition—"

"Dead?" Temeke offered, hoping the doc would get to the headlines and leave the boring bits for later.

"Fit. Apparent cause of death, homicide, gunshot wound to the left shoulder, one deep cut versus tear to the left front side of the neck, exposing cervical spine."

Malin stood on tiptoe and kept her distance. "You

said one deep cut, right?"

"Correct," Vasillion muttered more to himself than to her. "Definitely a fixed blade survival knife. Serrated edge. Not the Buck 110. But that did have blood on it. Different type."

"Do we have a name?" Temeke assumed the blood came from the assailant.

"I've got a rush on it."

"He must have been strong," Malin said. "Not saying a hunter isn't strong. They'd have to be. But this is precise, almost meticulous."

"Could have been a doctor," Temeke muttered, seeing Vasillion's eyebrows shoot up.

He wondered if he should go out for smoke, but gave his watch a pointed stare instead. He hoped they could get out before the old boy was gutted down the middle with a Striker Saw and the assistant began labeling jars of offal. He expected to ruin a perfectly good pair of underpants when he smelled the stench of burning bone.

"What's this, doc?" Temeke said, peering at a length of material lined in a silky twill and sealed in a bag on the counter.

"It's part of a double-breasted trench coat, Melton-style I think. The rest of it was recovered from the site, bloodstained rope in the pockets and a few hair samples. Forensics better take a look at it," Vasillion said, gazing down Ginger's throat. "Particles of soot in the trachea—"

"A heavy smoker then?"

"… consistent with smoke inhalation associated with the campfire. No further significant points."

Temeke huffed out a lungful of air and looked at the pathetic remains. He hoped the dead man wouldn't wind up in the National Missing and Unidentified Persons System. He hoped they'd get a name.

"Since we don't have antemortem data it could take a few days."

"Do you think he lived out there" Malin murmured, "in the woods?"

"Judging by the dirt under his fingernails, hair, teeth, I would say he did."

Temeke felt an icy cold wind across the room, a shudder that raised the hairs on the back of his neck. Someone must have opened a cold locker. He continued to stare at the scrub sinks and tables, wondering if the dead looked down from the ceiling and felt sad at what they saw. Why was it the place always made him feel so uneasy?

One of the ward doors was barged open by a stretcher and wheeled in by an Asian orderly. His eyes seemed to smile behind a pair of black-rimmed glasses and he nodded to Malin. As far as Temeke could make out, these were the remains of Danny Michael, recognizable only by the label tied to a toe.

Temeke flinched slightly; felt the prickle of tears. He hated death, but the terror of it was greater. Danny had left behind a wife and two small children. Bloody fantastic.

"Given that this is a homicide," Dr. Vasillion said, voice cutting through Temeke's thoughts, "and in the same area of woods, he could be related to your case."

Temeke watched that spatula as it hung between two fingers, saw the doctor's reflection in one side of the aluminum table.

"He could even have been shot in self-defense," Malin said.

Vasillion barely nodded and patted the upper right arm. "He's fit. When we get to the gross examination I suspect rabbits and squirrels in the way of stomach contents."

"We'll leave before you do," Temeke said, watching

the doc toss his instrument in a steel pan and pick up a scalpel. "What are we looking for? Got any ideas, doc?"

Vasillion played the scalpel between his fingers, eyes squinting at Temeke. "The shot to the shoulder was a warning. Maybe our John Doe overstepped the line, maybe he threatened his killer. It's the knife wound to the neck that fascinates me. There's a faint possibility, and I hope it's *faint,* that the killer might be ex-police or military. Some fail, some never fit in. Some join the armed forces to vent a rage against the foulest of humanity. And that cut, as Malin pointed out, is very precise. Only a high street butcher could have come close."

TWENTY-TWO

Tree limbs crackled in the fire, soot and smoke curling upwards to the ceiling. Adam could see them – his beloved braves – eating and laughing before the open fire. He kept his mind empty, so he wouldn't miss the visions that might be there.

Two days in the cave because of Ramsey's leg, two days without hiking onward in the open country. Two days and no sign of the rangers.

Adam explored the pit houses, towers and underground kivas, each carved into natural alcoves and painted with a skillful hand. He heard the wind as it shrilled through the chinking and, when the light faded in the many passageways, he thought he saw Tarahuma, the spear-thrower, carrying an atlatl.

Ramsey wasn't far behind pointing at this and that, and nursing that weeping wound. Sometimes he would pace and mutter, and sometimes he would chew the black stuff and doze off for a while. His eyes were circled in bruises or at least that's what Adam thought they were. Like he'd been popped with a fist. And he was up and down like a man with no way, whispering "Leave no man behind... leave no man behind."

It was late afternoon when Adam rinsed the saucepan at the mouth of the cave, set it beneath a natural runoff. He could hear the *drip, drip, drip*, and then a sudden downpour drumming against metal. And every now and then he would go and fetch it so they could bathe and wash their clothes.

"Close your eyes," Ramsey whispered, dipping his fingers into a multi-colored compact. "Need to camo your face up."

Adam closed his eyes, felt those fingers working the colors from nose to cheekbones, jaw to neck. It tickled his throat and he flinched a little.

"They won't see us coming out. *When* we come out," Ramsey said.

Adam knew Ramsey could move through the woods like a phantom, face flattened with paint. How else could he have survived this long?

"It's cool," Adam said, trying to think of things to say.

"What's cool?"

"All that stuff on your face. I've seen it in movies."

"Your dad would know all about that."

"He never talked about the military. He never told me what it was really like."

"It's about survival. It's about killing."

Adam felt a twinge in his belly, remembering something his pastor said. "Thou shalt not kill."

Ramsey snorted. "You don't give up do you?"

"No. Because God never gave up on me."

Ramsey tucked his chin on his chest and stared at the fire until his eyes began to water. "I don't believe in all that God stuff."

"But you can," Adam whispered. "We can pray if you like."

Ramsey shook his head. "There are things you don't know, things you don't need to know. I can't pray. It won't take away the filth."

"Did you kill that old man?" Adam had to ask, had to know. Ramsey frowned and looked away like he needed reminding.

"Men like that take young boys. They do things."

Adam could still see a skeleton in the woods when he thought about it. He had been hoping they wouldn't stumble across it any time soon. "Like the one tied to a tree?"

"Yeah, just like him."

"Did you know the boy?"

Ramsey nodded and sniffed. Said he knew the boy. He was dark skinned, like a nut, pretty-looking too. Always stood beside his mother in the hardware store, always helping her out with a smile. Then one day he was gone. But his face wasn't. It was all over the shop windows, bus stops, tacked to trees and posts. And when Ramsey saw that boy's face he vowed he'd kill the man who did it. He made an anonymous call to the police department. Told them where to find young Evan Trader. Wanted to take him down off that tree, but he knew better than to tamper with evidence. Only the police never found the man who killed him because he moved like a demon through the woods.

"It's dangerous out here." Ramsey wiped his eyes with the heel of one hand, looked like he was crying. "And I care."

"Is that why you took me? Because something bad was going to happen."

Ramsey began to take jagged breaths, and his hand was wiping some of that paint off. "It would be easy to say that. The world's not as bright as you think it is. And it gets darker by the day."

"What then?"

"I'll tell you when we get there."

"Promise?"

"Promise." Ramsey tried a smile, only it was lopsided, not really happy. "Finish your rabbit. It's getting dark."

He stood and kicked dust over the fire until the

flames were nothing but yellow rattails curling above a bed of ash. All those tears were because he was tired, that's all. Tired of running. Tired of waiting.

An owl hooted on a nearby tree, only Ramsey didn't think it was an owl. They would be herded in like cattle so he said, shut in by those rangers until they were starved out. He kept droning on about the old man with the thick red beard, kept saying he probably told the rangers where they were.

Adam knew Ramsey was dreaming it. The old man was already dead. And dead men don't speak.

They were warm and full of rabbit before the sun went down. Wrapped in their jackets, hoods up and lying on their bellies on the lookout ledge, they watched the opposite slope and listened to the grass murmur. After a while Ramsey fell asleep and that's when Adam noticed the figure, leaning against the trunk of a tree in the deep dusk. He was alone, or so Adam thought.

Not too tall, judging by the notches on the pine tree he stood against and looking across the canyon at the cliff. His face stayed that way for a time and then he looked about, slowly approaching the narrow track of shingle at the base of the slope.

A beam of light skimmed the trees. Twice it floated up the cliff wall and down again, making circular movements as it neared the bottom. There was a coyote somewhere on the slope chuffing and howling. That's what woke Ramsey.

Adam felt the hand against the back of his head, pushing his face lower behind the rock.

"Five," Ramsey grunted. "Maybe more."

Adam saw one man push up the sleeve of his jacket, wristwatch lighting up his face for an instant. He hooted to someone in the trees and another hoot came back. They all fanned out, ghostly pale in the moonlight and merging with the shadows.

Adam lowered his hood and listened, but he couldn't hear anything. He thought he saw something a little further down the slopes, a dark shape that seemed to bleed into the gray rock it was lying on. An animal stretched out for the night, waiting like a sentinel until dawn.

"The cave's sacred," Ramsey said, chewing that stuff again, spat a chunk of it on the ground. "They won't come here. So we'll wait for an hour or two. Then we'll make a run for it."

TWENTY-THREE

The growling in Malin's stomach was the alarm she didn't need at eleven forty-five on a Sunday night. The hollow between her breasts was drenched in sweat and she threw off the quilt in a hurry.

Thoughts of Hollister churned around in her head, how he seemed to lead her further and further down that foggy path without ever giving her some tangible hope. She'd already changed her name to AvantGuard.

A shiver ran down her back as she focused hard on the open door and the pale pink glow from the kitchen. The occasional sweep of car lights on the road outside the window reminded her that the world was waking up, people returning to their early morning shifts.

She padded out of the bedroom and stared at the laptop on the kitchen counter, a glossy lid illuminated by three puck lights beneath the kitchen cabinets. If it wasn't for that extra dose of curiosity she'd been born with she wouldn't have bothered checking.

There were four emails. Two were store receipts, one was spam and the other was an alert from Heartfree.com. Wingman had sent her a private message… to her new account. She blinked a few times to see if it would go away and when it didn't she signed into the website and there it was.

Wingman: Wanna talk?

Two words. It was the best he could do. Maybe he

was looking for women. Maybe he thought she was someone else. She looked down the right hand margin of the screen, saw only seven people on the list of chatters. His name wasn't among them.

Malin: Sure.

But she didn't press send. She wondered if it was too eager, too desperate. But she was a detective first and detectives don't hesitate. They ask questions and she had plenty.

Talking of lonely, she needed to hear a human voice. Spasms of panic hit her when she was alone, like the time when her mother died. The time when she realized there would never be another sympathetic voice. She noticed Temeke didn't picked up when she dialed his number. Left him a voicemail instead.

Two people came off chat and four more came on. It was like a revolving door, a pantomime of actors with false names and faces. Women with young faces, hopeful faces; faces with so many virtual nips and tucks did they really think they could ever get away with it? And men sucking in those overhangs and showing the pecs they had in their twenties.

She hit SEND.

Wingman had no idea who AvantGuard was, but he'd want to know, probably ask for her number because men like him trolled the dating sites, picking up chicks and scoring notches on their cupboard doors. Boy, was he going to be pissed when he found out it was only her.

Hollister was handsome, relaxed, confident, and women fell for him. Hard. He was never overtly lecherous or sexual, just a little suggestive. Listening was his strength and mystery was his forté. There seemed to be a never ending stream of relationships because on the internet you can cast your net far and wide, love a woman in Texas and another in Tokyo, or so he said.

In fact, the women on chat had no life. This was their escape from boardroom to bedroom where nothing ever changed and nothing ever would. This was the dating of the future where everyone sat in their own bubble, never feeling flesh, never getting sick.

It was surprising how intimate you could get without ever meeting, how flirtatious without ever really knowing. It was exciting and dangerous. And it was downright stupid because the risks were greater.

She wondered if he was still sore about the escort job she once had. Sore she'd suddenly changed into a prude. That was the word he'd used, wasn't it? Prude.

Malin made herself a cup of tea, ate a piece of toast and then she got to thinking. Perhaps the women on chat were all waiting to talk to Hollister, probably already met him, already kissed him…

She walked back to the laptop and nearly dropped her cup. It was the beep of an incoming message. Wingman was online. He was also on chat and he'd already left her a message.

Wingman: Like the new name. Cute.

Malin's heart nearly skipped a beat. How did he know? The picture was the same, a bland blue avatar that everyone used when they first signed up.

He's a cop, stupid, that's why.

It was true, she was always on Heartfree.com. He just didn't need to remind her that's all. As for the name change, she found it a little creepy he was able to find her among so many. But it was her own fault. She had fallen in the trap of what he called *desperation*.

She knew her way around the internet like a teenager. There were plenty of police officers trolling the same sites, basking in their easy chairs and having a good laugh. Some were just ordinary folk looking for an ordinary date, some were predators sitting on the sidelines, watching. So which one was Hollister?

Malin: New name?

Wingman: Don't go playing games, Malin. You know how easy it is to look up an IP address. We're all family.

Malin: It's not a coincidence you're on here is it?

Wingman: All singles use Heartfree. All lonely singles that is.

Malin: Are you lonely?

Wingman: Sometimes. You are. You're desperately seeking me.

There was nothing desperate about wanting to talk to him. Seeking you? she began to type and then changed it to: And you're seeking who?

Wingman: I'm here to find a way.

Malin: What do you mean a way?

He typed four more lines. This time poetry.

The many men, so beautiful!
And they all dead did lie:
And a thousand thousand slimy things
Lived on; and so did I.

She was about to google the first line when he carried on typing.

Wingman: I've been up all night thinking.

Malin almost smiled. It sounded like the old Hollister; the Hollister who did a lot of thinking, especially at night. He had to take melatonin to get his mind to stop scuttling like a hamster in a wheel, or he would lose his mind. Thinking about what?

Wingman: When in Rome.

Malin: Rome is about five thousand miles away.

Wingman: You're about five thousand miles away.

Malin narrowed her eyes and considered this. If he was saying he missed her she wasn't falling for it. Trouble was, she needed to unload, to talk to someone she trusted, someone she had been close to. And Hollister was always the first person who popped into her head. He was from a well-connected family. His father ran for public office, mother was a Hampton's socialite, and it never seemed to amaze her that he lived in the slummiest area of town without so much as a hint of embarrassment. He said it was because he didn't want women going hog-wild over his money. It was clever in hindsight, if indeed it were true.

Of course, she had done a little snooping herself when she lived in Camden. He had about sixty thousand in the bank, nothing to scoff at, nothing to get excited about either. He drove a white Toyota Highlander and bought his clothes from a dry cleaners down the road, the type that sold unclaimed suits. He had supernatural charm he could turn up on a whim and steely gray eyes that always appeared amused. And worse, he said he could never fathom why Malin—or any woman for that matter—wanted to get married. It was a tie he could do without, no back door to bolt through when things got tough.

Malin followed him to Alexander Avenue one night, to a neighborhood in Maple Shade. She shrugged into a dark ski jacket, hair scooped up in a beanie, duty belt, cuffs and a nine millimeter. The only thing missing was a hand grenade.

She parked around the corner on Martin Avenue, a block down from Alexander and walked to the house. A white 1950 Cape Cod style set back from the street with a gabled roof and dormer windows, and a large wreath hanging on a red painted door.

It was nearly dusk when she climbed over the wall between the houses, caught her jeans on a nail and ripped them from crotch to knee. She landed in a dense thicket of buckthorn, narrowly avoiding a square of light from a brightly lit window.

A dry hinge squeaked on the back patio and she caught snatches of conversation drifting out onto a wide lawn. The voice was female, accusing, asking why he hadn't called, why he hadn't visited in over a month and why he wasn't wearing uniform. She loved him, wanted him out there on the sun lounger in nothing but his black leather tactical boots. He could wear his insignia, those nice yellow bars, if he could think of where to wrap them. There was laughter then.

This woman was twelve years Hollister's senior and happy to provide large withdrawals every time he made a deposit. It was clear why he favored the back door. It paid the rent.

Nausea rolled through Malin's stomach and she tried to breathe. All she could remember was scuttling back to the car, jeans flapping around one thigh. She was thankful when the sound of an incoming message distracted her from that particular nightmare.

Wingman: Are you there?

Malin waited just a few more seconds, enough to unravel a ribbon of scenarios that were playing out in her mind. Yes, I'm here.

Wingman: Are you talking to someone else?

Was he actually jealous? She mulled over what to say, wanted to type *maybe* and then realized how childish it sounded. The delay alone would keep him guessing.

Wingman: Got more important things to do, right?

She quickly typed. Nothing more important than you.

Wingman: Glad to hear it. Glad to hear I'm still number one.

Malin: But I'm not, am I? Heard you were getting married.

Wingman: You got that wrong. No chance of me getting married. Sounds like a life sentence to me.

It was true. Hollister would be hard pressed to tie the knot, but then this stripper was pregnant wasn't she? Malin was fed up with typing, wanted to talk on the phone.

Seriously, can we… she began to type and he beat her to it.

Wingman: The Mayor's son. High profile case. Saw it on the news. You and Temeke?

As soon as she settled on a topic, Hollister seemed to change course and then he'd hit her with something new. She decided to let it go. Yes, yes and yes.

Wingman: Has the kidnapper called.

Malin: He called the victim's wife.

Wingman: How did he sound?

Malin: Calm. Middle aged. He said he had the boy, wanted three grand in ransom. Wanted half in hundreds, half in small denominations Said it better not be sequenced or the boy's dead. Malin blew out a loud breath. She didn't want to tell him too much. We'll find him. You know that.

Wingman: This one's different. You won't find him in the usual places. He's never killed, never kidnapped. Had a speeding ticket in 2006. Bought a house in 2008. His name won't be in the database. So don't bother looking.

It was one of those moments when everything became a blur. She opened her mouth, not sure of what to think. You know him?

Wingman: Met him once. Strange guy, closed off, a little angry. But then we all have an axe to grind.

Hollister had met him? Give me a name?

Wingman: Think, Malin. Most people who commit crimes aren't always smart. They're delusional, need money to drive their drug use. That's their motive. This guy's different. He's dying. So in the days to come, he'll lose the ability to plan because he won't be able to get the painkillers he's so dependent on. Ask yourself this. Why hasn't he called again? Why hasn't he kept in touch?

Hollister went silent. No little dots, no friendly bubble. How did he know who this kidnapper was?

Malin: Are you there?

He signed off then. Just like that. Malin sat in a fog for a moment clasping her head. She gave the computer a harsh, threatening look, picked up the phone and dialed his number.

"Listen," she said to his voicemail. "I hate to intrude on your privacy, but it looks like it's going to be a long night. I don't care what you're doing or who you're doing it with. You don't just leave me hanging there with a statement like that! I'm going to keep calling this effing number until you pick up!"

TWENTY-FOUR

It was midnight when they climbed down that ladder, wind buffeting the packs and forcing them along the path to the west. A round moon gazed down from the sky, shrouding the trees in a ghostly shade of silver.

Adam felt his belly tremble. He was scared alright. He was a bit sick too. The rabbit had done a number on him in the cave and he'd had to pull his pants down five times. Ramsey had caught him perched on a low stone wall, scooped him up with both hands and told him not to crap on an ancient monument. Said it was sacred and defiling it was a fine of two hundred grand or life imprisonment. Made him use the ladder and do his business down there.

Adam knew he'd have the trots again before the night was out. This time it was worse like his bilge was filling with sewage and he had no idea where it was all coming from. If only if he could just wait until they were beyond the cliffs and trees…

Ramsey raised one hand and they stopped for a while, staring at the track and the opposite slopes. Something scampered between the sand and rocks, stopped, and then went on again.

"Coyote," Adam whispered.

"You saw it?" Ramsey edged his way in the shadows beneath the cliff. He was limping a bit but that didn't seem to stop him. "Those rangers have gone on ahead."

"How do you know?"

"I just know."

Adam felt his nose run, wanted to blow it real bad so he wiped it on his sleeve instead. "Can they see us?"

"They'll hear us if you don't shut up."

Adam gripped onto the straps at his shoulders, felt a familiar stab of pain in his side. He'd have to ignore it for now until they were at least a hundred yards beyond the cliffs. There was wide open country then and only a few piñon trees to squat behind. His butt was sore and he was shaky and soaked with sweat.

He could hear the occasional rattle of pebbles beneath his feet, saw Ramsey lift his hand to warn him. The sky was darker in the west and so was the land and as they walked under a myriad of stars, Adam remembered the scout troop he'd left behind. He could picture the tents, a pulsing campfire and a pot full of beans. And he could hear the ghost stories that everyone liked best. He missed them all and he wondered if they missed him.

It was an hour before the cliffs became a flat-topped promontory fading out into a talon of rock. It was barely a glimmer now in the distance and they were walking through tufts of long grass tall enough to reach their shins. There was no sign of the rangers. Just a dark horizon ahead and a few scrawny bushes reaching upwards like dead men's fingers.

Ramsey stopped for a while to get his bearings. He didn't need a compass, nor a map. He pointed to the hull of an old boat, only Adam told him it wasn't an old boat. It was the hollowed out husk of a tree. It had been lying on its side for hundreds of years, smooth and calcified and dry.

They hung the tarp down from the top edge and weighted it with rocks, spread out their wet coats on the ground. Ramsey gathered what he could of the kindling, made a small fire and fanned it to life, sparks hurtling into the night sky.

"I need toilet paper," Adam moaned.

"There's no toilet paper. You can't want to go again."

"I do." Adam gripped his buttocks with one hand as if it would prevent a sudden blow.

He began hopping too. First on one leg and then the other, and then he dropped both the duffel bag and his pants before Ramsey could count to three.

"I feel better now," he said afterwards.

Ramsey's head was bent over and his shoulders were shaking. "By the laws of gravity your insides should have fallen out by now."

It wasn't funny. It was the rabbit that made him purge. "Give me some paper. *Please!*"

"You can have a pile of grass like before. And that's my final offer."

Grass wasn't half bad. It was leaves Adam hated the most. Prickly and cold against your skin and soaking from the rain. But it got the worse off and that's all that mattered.

Ramsey showed him how to hold a gun, showed him how to aim, except it was too dark to shoot it. They drank hot chocolate and ate marshmallows and talked about their favorite movies.

"*Jurassic Park*," Adam said. "That's mine."

Ramsey sighed and looked up for a time. "*The Deer Hunter*, that's mine."

The wind coming off the grass smelled faintly of corn husks and the faint susurration of the feathery tufts nearly put Adam to sleep. Ramsey left the jug out for the rain before they lay down for the night.

In the morning there was a faint rumble of thunder and a few spits of rain that pattered on the tarp. They ate the last of the venison for breakfast and buried the rest of that rabbit before striking camp. Adam knew Ramsey had been sick in the night, heard him retching too. He wondered if there were a few pages missing from that book and decided to ask.

"Of course I didn't use any," Ramsey said, giving Adam a drink of water before folding the tarp. "Paper's for girls."

Being with Ramsey was different to being with his dad, the tired old man who rarely smiled. It wasn't his dad's fault. It was his job, so his mom said. Being Mayor of Albuquerque had its downs, especially when he rarely came home. When he did, he was sleeping mostly; didn't want to play cards; didn't want to walk the dog. No, this was more like being with his mom, someone you could tell jokes with, someone who found the world a fun place to live in.

Ramsey shook out the cups and looked down at Adam's upturned face, then gave him a wink. "Wanna hear a joke?"

Adam nodded. It probably wouldn't be funny. Old people never made jokes funny. But it was funny. Side-splittingly funny and his body began to quake, breaths hitching. He must have laughed all the way to a clump of trees darkened from a forest fire. They recited cuss words to see who knew the ugliest and then they talked about the meaning and where the words came from.

"Course you mustn't use those words in front of a lady," Ramsey insisted. "Probably shouldn't use them at all."

He pointed at a low stone wall about fifteen feet from where they were. "Must be the foundations of an old homestead. There's a few round here, old and gnarled and burned to the ground." he said, unscrewing the cap off the water jug.

"Did all the people die?"

"Mostly," Ramsey nodded, looking around. "They died of cholera. Can't see any headstones. Can you?"

Adam shook his head. All he could see were dark shadows from horizon to horizon and acres of grass where the sun shone down. He hated the gray emptiness of death and he was scared of it too. "They're not underneath us are they?"

"Dang, you're not scared of skulls and bones are you?"

Adam didn't like the idea of skulls and bones wandering about and causing a ruckus. "Oh, no. I was just wondering that's all."

"Well that's good. 'Cause I don't want some crybaby worried about skulls and bones going on a scare bender."

"They do?"

"Do what?"

"Go on scare benders."

"There was a time when I used to sleep rough out by the volcanoes," Ramsey said, looking off in the distance. "But you don't want to hear about that."

Adam damn well did. And urgently. "The ones out by Grants?"

Ramsey nodded and handed the jug to Adam. "It was back in the 1900s. Three girls went hiking after church in the spring. Went all alone without a chaperone. Police didn't know what they were doing out there in their Sunday best. Couldn't find them. All they did find was a lace glove and a straw hat. And further up in a heap of ash, a pink ribbon. They were never seen again. But I heard them one night… screaming."

Adam nearly gulped on that water. "Screaming?"

"I often think of them when I go there. Sixteen, seventeen… too young to die. Pretty too. I dream of them sometimes. The wind blows ash tens of thousands of miles away… and it blew those screams. I wish I could have done something."

1900… Adam tried to do the math in his head and gave up after a few seconds. "How old are you?"

Ramsey grinned. "Old enough."

Maybe Ramsey was already dead. Maybe he was just a ghost limping about in the long grass and babbling on like one too. But he wasn't limping. He didn't seem to give that wound much mind and he was walking faster like it never happened, putting on a brave face.

They sat on one of those stone walls, ate crackers and drank water and then went on again. It was hard going with the duffel on his back but Adam wasn't giving up. He sensed ghosts in the sighing pines that grew along the route and wondered if Ramsey was just hallucinating with all that stuff he snorted. He hadn't smoked a cigarette since they left the lodge because he said the reek would give them away.

"Ever smelled a yellowbelly?" Ramsey pressed his nose against the thick, flaky bark of a Ponderosa. "It's like cinnamon."

All Adam could smell was wet earth and the occasional whiff of butterscotch. He was tired of wading through drifts of pine needles and patches of snow one day to clear blue skies the next, and he was tired of smelling like a porta-potty.

It was late afternoon before they reached a meadow of corn-colored grass and a hunter's cabin. Each stalk swayed back and forth in a fickle wind, whispering and chattering as if something lived in it.

"Can't see them, but I know they're there," Ramsey murmured.

"Who?"

"Better do it now. Better do it slow." Ramsey raised one eyebrow and flicked a quick glance at Adam. "Before the raptors come."

TWENTY-FIVE

Serena had called again and they'd talked. Only this time she wanted to see him right away and that made Temeke jumpy. He hoped it wasn't another round of accusations and torture, and he hoped she'd leave him with some furniture this time. Eleven thirty today. In the park. He wouldn't forget.

Temeke was wondering how to drop the news to Fowler about that jawbone he'd found. Everything was beginning to look prehistoric these days, even Hackett's suits. He had already interviewed the majority of the Mayor's staff the week before. There were only three left.

He looked at his cell phone, kept wondering if Serena would change her mind. There were a few unavailable numbers and some he didn't recognize. It was during one of those blind moments when he convinced himself it was her, too scared to identify herself, too scared to tell him how she really felt. It was a chance in a sodding million.

He was debating a second cup of coffee on that miserable Monday morning that wouldn't give him heart palpitations like the last one he'd had, when the quick chirrup of a siren in the parking lot shattered the silence.

"Hackett wants his car parked," sang Fowler from his office in his usual monophonic voice.

"Tell him to bloody park it himself," Temeke

chanted back.

He wasn't surprised to hear a round of laughter from the cafeteria followed by a bout of cussing from Jarvis. There he was, with his pink scrubbed face surmounted by tufts of blond hair carefully teased straight. He looked more like a cherub than a cop, sweeping through the lobby towards Hackett's car just to see how far he could grovel.

"Nice tie," Malin said, headed towards the interview room with a tray of coffee and cookies.

She noticed, Temeke thought, because he rarely wore a tie. Couldn't stand the pressure against his throat. "So you cussed him out?"

"I did more than that," Malin whispered. "I called three times. That should have made his night."

Temeke was almost beginning to feel sorry for Hollister, only he couldn't help feeling a tingle of salacious excitement. "Probably saw you on the caller ID and switched it off, Marl. One of those mine?" he said, pointing at the cups.

"For the gardener. He's already here."

Figures, Temeke thought. The old boy had likely parked in Hackett's spot.

Hackett breezed in and pushed through the opening door of the elevator. He gave a dry cough which was beginning to sound theatrical in light of the upcoming press conference. Temeke could still hear it as the elevator ground to the top floor.

Cesar Cruz had greenish-yellow eyes and a thin pencil moustache. He also had a limp, left foot turned slightly inward which didn't seem to impede his progress. He sat opposite Malin and that bag of cookies, flashing the best of three yellow teeth.

"Thank you for coming in," Temeke said. "Mrs. Oliver will be here in half an hour and the press can ask some pretty harsh questions. So tell me, how long have you worked for the Olivers?"

Cesar took a deep breath, fingers massaging his chin. "Eh… four years. Before, I work in Tijuana."

Temeke noted Cesar's voice was slow and clipped, every word spoken as if it were new. He didn't look much, but Temeke betted his mind turned over faster than a V-8.

"Have you found him?" Cesar said, eyes watering.

Malin patted Cesar on the arm. "Not yet. He's a scout. Remember that."

"His troop's out there looking for him and so are the police," Temeke added, seeing no visible relief on Cesar's face. He knew how he felt. The first thing he always noticed about people was their humility. You could see it in their eyes. On a scale of one to ten, this man was a firm ten. "You speak good English, Mr. Cruz."

"No, no, señor. I speak like the pigeons."

Temeke refrained from laughter and ran a finger down the resume on file. "It says here you were educated at the Instituto México. That's a private school isn't it?"

"Catholic." Cesar bowed his head where a comb-over revealed a gray painted pate. He took a sip of coffee and smiled at Malin. "My mother was a cleaner for Profesor Francisco. He pay the fees. She make him happy. He very good man."

Temeke gave a tight grin. "Do you like reading, Mr. Cruz?"

"A little." Cesar scarfed down a cookie and cracked his knuckles before eyeing the bag with renewed interest.

"So you like books?"

"I like poetry."

Temeke had never known a gardener to have a lexicon of leather-bound literature in his potting shed, but this one did. The field investigators found works by

Emily Dickinson and Theodore Roethke. "And you like gardening."

"Oh, yes, señor. I am a graduate of Foley's Institute."

Make that a V-8 on steroids, Temeke thought. "How did you come to work for the Mayor?"

"Because…" Cesar looked up to the ceiling and down again. "I am cheap."

"Cheap?"

"Yes, señor. I am from Mexico."

Temeke held back a snort and saw Malin cover her mouth. He was growing to like Cesar more by the minute. Truth was, the Olivers always found their gardeners through Foley's. Anything less would not have been good enough.

"You keep the garden shed tidy?"

"Ah, the shed. Yes, the shed. Very, very clean."

"Do you miss Mexico?" Temeke asked.

"No, señor. My father…" Cesar began and then crossed himself. He leaned forward and lowered his voice. "Had a violin."

Temeke snatched a look at Malin as if the word *violin* had some secret meaning. "He was a musician?"

"Couldn't play a note," Cesar said, peeling another cookie from the packet. "It is where he keep his… *stash.*"

"He was a drug dealer?" Temeke was momentarily speechless.

"Si, si. He talk in code. But every day I do crossword. I know code. One day, he get sick. Look like a naked Chihuahua. Still he work nights. He make money."

"How much?"

"Forty thousand dollars."

Temeke recalled the case. Cesar was ten years old when a car drew up outside their small house and someone lobbed a hand grenade onto the front porch. Cesar did what any ten year old would do. He promptly pitched it back. By all accounts it was a good shot, slipped inside that car through a crack in the driver's window. Big bang, lots of police. It was lucky he wasn't sent to juvie.

"How would you describe Mayor Oliver?" Temeke asked.

"He always say good morning… always take a rose for his coat." Cesar tapped at his lapel. "He say, 'Cesar, your roses are the best in New Mexico.' I very proud to work for him."

Temeke reached into the brown envelope and pulled out a syringe. "Wouldn't like to tell me what this is?"

"For the roses. They win the Albuquerque Flower Show every year." Cesar leaned forward and pointed at the syringe. "I take a white rose, put this in the stalk," he said, measuring about six inches with his thumb and index finger. "Water for seven days. Color of royalty."

"So you dye them purple?"

"Of course."

Temeke knew Cesar had visited the Mayor in hospital with a bunch of roses from his own garden. The officer outside the Mayor's room had counted over five visits since Sunday.

"Are you close to Mrs. Oliver?"

Temeke didn't miss the quiver of recognition, and saw the slight tilt of his head. It appeared that 'the Señora' spent a good deal of time on the phone behind closed doors. And when she wasn't indoors she was out shopping for haute couture.

"Sometimes," Cesar murmured, looking down at his clasped hands, thumb rubbing against thumb, "she sit in the gazebo and she cry. Sometimes she write many letters. But not when it rains."

"How does that make you feel?" Malin asked.

"When she cries."

"Sad… because she very unhappy."

"Unhappy?" Malin scooted the packet of cookies a little closer to Cesar's elbow.

Temeke gathered that Mrs. Oliver had a close friend she regularly confided in, someone she spoke to on the phone. She was now taking some form of medication and sleeping a good deal. The housekeeper often found her napping on the chaise long and had to rouse her with a hard nudge.

Cesar rustled the wrapper and popped three cookies onto the table with his thumb. "The Señora… she have two journals."

"Where?" Temeke asked.

"In the library. Look like books." Cesar wagged a finger. "But not books."

Temeke knew the sodding FBI hadn't found them because special agent Stu Anderson would have told him. He was a personal friend. He was also a notorious gossip. "Has the Mayor ever asked you to do extra work? You know, anything after hours?"

"Only the letters."

"What letters?" Malin asked.

Cesar chomped for a few seconds and then licked his fingers. "He ask me to post letters to Mr. Andrew Blaine. 522 Cragmont Ave, Berkeley."

Temeke reckoned there must have been a whole pile of letters to this person if Cesar could rattle off one name and an address. He also reckoned he needed to talk with the Mayor, but not before talking to Mr. Blaine.

"Any chance you know this guy?" Temeke hoped it would save a whole heap of time if he did.

"No señor." Cesar shrugged and examined the palm of his hand.

"Why were you at the Mayor's house last Sunday?"

"Mrs. Oliver ask me to sweep the driveway and oil

the gates. Mr. Art. He thirty-five last Sunday."

"Did you see anything unusual? Any activity outside the house?"

Cesar shrugged and shook his head.

There was a light tap on the door and Temeke made no attempt to respond. It was only the silhouette of Captain Fowler smeared against the glass. Just another wall of muscle and spiked hair he'd rather not deal with.

The door crashed back on its hinges and in bounded Fowler, eyes bright and wide. Looked like he was spoiling for a fight.

"Santiago," he growled. "Phone!"

TWENTY-SIX

Malin rushed out to the front desk. Sergeant Moran was doing his best to cover up a half-naked body builder on the front cover of Flex Magazine with the remains of his smoked salmon sandwich.

She pressed the phone to her ear. "Detective Santiago," she said.

"Good morning," a male voice said, punctuated by a few yawns.

It took her a second and she almost dropped the phone. "Hollister!"

"Got your messages. Wanted to talk before the dust settled."

"I'm sorry if—"

"You had no business cussing like a marine and leaving hate mail. What the heck did I do? And next time pick up your cell phone. Save me having to call Fowler. He's bound to think something's going on."

"Who cares about Fowler. And why do you think I called nine times? You can't leave a girl hanging like that. You did that on purpose just to get me all riled up."

"I didn't think you wanted to talk to me again."

"Course I wanted to talk to you," Malin said, lowering her voice. "It's my case. Now, who is he?"

"Who's who?"

"The man we were talking about last night. You seem to know so much about him. All that stuff about having a parking ticket in, what, 2006? You said we'd never find him. You said he's not even in the database."

She heard nothing but silence and a chill tickled up to the roots of her hair. What he said was not what she was expecting.

"I wasn't talking to you last night."

Malin felt like a cog in her brain wasn't firing properly. She muttered, "What?" and some other things as well. "If it wasn't you, then… who's Wingman?"

Hollister let out a loud sigh. "You better not be fooling about on those chat sites. Please tell me you're not fooling about on those chat sites."

Malin took a few seconds to gather herself before speaking. "He said he was you?" Well not exactly. He never really said he was anyone.

"Someone using my identity?" Hollister was raising his voice now. "First off, let me tell you something. If some little squirt's out there stealing a cop's identify I'll trace his IP address and cut off more than his connection."

"He knew about the case, asked if I'd heard from the kidnapper."

"And I suppose you told him everything. Suppose you gave him classified information." Hollister vented for three minutes, said a few things about federal crimes and a lynching. Said he was going to have her computer tapped, said she was a fatso."

"Who you calling a fatso?"

"I said FIASCO!"

Malin was making feeble movements with her arms and legs, felt like she'd just been struck by lightning. She must have gone through ten pounds of sweat in the last two minutes. He wouldn't stop shouting, wouldn't stop ranting on about how he was going to take this man down a dark alley and give him a shakedown he'd never forget.

"Who are you going to take down a dark alley?" she finally cut in. "You don't even know who he is. You don't even know if it's a *he*. It could be an old lady with senile dementia. It could be a minor—"

"With classified information!"

He had a point. "Maybe it was Fowler."

The line went quiet again and Malin had to ask him if he was still there. Hollister muttered an angry yes and said Fowler could be a hick sometimes, but he wouldn't mess on his own turf. Said her accusations would be better directed at herself since Fowler didn't use the internet to get dates. He didn't need to.

"I thought highly of you Malin," he said. "I really did. Thought you could do this job. Even gave Hackett a reference."

Malin felt her cheeks flash. He was mocking her now. First he told her she was fat and tried to wriggle out of it, and now this.

"Do your job, Malin," Hollister said with another deep sigh "And let me do mine."

He hung up then, left her standing at the front desk with a red face and watery eyes. Didn't give her an occasion to congratulate him on his promotion to Captain. Would have been OK if Sgt. Moran hadn't been listening to every word behind that magazine he was pretending to read.

She rushed across the lobby to the bathrooms, stared hard in the mirror. Tried to see herself through his eyes. A five foot five brunette with sallow skin and dark eyes smeared with make-up. She wasn't beautiful, not by Serena Temeke standards, but she was attractive wasn't she?

Dang! Hollister was such a brute. So typical to take Fowler's side. She wiped off a black smudge under one eye and would have cried harder if it hadn't been for the squeak of the door.

"Marl?"

It was Temeke.

"Can't a girl have some peace," she said, wondering why he hadn't knocked.

"Sarge said you'd had a call from Hollister. What did he want?"

None of your business, she wanted to say, leaning back against the sink, hands in pockets. She stared at the opposite wall and hoped her face wasn't as grimy as it felt. "Just an argument, that's all."

Temeke pressed a wrist against the doorframe and heaved a sigh. "About what?"

"About Fowler. Guess I can't stop thinking he's the enemy."

Temeke gave her a narrow-eyed stare and nodded slowly. "I wouldn't get on the wrong side of Fowler if I were you, love. He has subtle ways of making people pay up. Little nudges, that kind of thing. You'll wake up one morning and find your computer's been hacked or your hamster's throat's been cut. He can be ugly like that."

Malin held back a chuckle, looked into those black eyes and wanted to tell him everything. She could lose her job with one snap of Hackett's fingers if he ever found out.

"Called our Mr. Andrew Blaine. Course he didn't pick up so I left a message, told him we'd get a search warrant. Oh, and Mrs. Oliver's just arrived. Press conference starts in ten minutes." Temeke opened the bathroom door and flapped a hand. "Fowler's leading, poor old sod. Hackett thinks very highly of him. Wants to give him a medal in observation. Course, that's how he got his GED. Observation."

"What did you think of Cesar?" Malin asked as they cleared the lobby to the conference room in a few swift strides.

"He said letters—plural. When you left the room I asked him if the letters were sealed. He said yes. I asked him if he could remember what type of envelopes, big, small, window, self-seal. He said self-seal. So I got to thinking, self-seal can easily be reopened if you're quick. I asked him if he opened any. He said it's easy if you put the envelope in the freezer for a while. They open all by themselves."

The conference room was bulging with press as they worked their way through a crush of photographers and journalists to the podium. Mrs. Oliver sat at a nearby table with Cesar Cruz to her right. They were whispering, seemingly undeterred by the flurry of cameras in front of them. She was whiter than Malin remembered. Maybe it was just the maroon lipstick.

Fowler stood next to Hackett who was fighting hard to keep a rash of anxiety behind a sweaty face. He looked dogged tired.

"So, what have we got, sir?" Temeke whispered, leaning in and frowning at Hackett's frown.

"A dead man in the woods, no dental matches, nothing," Hackett whispered. "And why is he dead in the first place?"

Fowler pulled up his belt and tucked his shirt further down his pants. "He's dead because our kidnapper killed him. And our kidnapper is the Ringmaster. That's what we're going to tell the press."

"Got enough evidence to back up that statement?" Temeke said. "Cause you'll look like a right patsy if you don't."

Malin was enjoying the banter, wondering if Temeke was doing it for her benefit. He must have sensed her ego had been battered and Fowler only made things worse with that thin smile of his.

"For your information, the dogs picked up a scent in the woods," Fowler said. "Found the remains of a campfire and blood spatters on a nearby tree. There were rabbit bones and coffee grounds. It was him all right. Forensics are spinning out the DNA as we speak."

"Could take months," Temeke reminded. "So could the search."

Fowler wiped a trickle of sweat from his temple with the back of his hand. "Agent Running Hawk called it off that night. Wouldn't cross the river. Said there were only cave dwellings behind the cliffs. Said they were sacred."

"That's a big bloody shame because our killer was probably counting on that. Probably set up house in those ruins, nice big bed and place to call his own."

The line of Fowler's mouth tightened. "Running Hawk said the dogs were tired and so were the men. Said they'd go west in the morning. Remember he's a Shadow Wolf officer. He'll find them."

Malin didn't like the way Fowler was pandering to the press, occasionally turning sideways to catch a camera flash. He was far too pleased with himself for a man without an ounce of news.

"Oh, just in case you thought to mention it," Temeke whispered. "The doctor did confirm a match for that jawbone you found. Ovis aries. That's a sheep by the way."

Another deep sigh from Fowler and a roll of the eyes. Malin pressed her lips together and snorted through her nose. How like Temeke to keep that precious piece of information to the end.

Jennifer Danes sat in the front row, brown hair, slim body, immaculately dressed in black leggings and pumps. She was already scribbling something in that notepad and the conference hadn't even started. Cynthia Wrigley, Chief Editor of the *Journal* sat beside her. She was squeezed into a red suit, legs unshaved, little black hairs visible through a pair of sheer pantyhose. Cyn was a firm believer in the term *au naturel*. She even had the makings of a thin moustache to prove it.

Raymond Brewster from the *Daily Tribune* looked oddly ill at ease. His eyes flicked from one side of the room to the other, probably hoping he wouldn't run into Jarvis who was dealing out citations like a deck of cards.

Fowler walked behind the podium and raised a hand. Malin, Temeke and Hackett followed and stood directly behind.

"Good morning everyone. I'm Captain Fowler and with me today is Madam Mayor, Mr. Cesar Cruz, Unit Commander Fred Hackett, Detective David Temeke and Detective Malin Santiago." He managed to rattle off a few more department names before the press began to fidget.

Fowler raised his hand again. "The purpose of this press conference is to provide an update to the disappearance of Adam Oliver. Before I get into details, the last six days have been a tough and emotional time for the Olivers and I wish to add our sincere condolences to the family, friends and co-workers of Mayor Oliver. Here are the details of the most recent incident: Following our investigation, officers searching a stretch of woodland found human remains of a man thought to be in his late sixties, early seventies. There was recent evidence of a campfire, food and the like. Officers also found what appeared to be leather bindings attached to a tree. Further investigation is pending. The community can be confident that we will lead a thorough and transparent investigation. I would like to start with local affiliates to make sure their questions are answered."

Stan Stockard stood up and dipped his head. "Do we have any leads on the kidnapper? A name?"

"Not at this time, no," Fowler said, eyes flicking around the room. "Rest assured, the men and women of the Duke City Police Department are working around the clock—"

"I'm sure they are," Jennifer Danes shouted. "But our sources tell us the camp you mention belonged to the Ringmaster. Can you comment on that?"

"We have no evidence to say that it was."

"Was there excessive force?" she asked.

"There was."

"Which woods?" Jennifer Danes pressed.

"A tract of land at the west end of Gila National Forest."

"Can you be more specific?" she shouted.

"Not at this time," Fowler said.

"Can you tell us about the trace evidence?" Brewster yelled. "Who does the blood belong to?"

"I'm not able to give information on any trace evidence," Fowler said.

There was an uproar then. Cameras flashed, people yelled. Brewster accused the police department of hiding crucial details, of being anything but thorough and transparent.

Malin barely heard Hackett's voice in Temeke's ear behind a hurl of demands from the press. "Teenagers, that's all it is," he whispered. "A perverted ritual. They're always in the woods, smoking weed and having sex."

"A word if I may, sir," Temeke whispered back. "Old Ginger in the morgue might be something to do with these perverted rituals. For your sake I hope I'm wrong."

"Shut up and stop interrupting," Hackett wheezed behind a hand and gave another cough.

"I'll shut up, sir. But before I do, it's the campfire we need to concentrate on and the rabbit bones. I doubt a pair of horny teenagers had time to build a fire, skin a rabbit and eat it, let alone catch one. I'll shut up now, sir."

Hackett hung his head, finger massaging his bottom

lip. He didn't even look up when Jennifer Danes cut in again, shouting over the din.

"In what way do leather straps have anything to do with the disappearance of Adam Oliver?" she asked.

Fowler shot a brief look at Mrs. Oliver whose eyes were wide and searching. "We don't have all the forensic pieces and it would be wrong to speculate."

"What's the motive?" Cyn shouted.

"We think its money," Fowler responded.

"In exchange for Adam? Well, where is he then? Any news of Mayor Oliver? Is he still in a coma? Are the police really up for this?"

Fowler's response was drowned out by another volley of questions and the room was louder than the New York Stock Exchange.

Malin heard Temeke's whisper, warm breath tickling her ear. "Cyn'll be out stone-cold on the floor soon if she doesn't stop bleating. She'll also have a surprised look on her stupid face after Fowler's put his boot in."

"She's got a point," Malin hated to admit. "The first Press Conference didn't go much better. She accused the police of hiding information she thought the public should be made aware of."

"When you look at Mrs. Oliver. What do you see?"

Malin saw a woman who should have been the face of Yves Saint Laurent. She was talking to the press now, pleading for the kidnapper to bring Adam home safe. "Confident, determined. She's looking right at the cameras like a news anchor."

"She was a model. She knows how to work them."

"She's gripping that cell phone, keeps looking at it like she's expecting a call."

"Wouldn't you if you lost your son?"

"You've always said concentrate on the facts. Boy goes missing. Fact. Father gets shot. Fact. Kidnapper calls the wife. Fact. Police are no further in their investigation in the five long days since Adam disappeared. Fact."

"That's why Hackett's called this Press Conference, Marl. To see if the local rag can get the ball rolling since we've managed to come up with bugger all."

"But Fowler's telling them the motive's money."

"Good. Then if our kidnapper's watching, he'll have a bloody good laugh."

TWENTY-SEVEN

Ramsey was laughing again. Long drawn out sounds that seemed to scrape and churn in his throat and echo around the hunter's cabin. Sometimes he spat that laugh right out where it left a glistening trail in the carpet. Sometimes he clutched his chest where his heart was because he said there was a tear in it.

It was the grass and tobacco he rolled, smelled like burnt hay every time he took a drag. Said it was safe to smoke inside, said the walls were thick enough to hide the smell. Sometimes, he would grasp his thigh with both hands and then he'd lie back in that chair with a glazed look on his face.

It was Monday morning. Had to be. Adam counted the days off on his fingers and he was on the fourth finger on his right hand when he heard the rise and fall of Ramsey's voice. He was on that phone again, only this time he was talking to himself, leaving a message that nobody heard.

Something about Midsummer's Day and how he should have been there. The rest was muffled behind a hand, like he didn't want Adam to hear. The phone lost its juice after that and Ramsey turned the volume up on the TV, sat smoking that thing until it was no bigger than a child's tooth. He muttered to the wall as if there was someone else in the room and then he sighed, shoulders jigging in a sob.

It was the tears that made Adam shudder. He'd never seen a grown man cry, slumped in the chair with his head in his hands. It went on for a while until Adam could hear no other sound but the wind. He wanted to run away, wanted to charge through the front door. The deadbolt was engaged, he could see through the gap in the frame and there was no key in the lock to open it. The cabin was old, its plaster stripped down to the wall studs, and the wind whistled through dirty panes of glass.

He felt sorry for the man, felt a clawing at his heart. Ramsey had been a little harsh in the beginning. But he hadn't tried to kill him, hadn't tied him to a tree and left him there for the wolves. Brought him to the cabin… house… whatever it was, and lain him in the bed. Even put a thick blanket over his shivering body. Adam had been crying then, missing his dad, and Ramsey stayed until he fell asleep. But there was something that bothered Adam, something he needed to ransack from that cluttered mind of his.

It was his sixth birthday when they were living in the big white house, the one by the sea. He remembered the cake, the candles. He even remembered the walk down to the beach, the rush of wind across the dunes. He could still feel the warmth of his Dad's arms around his thigh like he'd never let go.

They walked in the tideline that evening, watching their footprints as they dimpled the sands. He remembered the thud of the waves, the swell and the foam, and he remembered the man. A figure in the distance at first and then a solid shape as he came up close. His hair was cropped short like the men his dad once knew.

You always remember things like that, when a sharp yellow sun rides along the coastline and stretches out of sight, and all the rest is gray sea, sand and sky. Before they said goodbye, the man crouched down and gave Adam something and said something too, only he couldn't remember what it was. But there was one thing he remembered. A raw red line that ran along the man's left temple.

Adam looked over at a pot belly stove in the corner of the room, coals flickering through the fire door. A kettle began to steam on the hotplate, a shoot of it almost to the ceiling. Ramsey pulled his sleeve down, grabbed the thing by the handle and poured two cups of water.

It was the sound of thunder that made Adam flinch. Rain rattled against the roof. He came out of the bedroom and sat down on the floor next to Ramsey, looked up at two wide eyes.

"You knew my dad from before, didn't you?"

Ramsey took a sip of that tea and offered a slight nod. "Well, that would take all night. It's nothing you need to worry about."

"But I do worry." Adam was worried Ramsey's leg would fester and he would die out here, and Adam would never find his way home.

"A lad like you has a mother for that stuff."

"Yes, but she's not here is she. And I'm worried now."

Ramsey sucked in his bottom lip like he was thinking real hard and he seemed to study the cracks in the floor. "There was a time," he said, "when I worried a lot. Thought I'd die once, but I didn't. Better to laugh, remember a few good jokes. Awful world to be sad in."

Adam smiled at that. He'd laughed about the raptors in the long grass, the stupid growls Ramsey made all the way to the cabin. They'd run like two madmen anyway.

"Got us here, didn't you, Mr. Night Eyes?"

"You got us here."

"Between those eyes and my belly, we got us here. Eyes to see, belly to sense. That's what it's all about.

Teamwork. So tell me about the girl you like at school."

Adam told Ramsey her name again, told him how he liked her hair and the way she rocked her head from side to side when she spoke. "She's Indian. They do that, you know."

Ramsey glanced down at the phone on his lap. "I like someone too. Well, love, actually. There have been others, but no one like her."

"Did you ask her to marry you?"

"No."

"Why?"

"Because it wouldn't have been right."

"Why?" And when Ramsey didn't answer, Adam remembered the photograph. "It's that girl isn't it? The one in a bathing suit. Why do guys look at girls in bathing suits?"

"You wouldn't understand—"

"Why won't you tell me?"

"Well, it's hard to explain. So I'll leave it for now. Until you're older."

"What if I die before I'm older. You promised!" Adam was kneeling now, fists by his sides and shaking too. There was something Ramsey wasn't telling him and that made him mad. "It's all that sex stuff isn't it. The kissing."

"It's more than that."

"You did something… you did something bad."

"Now, son—"

You killed my dad!"

Adam started thumping Ramsey then. On the cheeks, on the head, on the scar. He thumped Ramsey in the chest, on his thighs until he crumpled to the floor. He felt the hand on his head as he sobbed. Felt so wretched.

"Who are you?" Adam whimpered.

"Just a small piece of your life, son. That's all. I made you a spitfire when you were a kid. Painted it too."

Adam shook his head at first and sobbed some more. And then he remembered the old plane in his bedroom, the one high up on the ledge, the one with the tattered paint. He recalled running around the garden with his arm in the air, plane banking first to the left and then to the right, tongue bouncing off the roof of his mouth in a stutter of gunfire. He kept it on his windowsill at night, watched the moonlight spill over those gray and green wings and dreamed of it bursting through the clouds. He was proud of it.

"It's still in my room," he murmured.

The little plane was no longer in pride of place and half hidden behind a larger Spitfire, a few Junkers and a couple of Messerschmitts. But it was still there.

"That's one of the small pieces," Ramsey said. "Maybe you'll have a good laugh at some of the things we did. Maybe you'll find it in your heart to forgive me. And maybe you'll marry Runa and tell your kids about me. I'd like that." Ramsey always looked at him with squinty eyes, face tilted to one side, mouth almost a smile.

"You never taught me how to shoot a gun. You only taught me how to hold one."

"I'll teach you how to shoot. After you learn how to load and aim."

"And you said you'd tell me everything."

Ramsey agreed. Said he'd already started writing it down in his blue book. Said he'd give it to Adam as soon as he'd finished writing it. "Do you remember what I said to you that day? On the beach?"

Adam shook his head. It was always blur.

"I said I was proud of you. That you looked like your grandma. Same eyes. Same nose. It used to tilt up like this." Ramsey pressed one finger against his nose and pushed it as high as it would go. "Looked like Miss Piggy."

Adam sucked in a smile, wasn't going to let Ramsey get off too lightly. "Is Ramsey your real name?"

Ramsey pursed his lips and narrowed his eyes. "Ramsey… Gray Fox, whatever comes easiest." He rubbed his leg then, gave a wince now and then. "You want to aim that gun?"

Adam nodded. They were outside before he could count to six. He was scared, but he was excited too. Ramsey checked if it was loaded, told Adam to do the same.

"It isn't loaded," Adam said.

"How do you know?"

"You just checked."

"But did you?"

Ramsey told him to make sure the safety was on, told him to hold it downrange. He shouted a few times, made Adam jump until he forgot which way was right.

"You won't load it until I tell you to."

Adam nodded. He just aimed and steadied it a few times, forefinger below the trigger guard. Something about being bitten by the slide and how painful it was. And there was a story to go with it.

It was fun in a dangerous kind of way and Adam wasn't sure he wanted to pull that trigger when the time came. Didn't want the thing to go off and make him deaf. His heart nearly missed a beat, tried to aim at a notch on a nearby tree. Something about sights moving and could he see his aim point. The gun felt heavy in his hands and there was sweat pouring down the side of his face.

"Take a deep breath and hold it," Ramsey said.

Adam thought he would pop and it wasn't until Ramsey took that gun away that he let out the breath he was holding. Then Ramsey told him about flying shells and hot gases, how guns were all different. Made him feel important. Made him feel like a man. Told him they'd practice again tomorrow.

It was late when they finished all the food, drank all the tea. Ramsey said there was a town two miles to the north where they could buy more food. They'd stay the night there in a motel, take showers, change clothes. It was something to look forward to.

That night, Adam dreamed of a dark gray sea lifting and falling behind the breakers, and of a man walking through the water, legs frothy from the swell. He woke up once shouting for his dad until a voice soothed him back to sleep.

It was the sound of a dog's bark that woke him up at dawn.

TWENTY-EIGHT

Temeke drove into his usual parking space to the right of the dumpster and turned off the ignition. His cell phone gave him a jolt. Serena.

It was her voice that made him tense and for some reason he couldn't stomach her today. He missed her but not enough to bear any more pain. He knew what she wanted. Just couldn't bring himself to agree to it.

"Yesterday?" Temeke almost smacked his head and dropped the phone. It was Tuesday. He had completely forgotten. "I'm so sorry, love."

She said she was sorry too. Said he should have been there to hear what she had to say. There was always a sob in Serena's voice, a tremor that sometimes darkened his dreams and caused him to wake up sweating. He knew he wasn't good enough, knew he couldn't fill that husband-shaped hole. Couldn't have kids either.

And she'd waited for him in the park. Half an hour she said. Then her tone was caustic, one that told him she wasn't going to repeat any of what she wanted to say that day. He'd quite simply missed the boat, which was lucky really, because it meant she'd have to wait another month for a signature on those sorry-ass divorce papers.

"Luis is looking forward to his new job," she said.

"New job?" Temeke hated to sound so puzzled but the truth was nobody had told him.

"Watch Commander. He's been promoted."

Watch Commander? Hello... Fowler was after that position and the poor old git got pipped to the post.

"Score!" he said a little too loudly. "Couldn't have happened to a nicer person."

Couldn't have happened at a better time. If Temeke played his cards right, he might be reporting directly to Luis. Serena ended the call after that. Said she didn't feel like talking anymore.

Temeke poked a cigarette in his mouth and grabbed a book of matches from the dash. Two long drags and he was in heaven except for the ash stain on his pants which he worried away with a spit-moistened finger. The wind hurled a handful of leaves in his face, and despite the lateness of the morning, there were only a few cars in the parking lot.

Hackett was going to love Fowler. After more than a week, he still hadn't come up with any leads and the smarmy bastard was making shoddy excuses due to the lack of manpower. Temeke tried to keep the delight from his thoughts. He'd show the yokels how to get a result.

His military jeep was covered in a brown slush and it was time to take it to the carwash. A raccoon had once taken to lying in the sun on the canvas roof. Temeke had no idea how much trash was left up there until he drove home one day and a passing driver gave him the finger, complaining of a windshield full of candy wrappers.

Temeke liked that raccoon. He was the only friend he had these days. Smart those raccoons. They had sharp eyes that burned into your mind like they could read it and they could pick a lock no matter which way it was turned. Must have had a den in that dumpster. Looked better fed than he was.

He puffed a smoke screen out into the parking lot, dropped the cigarette and gave it the full weight of his foot. Sarge was in the lobby on the phone and staring blankly at his clipboard. "Round nine thirty? Very good.

I'll tell him." He hung up and nodded at Temeke. "Megan Sterling. Housekeeper. She'll be here in ten minutes. Good news. Seems Mrs. O got a phone call yesterday from the kidnapper."

"Did they get a trace?"

"West Fork Gila River. It's a wilderness up there."

Temeke lowered his voice and leaned towards the desk. "Is the old git in?"

Sarge's eyes snapped over Temeke's right shoulder, gave a smile and widened his hands.

"The old git is in," a loud voice confirmed over a theatrical cough. "And he's going home."

"Bad cold?" Temeke said, turning around only to be greeted by a filthy rag bunched up under Hackett's nose. He'd snuck down the stairs this time in those soft whispery shoes.

"I've had it since Christmas."

"Might I recommend a good dose of whisky, sir. And by a good dose, I mean more than just an eyebath. Good news about the phone call."

"Freakishly long river. We'll be lucky if we find him. I've emailed you the file."

Hackett paused by the front door, watching a small white Cavalier as it crossed the parking lot and splashed through a puddle right in front of his nice clean car. "It's been twenty-two years," he muttered. "Twenty-two *long* years in this dried up hell-hole and it's never rained this much."

"Good for the reservoirs, sir," Sarge piped up. "Just think, no water ban this summer."

"He's got a point," Temeke said, hoping to get shot of the boring conversation. "Course it makes no difference to me. My lawn's plastic."

They both looked at him with empty stares, the kind that told him he was a traitor to nature. Temeke was partial to his tacked down grass. No mowing, no watering, always green no matter the season. Just needed a little vacuuming now and then.

Hackett buried his nose in that oily rag and braved a slanting rain. When he was gone Sarge gave a big sigh and opened his desk drawer. He held up a pile of telephone messages addressed to Captain Fowler from Gloria Pacheco.

"She's called three times and he won't talk to her."

"Do yourself a favor, don't show any of these to Fowler on account of his bad temper. Rumor has it, he's been ghosting Gloria after he found out it was a pair of old socks down her sweater." Temeke tapped his nose. "Nothing special about her weapons."

Temeke barged his way past Fowler and Jarvis on the stairs and shut himself in his office. Logging into his computer, he found the sound file from Hackett. It was clearer than he expected, voice deep and homely. Couldn't think of any other words to describe it.

Midsummer's Day... I should have been there. I wanted to be. He's a good kid. Knows how to shoot and fish. You know how they made us. Rock hard inside and out so our hearts don't feel anymore. It wasn't right... just wasn't right....

The phone went dead after that. Adam was still alive and still very real to his kidnapper. But there were two things that kept nudging at Temeke's subconscious, things he needed to talk to Mrs. Oliver about. Accessibility to a private number. And the word's *I should have been there. I wanted to be.*

Temeke checked his watch and found an empty interview room near the front lobby. Closing the blinds, he cracked two slats open with a finger to see a ginger blonde by the front desk. She was clutching a small yellow purse in both hands.

"Can I help you," Sarge said.

"Detective Tamale?"

"Temeke," Sarge corrected. "And you are?"

"Megan Sterling."

"I'll tell him you're here."

Sarge drifted across the lobby and tucked his head around the door. He gave a slight chin jerk and a long drawn out, "Housekeeper's here."

"Get Santiago," Temeke said, both hands raised.

He didn't relish the thought of being shut in with a girl whose rear was squirming to get out of those spray-on jeans. As for the accent, he'd need subtitles.

Temeke held out a hand and showed Megan a chair. "We appreciate you coming in today."

Malin arrived shortly after, hugging two cups of coffee. She recorded the date and time and all the people in the room.

"Do I need an attorney?" Megan asked.

"You're not a suspect. But if you would prefer to have an attorney—"

"Oh, no, that's OK."

"So, how long have you known the Olivers?" Malin pushed a cup of coffee across the table.

"Nine months." Megan gave that small yellow purse a chair of its own. "I came straight from college."

"What was your degree?"

"Cooking." Megan lightly cocked her head towards the handbag. "With a minor in shopping."

Temeke studied the cat-eye makeup and the pale lipstick which appeared to have been smeared on with a generous helping of lube. Her lips were full… full of dermal fillers, he guessed, unless someone had booted her in the kisser.

"Was there anything unusual you might have seen or heard leading up to Adam's disappearance?" Malin asked with a terse smile.

"Yeah," she said, drawing the word out like it was obvious. "Mrs. Oliver was mad, always shouting at

Adam to put the seat down, clean his room, do his homework. He's a good kid. But honestly, she was, like, a total bitch. I wouldn't be surprised if he ran away just to get away from her."

"How do you explain the shooting?" Temeke asked, listening to the modulation of her voice, marked by a rise in pitch at the end of every sentence.

Megan sipped her coffee and pulled a face like she was drinking sewage. "Probably an accident. Who knows. Boys and guns. Mayor's not dead is he?"

"No, he's in ICU. But don't let that bother you." Temeke noticed the pressed shirt and the navy woolen blazer. Even her jeans were designer and he wondered how a housekeeper could afford all that.

"Tell me about Art Ingram's birthday. Sunday was it?"

Megan nodded. "You wouldn't think he's thirty-five. Nice looking. Single. So, she called me in to cook lunch. I didn't mind. It's, like, overtime."

Malin looked up at the ceiling and down again. "You were saying something unusual happened."

"That afternoon, Mrs. Oliver was on the phone. She was scared."

"Do you know who she was talking to?" Malin said, lowering her head towards the file.

"Know? Of course I *know*. It was some guy. The volume was turned up so high you could hear it in Roswell. But see, it was really sketchy 'cause he was talking in code."

Malin's head came up. "Code? Can you give me an example?"

Megan had a tongue stud which occasionally popped in and out of her mouth. Since she yawned repeatedly, it spent a good deal of time out rather than in. "Something about PST and LSD. I guess it was drugs. Then he was talking about goals and buds."

"Where was she when she made this call?"

"In the gazebo."

"Where were you when this happened?"

"In the kitchen. Only I had to open the window."

"Bit cold to have the window open at this time of year. Did you burn something?" Temeke asked.

Megan gave a tightlipped smile. "I just wanted to hear what she was saying. See if she was OK. So Cesar and I went outside and hid behind the shed."

"What else was she saying?" Malin asked.

"She said she was being followed. Said he was angrier now, didn't want it all to get out."

"Do you know who she was talking about?"

"Who the *he* was, you mean?" She shrugged. That was the part she didn't know. And she didn't have a clue who the voice on the phone belonged to either.

"How far away were you?" Temeke asked.

"Behind the trellis."

So not behind the shed. The trellis was at the back of the gazebo as Temeke recalled. They would have been closer to Mrs. Oliver than he was to Megan now.

"Anyway I'm thinking she must have had a stupid-ass mental breakdown with all that crying and carrying on. And I'm, like, wondering if she's going to pass out, when all of a sudden she starts cussing him out. She said, 'Don't tell him, 'cause if you do, I'll get an attorney.'" Megan was stabbing the air now with a fingernail. "And I'm like… calm down! 'Cause she was really yelling and the Press Secretary was coming around the side of the house."

"Did he see you?" Malin asked.

"No, silly. How can he if he's on the other end of the phone?"

"The Press Secretary."

"Oh, Art? Just 'cause he wears prescription Louis Vuittons doesn't mean he can't see."

"You remember the entire conversation?" Temeke said. "Word for word?"

"Word for word. Another thing." They all leaned in a little closer now. "She's got a couple of journals."

"Anything interesting?" Temeke asked.

Megan grimaced for a few seconds and then rattled an array of gold bangles as she brushed an imaginary piece of fluff from her jeans. "Tried opening one with a paperclip. Lock wouldn't budge."

"What made you think there was anything worth reading?"

Megan sucked in her bottom lip and frowned. She took the yellow purse off the chair beside her and placed it in her lap. "Mrs. Oliver said something about it to the man on the phone. Said everything was there. All the proof."

Temeke waited for her to continue and when she didn't, he said, "Proof?"

"That's it." Megan lifted her chin and gave an easy nod. "I thought you should know."

Blimey, Temeke thought, wanting to give Megan a mental clap around the ear for not opening the wretched thing. He sneaked a look at his watch, stood up and walked towards the door. "I need to make a phone call so I'll leave you with Detective Santiago. If there's anything else you need, you let us know."

He wanted to call Andrew Blaine of 522 Cragmont Ave, Berkeley, before the crafty old bugger went missing in action. And he wanted a search warrant for those journals before someone else got to them. He slipped out of the door, made a mad dash for the next room and peered through the observation window. Malin knew the drill.

"Between you and me, you don't happen to know where those diaries are?" Malin asked, barely giving the tape recorder a sneaky glance.

Megan was quiet for a few seconds and then looked Malin directly in the eye.

"In the library," she said, blowing out a loud breath. "Third shelf down. Between *Huckleberry Finn* and *The Last of the Mohicans*."

TWENTY-NINE

Temeke called Judge Matthews' office and it took almost a minute before somebody answered. He told the secretary he needed a search warrant, told her why. Judge Matthews refused to issue one, said the information was unreliable and that Madam Mayor's private journal could hardly be connected to a crime. Matthews and the Mayor were as tight as thieves.

Temeke shook his head, struggled to pull his coat on and rushed downstairs to the lobby. Fast fingernails tapped against keyboards, chattering printers and the sudden shriek of a cell phone. Sarge was reading the newspaper with his feet crossed on his desk, eyes red from scanning his computer screen. "You off again?"

Temeke let his gaze swing towards the voice. He gave a nod and shouldered the front door. The smell of fresh air and a cold wind that hadn't lost its bite, and the afternoon sun covered the mountains in an eerie glow.

Key in hand, he hurried past four police officers, a cluster of uniforms leaning against a unit and who seemed to be sharing a joke. He cleared the snow from the windshield of the Explorer with his jacket sleeve and put on his sunglasses.

The traffic was thin on Coors and so was the sun. He had to take those glasses off again to see all the way to the Mayor's mansion. Looked like someone had scattered confectioner's sugar all over the driveway.

Looked like Christmas all over again.

"Let's get this bloody farce over with, shall we," Temeke muttered to himself, rang the bell and glanced up at the front façade.

He felt lightheaded as he showed his badge to a young woman, five feet two inches tall, hair tied in a bun, unreadable eyes.

"Your name?" he said, staring down at small feet wrapped in gray moccasins.

"Francisca, señor."

"May I speak to Madam Mayor?"

"She not here, señor. She back at two."

He was hoping as much. "Can I wait?"

Francisca showed him into the library, left him sitting on an easy chair with a folded newspaper that looked as if it had been ironed. She wouldn't ask for a search warrant, didn't know he wanted to take anything.

He lifted his head and squinted out of the window, trying to make out a line of trees beyond a veil of snow. Some of the wild shrubbery on the south wall had been cut back, trees trimmed so that the sounds of Paseo encroached in a way that they hadn't before.

Temeke scanned the bookshelves and spotted the journals exactly where Megan said they were. Two embossed leather books both fastened with leather straps and locks.

He gave the hallway a cursory glance, dark and deserted, illuminated by two windows either side of the front door. The distant moan of a vacuum cleaner drifted from upstairs and he retrieved both books in a one handed grip.

He checked his watch. Quarter past one. The heater hummed gently in the background, air filtering through the air vents, giving him a tentative sense of calm.

It had been a long time since he used two paperclips, one fashioned in a straight line as a pick, the other bent into the letter 'r' as a tension wrench. It took three tries before he timed it just right and the lock released.

He flicked through the pages and tried to picture each scene. The writing alone could tell him what Raine Oliver was feeling; the neat layout, the thought that went into each entry. There was something sad about them, something he couldn't put his finger on.

He leafed through a few more pages until he found what he wanted. The dates started as far back as December 1999 before Adam was born.

Sunday 23rd December, 1999: Party at the Olivers'. You weren't there. I wanted to tell you the good news.

Monday December 24, 1999: I left a letter for you under the tree. We've set a date. If you ever want to know how it all happened. It was just this. He captured me.

Tuesday December 25, 1999: Maybe you just wandered away and can't find your way home. Is your heart breaking like mine?

Wednesday December 26, 1999: Bill wants to move after the wedding. Colorado or New Mexico. I rather like the idea of New Mexico. A promise is a promise. Middle name. Just as you said.

The last entry was resigned, almost cold. Perhaps the language was different in the late nineties for her, perhaps she was just trying to be brave. If he read between the lines, it was someone who didn't approve of her marriage to Bill Oliver.

Felt like a man. Could have been a woman. And as for the middle name, his guess was as good as anybody's.

Temeke took a cigarette out of his top pocket, played it between his fingers and then put it back.

The sound of the wind tugging at a rose bush outside, thorns scraping against a window pane, made his muscles jump. He looked around the room again, this time settling on another photograph of Adam, a concerned little figure with skinny legs and a model airplane in one hand. The mere thought of the boy being out there with a kidnapper made him shudder and he swallowed hard, laid a flat hand against the pages of the journal.

The vacuuming stopped.

Temeke looked towards the hall, listened hard, and heard a muffled voice upstairs. Francisca was on the phone, voice raised one minute and low the next. It was likely she wouldn't have heard a phone over the vacuum cleaner, suggesting she must have made the call herself.

Light seeped in through the library window and arced across the floor. Headlights outside. Temeke realized how dark the afternoon sky had become, recognized the sound of a van.

A sudden adrenaline spike seemed to send his brain on overload and he broke out in a sweat. Francisca was likely watching out of a window upstairs, just as he was watching downstairs.

Fed Ex. He relaxed his shoulders and realized he hadn't taken a breath for nearly a minute, slipped the journals back where he found them and sat very still.

A shadow fell across the window, short and wiry and likely dressed in a brown suit. Temeke heard a scuffling, heard the doorbell and a few seconds later, the growl of the engine.

Shoes pattered on the staircase and Francisca peered into the library first, eyes scanning the entire room as if there was some filter of doubt. "You want coffee, tea… something to eat, Detective?"

"No thanks, love." The shrillness of her voice struck a chord that made him clench all the muscles in his face. He needed that search warrant. "Tell Mrs. Oliver I'll call again."

Francisca opened the door to retrieve the package, gave him a curt nod as he slipped past her to the driveway. The wind reached him through the trees and so did the smell of traffic fumes. The chill from the icy ground worked its way through the soles of his shoes, snow crunching underfoot.

All the way back to the office, he kept wondering about the Tuesday entry and the one question that scratched away at his subconscious. Whose heart was breaking like hers?

Malin tapped the keyboard and squinted at the computer. He knew she could hear him over those loud frustrated clicks. "What time did Megan leave?" he asked.

"Ten minutes ago."

If Megan was on her way back to the mansion, he would have just missed her. "How long ago did she try picking the locks on those journals?"

"She said she was alone in the house during the Annual Mayoral Luncheon, so... two weeks ago," Malin said without looking up. "After everyone left, she went snooping in the library. She was worried about Mrs. Oliver."

Temeke straightened his chair, scuffed it away from his desk and rocked it back and forth a bit. "And Cesar? 'Cause he's not exactly squeaky clean. Imagine two members of staff going through your stuff. Just because they're worried about you."

"Apparently, the Mayor shouted at his wife several times, only one time he slapped her. Megan saw it all through the living room door. She was certainly frightened enough."

Temeke began to imagine two dark silhouettes in front of the fire, one leaning over the other and shouting at the top of his voice. The whole house must have heard them. "Did she say what they were arguing about?"

"A letter. Something to do with a test."

THIRTY

An afternoon of studying the Mayor's resume and making phone calls of all the references listed had given Malin an appetite. She tore the lid off a microwavable lasagna, inspected a few steaming strings of cheese and took a bite.

"Judge Matthews called yet?" Temeke asked.

Malin shook her head and shaved another slice of lasagna with a plastic fork. She knew he was itching to get back over to Mrs. Oliver's house to get those journals. "What are you working on?"

Temeke smeared a layer of paste on a thin slice of toast. Gentleman's Relish, he called it. "Checking with the Chief Administrative Officer to see if any of the Mayor's staff were absent this week. So far, all present and accounted for. The Media Enquiries Director had to set up a 'Mayor Oliver update' line."

"That's a bit impersonal, isn't it?"

"Not after they received three hundred phone calls in less than an hour. Jammed up the front desk."

Malin read the Mayor's tweets out loud, the most recent of which commended Unit Commander Hackett as employee of the week. The rest were return to work bills, donations, youth ambassador promotions and a celebration of the legacy of Martin Luther King, Jr.

There was also a picture of the Press Secretary on the Fox News couch giving a brief update on the

Mayor's health, concluding with legislative priorities for the coming year. Malin looked up and realized Temeke had already glazed over, couldn't care less about Twitter.

Pressing the sticky lid of her lasagna back in place, she threw the remainder in the trash. Temeke opened his desk drawer, pulled out the piggy bank and peeled off a rubber seal from its belly. He shook it a few times until a handful of change clunked onto his desk.

"What?" she said, knowing he was jumpier than a housecat.

"When Mrs. Oliver called the police on Sunday night, she insisted she read the time off her cell phone. That means she had the cell phone in her hand. Yet she chose to call 911 from the landline instead."

"Maybe she was expecting a call on her cell," Malin said. It was the only explanation she could think of.

"That's why she chose to be with the Mayor… in hospital. It wouldn't have mattered where she was if the kidnapper had her cell phone number."

"But he called the house. The police were there and so was she." Malin felt the room spin. There was something in what he said. "I have a list of all her contacts."

"Call them, will you. Find out if any of them had an appointment to call her on Sunday night."

Malin found the list, but not before noticing Temeke had something else to say. He was nodding his head vigorously and yawning at the same time.

"I got to thinking, who's this Andrew Blaine? He's a sodding PI, that's what. Said he wouldn't talk to me when I got through finally. Client attorney privilege, my ass. I asked him why he didn't call me back the first time and he said he couldn't understand the accent. Accent? I don't have a bloody accent."

"Yes, you do." *A real sexy one*, Malin wanted to say

and thought better of it.

She called the Berkeley police. Asked them to get a search warrant for Andrew Blaine's house and then checked her messages for the third time. There was still no call back from Judge Matthews' office. She didn't really expect one.

Two more hours of calling Mrs. Oliver's contacts, most of whom had no scheduled phone appointments with her. Malin checked her watch. It was just after six. The next ten minutes was spent nagging the receptionist of Kim Tzu's Nail Place for Kim's home number. Malin's hands were damp with sweat as she listened to the phone ring, with a sense of foreboding in her stomach. It was the same response she had learned to expect. Kim had not made a phone date with Mrs. Oliver that Sunday night.

Temeke leaned back in that creaky chair, hands behind his head. There was something feral and graceful about him, something otherworldly that made her skin tingle. He cleared his throat a couple of times as if he was about to speak, slipped the pack of cigarettes from his top pocket and flicked open the lid. A match flared and she saw him suck on that cigarette and slowly exhale a lungful of smoke. It always amazed her how he got away with it. The only employee allowed to smoke at work, the only detective Hackett really depended on.

Hackett never told Temeke, of course. He only wrote it in a memo to the Chief of Police that Malin had delivered a few weeks back. Praised Temeke as a tactical thinker, said he'd put up with anything as long as Temeke was given a second chance.

"Who does he look like?" Temeke said.

"Who does who look like?"

"Adam?"

Malin looked up at the cork board and studied the photographs. "Favors his mother. Same build, same coloring. Except in the eyes. Difficult to tell from a picture."

"You know what bothers me?" Temeke said, fingers pulling at his bottom lip. "How do you think it makes us look if we can't come up with a single witness? All of them suddenly gone deaf and blind? You go home, love. Get some rest."

Malin wasn't about to argue. She grabbed her coat and looked up at the clock. Eight thirty. Not bad for a weekday. She would have called in on Sergeant Moran's wife for a coffee on the way home, but there was an ache in the back of her throat and she had trouble swallowing.

The apartment felt different. Cold, uninviting. The blinds to the patio doors clattered in the wind and she wondered why she would have left the sliding door unlatched. No one could have opened it from the outside without shinning up two storeys and vaulting over the railings. She swatted a drift of blinds and closed the latch.

The laptop took a while to boot up and she noticed Wingman wasn't in the chat room. No use talking to an imposter. Maybe one last message to vent the anger she now felt.

All singles use Heartfree, you said. All lonely singles you said. Lonely? Who said anything about lonely? I know who you are.

She tapped SEND, heard herself laugh and the sound caught her by surprise. She was thinking about what he would say when he saw that message. He'd be biting his nails that's for sure, right down to the quick. Probably wondering if she had state-of-the-art surveillance equipment to find him with. Probably scared she was already standing outside his window.

Darn it! She should have typed that.

There was nothing on the TV except Jennifer Danes reporting live outside the university campus. A student had been arrested for spray painting *Professor Reid is a pederast* on the front door of the Law Library. Cyn Wrigley had been nominated for the American Journalist Award for the third time and there was a photo of her getting out of her car, registration plate PMS24-7. And Farmer Capra who had been breeding goats with sheep for four years had finally produced a pair of black and white shoats.

Malin yawned and glanced at the laptop. "Get a grip," she whispered, flicking on the switch to the gas fireplace.

Blue flames fluttered between a pile of faux logs and there was a cloud of condensation on the glass. She sat on the couch and stared at it for a moment, wondering why Wingman pretended he was someone else.

It was the whine of a police siren on the television that woke her up at one seventeen in the morning. All the moisture had been sucked out of her tongue and it was stuck on the roof of her mouth. Gulping down a glass of water, she remembered the laptop.

There was an email in her inbox.

Wingman: The way I see it is this. Your neck's on the chopping block. A good detective like you telling a complete stranger about the Oliver case? My, my, that's worth a firing. You say one word to Temeke and I'll tell him what you told me. If you don't, I'll tell you who took Adam Oliver. So sit tight and wait for my next email. You're really going to love this.

THIRTY-ONE

Ramsey was looking real bad now. His skin was gray and his eyes were wide and staring, and he could hardly move. Kept mumbling about painkillers, about the village, about the stores. Kept pointing at the front door.

"You have to go," he said, slipping off his watch and handing it to Adam.

Adam was too afraid to go. He knew the rangers weren't far away. The howling in the night woke them up three times and Ramsey threatened to shoot the dog with all he had. He said it was a black Tervuren, whatever that was. Seen it out of the window scurrying away towards the woodshed, said it was big and dangerous.

Ramsey found cans of food in the hut, found spoons, toothbrushes, oil, can openers and tin plates. He'd found a black and yellow can of gun solvent and a cleaning rod, at least that's what he said they were.

Adam knew what Ramsey wanted. He just didn't think he could do it. Staying in the house wouldn't help either of them so there was only one thing for it. He found the key on a hook under the kitchen sink and he found the duffel. Some of the money was scattered about and some was wadded and sealed. Twenties, fifties, looked like a lot to him. He stuffed a few notes in the pocket of Ramsey's coat and zipped it up to his chin.

It was all his fault anyway. Ramsey wouldn't have

got sick if he hadn't pounded that leg and made it bleed again. His mom said hitting came from hatred and hatred was an ugly thing. If you have a problem with someone, she said, look for whatever is true, good and praiseworthy. Ramsey was good as good goes. As for the true and praiseworthy, Adam wasn't quite sure about that.

"You've got a good compass now. So head west. And don't talk to anyone," Ramsey said, barely lifting his head.

"How am I supposed to get you stuff if I can't talk to anyone?"

"You know what I mean." There was a rattle in his throat that sounded bad, like it was thick with spit. "Make sure you're not being followed."

Adam frowned and opened the door. "I won't be long."

Ramsey just lay there shivering in that sudden blast of cold air, raising a hand towards the door. He'd made a nest in a pile of blankets in front of the wood stove, hat pulled over his eyes and mouth opened a slit to breathe. Looked like a homeless person, looked like he wouldn't last much longer unless Adam hurried back.

Adam slipped outside and shut the door. Looked up at the eaves and saw an old bird's nest wedged into the siding. There were gray and white droppings splattered down the wall and the smell of mold in the wood. Fresh air stabbed his lungs and made his eyes water, and he didn't know which way to go.

The wood shed was to his left now, kindling barely covered by a rotting canvas. He took out the compass and followed the needle west between the trees to a furrowed field. He'd have to be quick in case the rangers spotted him.

He missed Ramsey to be honest, missed his cheery tone and the way he did things. He could look after himself in the desert, find food and water where nobody else could. He'd saved Adam's life, hadn't he? Now it was his turn to save Ramsey's.

Markers, watch for markers.

The leaves were soft underfoot from the recent rains and there was a haze between the trees. It was the shifting winds that spooked him and the occasional flutter of a bird. He thought he heard someone calling his name. He thought he heard drums in his head.

It was several hours before the sun broke out of the clouds in a long, thin line, striking a puddle in the rut of an old farm track. It seemed to reflect a myriad of colors like a prism and Adam ran towards it, breaking through a hedge of dried out corn husks. There were no cars, cattle or barns. Just acres of land now beneath a birdless sky. With the sun so high it had to be noon.

Something moved between the trees. A shadow in the mist, head nodding from side to side and feathers spinning in the wind.

"Tarahuma," Adam whispered, pausing there in the road, "is that you?"

He thought he saw a man wearing a gray beaded bodice and leggings with two others behind him. One with a flute and one with an eagle feather, yipping and wailing and pounding the ground. When an eagle shrieked in the distance the drums stopped. There were no shadows in the dew-soaked grass and only his footprints marked a light dusting of snow on the road.

The road. He'd found the road.

It had been so long since he'd had a shower, slurped a coke or tied his shoelaces. Pushing one hand further into his coat pocket he reached for the money. He'd call his mom if he could get some change. Wednesday. Must be Wednesday.

He walked that bleak road for an hour, maybe two, turning around occasionally to map the trees and the rutted landscape. He counted the clouds and guessed their shapes. He tried to sing a scout song, only he couldn't remember all the words. Whispering pines… eagles soaring … purple mountains… azure sky.

Sand and leaves skittered this way and that, and somewhere in the distance he heard the soft jingle of a wind chime. Then the scent of burning cedar and smoke spiraling behind a rise in the road.

Picking up speed, he climbed the hill, a cold sweat pricking the back of his neck. Just before he tipped over the rise, there came a familiar sound. A high pitched whine.

It could have been the wind through a blade of grass or a herder's whistle. It wasn't a threatening sound. More like a dog's version of hello. He turned sharply and there in the middle of the road about ten feet back was a dog. Black coat snagged with mud and leaves, head lowered to the ground.

Adam stood there for a while, hand flat across his brow. It was a large dog with a square head and tail thicker than a rudder. Could have been a Newfoundland or a long-haired retriever. Could have been… no, it couldn't…

Adam walked back a few paces, and then some more. Crouched and held out a hand. His fingers tingled against the cold muzzle and then he hooked his arms around that neck, smelling wet fur and grass and other things he couldn't describe.

He sobbed harder than he did the first night he was taken and Murphy just made those grunting sounds dogs do. His whiskers were damp from the puddle back there but God only knew what he had eaten. Probably dug himself a den near a stream, probably ate a rabbit or two. Probably followed Adam's tracks. But he was alive.

Thank God, he was alive.

"Your dog, son?"

Adam twisted around to find an old man, leaning on a wooden hiking stick. It spooked him at first. "Yes, sir."

"Looks hungry. Got a nasty limp. If you want, I can give him some food. I can give you some food and all."

Adam slicked back his hair with one hand and bobbed his head. "I'm a bit thirsty, sir," he said, standing.

"Where you from?" The old man inclined his head, but he never stopped smiling.

"Albuquerque."

"You're a long way from Albuquerque. I'd say you were lost."

"My… my dad's sick. I had to leave him back there. He needs help. Real bad."

The old man nodded his head. "Follow me, son. And bring your dog. We'll call an ambulance—"

"Oh, no, sir. He doesn't need an ambulance." Adam dangled his hand for Murphy to sniff, urging him on with a pat.

The old man walked him to an adobe house with blue painted shutters and small courtyard. There were ristras hooked to a porch truss and wind chimes that twisted slightly in the wind.

There was a shake in the old man's hand and a wheeze in his voice. He coughed a lot too. "Is your dad coughing? Course if he's coughing I can make a mug of hot buttered rum. Opens up the chest. He'd like that."

Adam nodded. Ramsey would like more than one. "No, it's his leg. He fell. It doesn't look good."

"Scrapes get infected. He'll need bandages. Where are you headed?"

Adam had no idea. Ramsey had never told him. He felt a tightening in his stomach every time he told a lie. "We're doing an orienteering exercise. For scouts."

"Now you're talking. Which troop? I used to do scouts. Course I was a bit older than you when I got my orienteering badge. Ever been to Philmont? Climbing Baldy Mountain's bad enough, only we had to do it at a run. Course when you're on the top it's like riding the clouds. Name's Jim Trader, but everyone just calls me Trader. You have a name?"

Adam knew he couldn't give Mr. Trader his name, couldn't tell him anything and he felt bad about that. "James," he blurted out. It sounded like an honest name.

"Good and biblical." Another rough cough. "Jesus' brother eh?"

"Yes, sir." Adam didn't want to talk about Jesus, not in the same breath as lying.

"Here we are then." Trader opened the front door and brought them into a small parlor. It had a long wooden table in the middle of the room and a range behind it. "There's some stew on the stove. My Nan used to make a mean stew, only she's been gone two years now. I'll get a bowl for the dog."

Adam looked for a phone. Couldn't see one among the old newspapers on the counter and there wasn't one on the wall. Just a picture of a boy wearing a scout uniform and a second class badge like his.

Old people didn't have cell phones. They didn't have much of anything, except boxes of nails and old car parts and rusted out tins of who knows what.

He could smell that mean stew and he licked his lips just thinking about it. Trader said a blessing. It went on for a while and in the background Murphy made slurping noises and crunched on a few pieces of dried toast he found in the grate.

After dinner Trader fetched the first aid box down from a shelf in the pantry. Painkillers he said. About six months old. Didn't need them where he was going.

"Better stay until the morning, son. It's going to be dark soon. Storm's coming. You'll need to see to your dog."

There were three goat's-heads in one paw, deep down between the pads. Trader took them out with a pair of tweezers, fingers rough from all the work he'd done.

"He'll need to rest," he said, "and so will you."

Trader made a bed on the couch in the parlor and spread out blankets for the dog. He let Adam take a bath, washed his scout clothes too. Told him about his grandson, how he always wanted to get his Eagle.

"Did you get your Eagle, sir?" Adam asked.

"I did, son. Evan would have too… if he'd lived."

"What did he die of?"

"God just takes some folk young, I guess."

Adam slipped in and out of sleep that night, happy to smell the dog beside him, happy to hear his snores. He could hear deep throated coughs in another room and his own frail breath in the blackness.

It wouldn't be wrong to write a note, something Trader could give to the police. Adam could leave it on the kitchen table with his mother's name on it.

He would leave Trader some money too. He penciled a few lines on a scrap of paper, wrapped it around a fifty dollar bill and left it peeking out under the tea caddy.

The old man was up at dawn, scraping out a pan of oatmeal into a china bowl. "Sleep all right, son?"

"Yes, sir." Adam licked his lips. He looked for the note. It was still there.

"Seen any woodsmen in your travels?" Trader asked.

Adam shook his head. Didn't want Trader to know about the old man. "No, sir."

"Where exactly is your pa? He's not in the woods is he?"

"Not far. Just over the hill."

Trader nodded slowly, eyebrows drawn together. "Sure you don't want me to walk you?"

"I'll be fine. Promise."

Adam ate most of that bowl until he couldn't hold the hurt in any more. It was like when his grandpa was alive, how when they visited him hospital that last time. How those bony hands clawed through Adam's hair as he said goodbye.

"My chest," Adam patted the place where his heart was and he began to sob. "It's bursting. I… I—"

"It's alright, son." Trader put an arm around him, strong and warm and full of love. "I prayed for you in the night and I prayed for your pa. There's a flask of hot buttered rum in here," Trader said, taking the pack and slipping over Adam's shoulders. "A few things I thought you might need."

"Do you have a phone?" Adam asked, wiping his eyes. "I need to call my mom."

"You can have it," old Trader said. "I won't be needing it no more. It's charged. Should last three days."

"I can't—"

"Yes, you can, son. Here," he wrapped Adam's hands around a black cell phone and nodded. "It's yours."

Adam dialed the number, heard a click and a sharp intake of breath. "Mom. It's me."

She sounded different, strained. "Adam… Where are you? Is it really you?"

"It's me, Mom."

She cried some and then asked the question Adam hoped she wouldn't. "When are you coming home?"

"Soon mom, we're on Operation Gray Fox—"

"Are you eating OK?"

"Squirrels, birds—stuff. Everything's fine, Mom." He wanted to cry, felt a lump in his throat. He wanted to ask about his dad, about the funeral. But Trader was listening, head cocked to one side. "I have to go, Mom. Love you."

Trader gave him some gloves and a wooly hat. Told

him there was enough water for him and the dog. Told him to be careful out there. Sent him out that cloudy day with a wave and a smile.

Shouted *Godspeed* at the top of that grainy voice.

THIRTY-TWO

The ground stank to high heaven in the pouring rain, all moldy and full of ancient rot, and Temeke cursed his luck for venturing out on such a lousy morning. There was a smear of excrement on the hood of Hackett's car. It was a sod of a day.

"Since when," he said to Sarge, as he walked through the front doors, "did Fergus the Flasher start using that as a bloody toilet?"

Sarge shook his head and looked down at the slop bucket, suds seeping over the rim. "It all started when Hackett caught him under that tree. Said big trees like that didn't need watering. Told him he should have gone before he came. Fergus doesn't own a toilet. Doesn't have a home."

Temeke could see how that would handicap the poor old bastard, but what he couldn't understand was Sarge's endless sympathy. He was glad he didn't have to scrub *poo* as Malin called it. "It's flaming whiffy in here. I'd give him the bleeding scrubbing brush and tell him to do it himself!"

"What's that racket down there?" Hackett shouted over the banister.

"Just a little situation, sir. But we're handling it." Temeke craned his neck up to a big silhouette whose shoulders were slumped with the weight of an unsolved case.

"Handling it!"

The words were followed by a barrage of cursing, most of which Temeke had hardened to over the months. He kept saying how sorry he was the press had hacked the Northwest Area Command to pieces and how embarrassing it was that he was being blamed for the incompetence of the entire police force. There would be layoffs in the morning.

"That's a bit unfair, sir. I mean, it's hardly your fault. It can take months, years to solve a case—"

"You'll be going with Fowler to the Mayor's mansion. I want to know about that call she got."

"What call, sir?"

"Two of our boys were with Mrs. Oliver this morning. Listened to a call from Adam. Apparently, the boy told his mom they were fine. And who's *they*? I want to know what special ops he thinks he's doing, cos eating squirrels and birds sounds like a frigging camping trip to me."

"Well, that's a stroke of luck. We can all go home."

"Not so fast, Temeke. The boy's disappeared again. And what's more, the number's registered under a Mr. Jim Trader. Ring any bells."

It did. "Anyone called it?"

"Of course someone's called it. Several times if you must know. Either it's on silence or someone's screening the calls."

"Let me get this straight. On the caller ID, do we come up as Duke City Police Department? 'Cause if we do, that might be the reason why he's not picking up."

"I've noticed a change in you, Temeke. Even the admins are offended by that brash cockney attitude. Any more dirty jokes and you'll be suspended, you understand? And the parking lot's full of half-smoked cigarettes. It's a fire hazard."

"If it's not too much to ask, sir, could I have that

number? Might speed things up a bit."

"Captain Fowler's got it. Ask him." Hackett raised his chin a little and narrowed his eyes. "He'll be picking you up in ten minutes. What's that on your lip?"

"Lip, sir?" Temeke picked at the scab where a cigarette had burned dangerously close after he'd fallen asleep in the bath. "It's a burn."

"You smoke too much. Your lungs will catch on fire and so will your house."

Hackett began to slide dangerously towards the elevator door and Temeke hoped Sarge had enough time to scrub that car since the odor out there was worse than a turkey farm.

"When you talk to Mrs. Oliver." Hackett's big thumb was squished against the down button. "Make sure you don't interrupt. Better results if you don't interrupt."

Temeke had never ridden in Captain Fowler's car. It was cleaner than a doctor's office and reeked of freshly laundered linen. There was a Hawaiian doll stuck to the dash, another peculiarity that separated Fowler from the boys. Temeke pressed down on her shoulders and a squirt of air freshener shot out of an orifice he couldn't see.

"Women love that," Fowler said, spinning the wheel for an illegal U-turn and bumping down a puddled lane. "Like the piggybank in your desk drawer."

"Bloody marvelous!" Temeke said, wondering if they were going the right way. "The police can't find a kidnapper but they've got the resources to find a piggybank. Are you going to give me Adam's number or do I have to hold you at gunpoint?"

Fowler made a left turn in the Mayor's neighborhood and then a right, and then stopped in the middle of the road. "Where are we?"

"Buggered if I know."

"I made a wrong turn."

"You mean the first turn, the second or the third?"

Fowler refused to comment, shot through a gap in someone's nicely clipped hedge, fender dipping into a concrete arroyo. They bounced through a narrow stream of water and up the other side.

The lane was recognizable by a border of honeysuckle draped over an adobe wall. After a few terse ripples of that siren, the gates swung open to the Mayor's mansion and Fowler released the gear stick in a triumphant flourish.

"What about that hedge and the tire tracks in the neighbor's lawn," Temeke said.

"Keeping secrets is part of our civic duties." Fowler put the car in park and turned off the ignition. "Let's make one thing clear. If Hackett won't remove you from this case, I will. If you say anything, *anything* about that hedge, I'll even kill you with my bare hands, and that's a promise. And don't go complaining to Hackett about death threats, Temeke. He won't believe a word. Trust me, they're real."

"Real? You'll feel a nasty pain in your groin in a minute," Temeke snapped, "and that'll be real."

Fowler pressed a fist against his mouth and puffed out his cheeks. "Here's the number for what it's worth. I've tried several times, no answer."

Temeke stayed where he was. "You know what your problem is? You're scared I'm going to solve this case just like I did the last one. You're scared I might get a pat on the back from the Unit Commander, two Watch Commanders, Homicide and the Chief of Police. You're scared Gloria's pregnant. Since her husband's a high court judge he's bound to find out. And just one small detail. He's black. For someone so good at keeping secrets, you made a right ass of that one."

"Gloria?" Fowler's Adam's apple clunked up and

down as he swallowed.

"Yes, Gloria."

There was a long period silence when nobody said anything. Temeke fumbled for his cigarettes, wrapped his fingers around the pack and sighed. "Let's listen to that tape again shall we?"

They listened to the short tape of Adam's voice. There was nothing in the inflection to say he was under duress and nothing to say he wasn't out enjoying a few days hiking with his troop.

They were interrupted by a belch of static from the radio and Hackett's voice tuning into Westside Dispatch. Fowler gave their position and listened to a short report. Apparently, Mrs. Oliver had been prescribed a course of anti-depressants by her loyal and very dependable physician. She wasn't in the best of spirits and Fowler was to do all the talking.

Temeke shook a cigarette from the packet straight into his mouth and leapt out of the car. He walked towards the front door and scraped a match down the stucco. He watched Fowler pulling out the best of a box hedge from the front bumper, footsteps clacking on the driveway towards him.

"You always seem to screw things up in ways nobody's ever heard of." Fowler said, walking through a puff of smoke, face deadly white like a corpse. "Why do you have to tell everyone about Gloria?"

"Tell everyone? What do you mean tell everyone? Everyone told me. It's like Chinese whispers in the sodding toilets." Temeke pointed two fingers wrapped around a cigarette. "Calm down. It's all part of the learning process and you know what a dim old sod Hackett is. He thinks the light shines out of your ass."

Fowler seemed preoccupied with his shiny shoes, probably admiring his face in them. "Put that out and let's get on with this. I'll do the talking. You see what you can find."

Temeke wheezed in a long drag and squeezed out a little smile. "My pleasure."

They rang the bell and listened to the first few bars of a well-known theme. Mrs. Oliver was dressed in black satin pants and the cobweb of a gauzy sweater. "I'm sorry, I wasn't expecting you."

"That's OK, Mrs. Oliver," Fowler said, and there was no doubting the sincerity in his voice. "Can we come in?"

"Please," she swept a hand towards the kitchen, closing the front door after them.

Temeke could hear her slow ambling gate behind him and the click of heels against the tile. "Nice place."

"We've lived here for nearly four years," she said. "The house is older of course. About ten, fifteen, I think."

"It's a sod about your cameras. Just when you think you're safe and some jackass comes along and covers them with duct tape."

Fowler gave him a testy look, if you could call one raised eyebrow and a half-snarl, testy. His flashy good looks didn't allow the expression to last and he gave Mrs. Oliver and that sweater a generous smile.

She showed them into the kitchen, a large room which was surprisingly warm from a morning of baking. Two white fans whirred on a large granite countertop, turning in unison like the telescopes of the VLA.

"We'd like to talk about the call you received from Adam," Fowler said, nodding at two officers who were sitting at the kitchen table, yawning and staring at the landline phone. "Can you tell us exactly what he said?"

She pulled the sleeves of her sweater down over her hands, exposing only the tips of her red painted nails. "Aren't you monitoring all my calls?"

"Yes, ma'am." Fowler moved in a little closer,

looked down at her with a brittle smile. "I just wanted to know if you found anything odd. Anything at all."

Found anything odd? It's all bloody odd, Temeke thought, watching her face and those delicate hands reaching for a tea towel. She was keeping busy all right, probably trying hard not to think about it all.

"I… I don't know exactly."

Fowler wiped the palms of his hands down his trousers and rephrased the question. "How did you feel when you heard Adam's voice?"

"Relieved."

"So, he didn't sound upset to you?"

"No… not at all. But I wanted to ask—"

"Wanted to ask what?" Temeke butted in. He wanted to understand why she kept frowning and looking at the floor every time he did. He wanted to know why his foot didn't clunk against a china dog bowl.

"I wanted to ask him where he was."

"But you asked him something else?"

Mrs. Oliver merely nodded. "I asked him what he was eating."

"You asked him when he was coming home." Temeke watched those eyes flicking from Fowler to him, watched a small intake of breath. "When you said you felt relieved, was there anything particular that made you feel that way?"

"Hearing his voice." Her hands were worrying at that tea towel, twisting it into a tight ball. Her eyes kept flicking to a small red cell phone on the kitchen counter.

"Does the name Jim Trader mean anything to you?"

"No."

Her fragile smile was on the verge of crumbling and Fowler moved in with the stealth of an alligator.

"I don't know what to do… I'm so confused," she said, voice hitching.

Fowler gave a few encouraging murmurs, patted her on the back like he was burping a baby. She just stood there, head against his chest, arms reaching around his back.

Temeke studied Fowler's belly and wondered if the slimy bastard had put on weight. The once ripped abs had turned into a slush from too many good dinners and he was beginning to look like a retired lifeguard from *Baywatch*.

Fine time to start blubbing, Temeke thought, edging his way towards that cell phone. He clicked his way through four calls received since Tuesday afternoon and found one registered under the name, Ron King. He made a mental note and put the phone back on the counter. It didn't feel right. Two big losses in her life right now and not one mention of the dog. Not one flyer down her street either.

Temeke made his way to the library, stared at the shelves, the embroidered chair and the reading lamp on the table beside it. Third shelf down, between *Huckleberry Finn* and *The Last of the Mohicans*. Just as he thought.

The journals were gone.

THIRTY-THREE

Interview room 4 stank of stale milk and heave from an arrest the night before. The table was clean, tape recorder stacked on a phone book and flushed against the wall.

Malin dropped the file labeled *William Stanton Oliver* on the table. All she could see was the blur of his son's face, eyes bright beneath a fringe of hair. She hoped Adam was still alive, hoped he wasn't defeated into thinking no one cared enough to find him.

Taking a deep breath, she rubbed her forehead with the heels of both hands. Wingman had been on her mind for the last twenty-four hours, only she hadn't opened her laptop, hadn't bothered to see if there was an email. He was probably out-there, you know, a psycho. She wasn't going to let him off that easily, not after signing off without saying goodbye. She'd make him wait.

"Hot chocolate?" Temeke asked, hooking his jacket on the back of a chair and grabbing a handful of change.

"I'm OK."

"You don't look OK." He reached into the cupboard and pulled out a jar of lollipops. Slapped a couple on the table in front of her. "Here, gnaw on one of these."

She could hear him thumping the vending machine in the corridor, tipping it forward and back until a rubber seal popped out from the bottom right-hand foot and bounced across the floor. He left the machine tipped forwards slightly like one of those statues on Easter Island.

"Who have we got today?" he asked, tearing into a bag of M&Ms.

"There's only one name left," Malin said. "Art Ingram, Press Secretary."

"And here he is," Temeke said, peering through the blinds. "Six foot four. Looks like a professional footballer. Bet that's an Armani suit."

Malin thought Art Ingram smelled even better close up. Probably a cologne worth several hundred dollars a squirt. Handsome wasn't really the word. Charismatic, charming, funny. Well educated.

"So, how long have you been working for Mayor Oliver," Temeke began.

"Four years. Has it been that long? Wooo! Seems like ten years. He saw me on TV when I was playing for the Oakland Raiders. Got my number from the coach, called me up and was like, it's me – Uncle Bill. Nah… just kidding."

Art had a laugh that came from the back of his throat and a soft hissing sound when he spoke. He was nervous, hands tapping on the table, chair creaking underneath. His mouth was like a steam train, never drew breath, always cracking jokes. How Temeke kept up with it all Malin couldn't imagine. All she could think about was lunch and that heavy cologne was making her hungry. She peeled the wrapper off a lollipop and stuck it in her mouth.

"I look at the jobs I've done," Art said, "the places I've worked… I mean, you have to be the stereotype. The suit, the Gucci shoes. It gets you paid, it gets you laid. It gets you in the business."

Temeke was just nodding, taking the odd note in that yellow college lined pad. He looked engaged but somewhere deep in that head he was thinking things, sizing Art up, deciding who he was.

"Don't get me wrong, I love my job. But we've had our ups and downs. Especially the downs. He tried to get me fired last year. Happened faster than a knife fight in a phone booth. Wooo, this isn't going to be easy, I thought. If it wasn't for my pilot's license and several additional ratings, I wouldn't be here. I flew Governor Bendish's Bell 430 five years back. Black it was with a gold stripe down the side and the commonwealth seal on the doors. Hell—you could roll that bird like an F-sixteen."

The thought of being upside down in a helicopter gave Malin a brief jolt. She bit into that lollipop with a loud crack.

"I only did it once," Art was quick to add. "Flight simulator at the training academy. That's how I met Mayor Oliver. If you ask me whether I like him, I'd say not really. He can be right asshole when he wants to be."

"That's no way to speak of His Honor."

"I do everything. I mean *everything*. Yes, sir, no, sir, abso-fricking-lutely, sir."

"Isn't that what Press Secretaries do?" Temeke said.

"Yeah, only Brady did everything for Ronald Reagan and look what happened to him."

"Do you like Mrs. Oliver?"

"Not many people do. I think she's a doll. She's been through a lot. Not so as you would know. Hides it all behind a brave smile. But you can sense it, feel it. And I never touched her if that's what you're thinking. We just talk sometimes."

Temeke crossed his arms and raised his chin. "But you touched a woman four years ago. Rape, she claimed. An administrative assistant to the Mayor's Chief Executive Officer. Course, she's not working there anymore. Got the old heave-ho."

It was like a slap in the face for Malin as she took

another bite of that lollipop. Here was a hulking one hundred and ninety pound African American playing the heavy, the funny guy who couldn't sit still, and looked like he had a permanent itch in his rear. But nothing would have prepared her for 'rapist'. She should have done the research and, as usual, Temeke had beaten her to it.

"She touched me," Art said, tapping his tie pin. "Kept groping me at meetings, in the corridors, at the courthouse. It was like, hands round my meat stick whenever she had the chance. I can't believe she did it under the table at the Annual Gala Charity."

"April was it?"

"Barbara, I think."

"No, the Gala. April. The month."

Art nodded. "Anyway, I went to the bathrooms and when I came out, there she was, all naked and splayed out on a chair. What's a man supposed to do?"

"I don't know. You tell me."

"I told her to get lost, that's what I did. She just laughed. Said I wasn't the man she thought I was. Didn't have the balls. She wasn't much of a looker and I have taste." Art looked at Malin and winked. "Now if it was you, darlin'—"

"If it was me," Malin snapped, "you'd have nothing left to rape with."

Art held up both hands. "I didn't touch her. Promise. I just showed her the biggest rack she'd ever seen and she screamed. Called the cops after that. And bang! There goes my ratings."

Malin felt her jaw drop. Wondered if he was joking. But he wasn't. Just went on talking like it was nothing.

"The Mayor and Mrs. Oliver were fighting in the library the other day. I thought it was on account of the Darjeeling 'cause they'd run out and he's addicted to the stuff. Only it gives him the runs. That downstairs bathroom ... Wooo! Stinks like rotten eggs. Mind you, he was doing all the talking at first because he didn't want to listen to something he didn't want to hear. She said nothing had happened and how would he feel if she put him on the bricks for a month. He said she wasn't fit to be first lady."

"When did all this happen?"

Art looked up at the ceiling, took a deep breath. "Three days before my birthday."

"Thursday?"

"Around two thirty. I remember because it was when the security man came to check the monitors. The Mayor said if she didn't give him up, he'd pack her off to California and tell the press."

"What did he mean when he said 'if she didn't give him up'?"

Art formed a steeple with his hands and shook his head. "There's someone she talks to on the phone. He's got to be someone important, 'cause one minute she's all soft on him, the next she's telling him where to go." Art gave a resigned shrug. "Listen, I don't know diddly-squat about the guy. All I know is he reacted badly to something she said. Said he was on his way to Albuquerque. It all went tense after that."

"Do you usually listen in to her conversations?"

"I am the Press Secretary, that means keeping as much from the press as possible. Mrs. Oliver's a little hard of hearing. Volume's turned up all the way."

"What do you do in your spare time?"

"Running women and watching TV."

"You do chat sites, blogs, Pinterest?"

"I have no idea what that is but that's never stopped me before. I'm in."

Malin could read Temeke like a book, lip curling, playing that pen in his hand. She knew the signs when he felt threatened, envy had a way of creeping into his tone and very soon he'd be putting Art down.

"Think a lot of yourself don't you?"

"Hell, no. It just goes with the turf. I used to do acting at school. Loved it. My dad wanted me to work in his solvent factory. But I joined the army instead, learned to fly helicopters and earned a bachelors in criminal justice. Sent my dad an autographed picture of the Governor and me in that helicopter just to rub it in. Nah, I'm no pool shark. Just like to party."

"On Sunday you were partying with the Mayor." Malin wiped a wisp of hair from her forehead. "How was it?"

"No one would have guessed they had such a messed-up life. She was sitting at one end of the table staring into space. The Mayor was in a mood because he was missing the football. I was cantering one of those silver horse salt cellars all over my dinner plate and Megan was having a smashing time in the kitchen from the sound of it. Wooo, I thought. Something's up. Then the Mayor took a phone call, went into the library and shut the door. Mrs. Oliver beckoned me into the kitchen. Said she needed extra security. I told her I'd look into it. To be honest, that house has more security than the National History Museum."

"So you let it go," Temeke said.

"I checked with surveillance. All the cameras were working fine."

"What time did security come to do the monitors on Thursday?"

"Around two thirty."

"Anyone reposition the cameras in front of the house, dab a little Windex on the lenses?"

"Not as far as I know. I was in my office."

"Correction, your office is behind kitchen. You had your big fat ear pressed to the library door, remember? What time did you leave on Sunday?"

"About four o'clock."

"How would you rate Mrs. Oliver's state of mind?"

"I would say she's been very stressed."

"Do you ever call her Raine?"

"Wooo—no. It's always Mrs. Oliver. To the house staff that is."

Temeke gave that slow nod he always did at the end of every interview. "You've been very helpful Mr. Ingram."

THIRTY-FOUR

Adam left the road and walked towards the cornfield, kicking up a shower of dead leaves as he went. Slats of sunlight passed between the trees and his eyes were almost shut against the glare. He thought of running away, only when the feeling came his heart was heavy like it was the wrong thing to do.

Ramsey was too sick to move and besides, the rangers might have killed him in the night. Even the dog knew what Adam was thinking, black eyes searching in that way dogs do. If he could speak he would say something fun like, 'race me to the woods,' or 'what's for dinner,' or 'you throw and I'll fetch,' because he was already gripping a gnarly old stick in that mouth of his.

Adam could hear the rumble of traffic on the highway and he wondered how far it was. How wrong would it be to stand on the hard shoulder and stick your thumb out? Grab a lift from a passing stranger. Tell them to call the police. In those three hours he had jostled with the idea of leaving the meds outside the hut and making a dash for it. But Ramsey was lying there all alone. He needed those pills, he needed a clean bandage.

Adam took out that phone, dialed his mom again. A dialing tone and sometimes a lady came on and said the call could not be completed as dialed. There was only one bar out there in the woods and he couldn't hold the phone high enough to get any more. Least, that's how they did it in the movies. Stand on rocks and wave it about. He snapped the thing shut and slipped it back into his pocket.

Murphy stopped and lowered his head and dropped the stick, taking a scent of something he couldn't see. He was an old dog. A smart dog. He'd found Adam, hadn't he?

And that was strange. Or a miracle. Or a bit of both. When Adam got to thinking, Murphy had appeared just after he had prayed. God must have had a hand in it like He had a hand in everything. God was old and God was smart.

Snap!

There was a ridge along the old dog's back now, one foot lifted, body half-hunkered down. Adam squatted behind a tree, pushed his hand out against the bark to keep his balance. There was something up ahead where the path rolled away, a blackened shape rising up and down in the murk, moving unseen between the sun's tracks.

There was no sound but the wind in those bare trees. Leaves twisted and fell from a dark gray sky and snowflakes gusted off a branch overhead. Silly isn't it when you're walking alone in a wood how you can see things, hear things, and you get to wondering if there's someone else out there. Watching.

Angels watch, Adam thought. He wasn't sure what they looked like, whether they were frightening or just covered in sparkles with feathery wings. Whether they were seven feet tall or just as ordinary as your next door neighbor. But whatever it was had gone. There was no sign of it now.

He had the uncanny feeling it was hiding, but he plodded on as far as the curve in the trail. Murphy's head was soft, especially that part between his ears and Adam wanted to take off his gloves and stroke him. But it was too cold. The air smelled of ice just after you've opened the freezer and it was sifting down his neck and into his bones.

Snap!

Adam held his breath, wrapping one hand around Murphy's grunting mouth and pressing it to his thigh. He only had to do it once. The old dog knew he had to be quiet. A sheer mist of snow seemed to hang over a tangled hedge and then it was gone.

Snap, snap!

Adam looked behind him and to the left and right. There was no moisture in his mouth now and he tried to swallow. It could have been a wolf sauntering along the path ahead. It could have been a dusky grouse. He took cover behind an aspen, each breath keeping time with his thumping heart. Straight ahead was a bristlecone pine and he focused between the leaves at a clearing beyond.

There… between two white-skinned trees about twenty feet away was a man, glossy hair tied back in a ponytail beneath a black cap. He stood waist deep in buffalo grass, one hand nudging the rifle on his shoulder, the other splayed out like a divining rod. He wasn't alone. There were four more nearby, chins raised, like they were watching something they didn't believe. One man seemed to be studying a limp map, anchoring the page with one hand, lips moving.

Adam wanted to unsnap the throat of his coat and peel off that wooly hat. He lifted the rim up over one ear instead, wanting to hear. But the air was thin and biting, and it was getting darker. The first of them tilted his chin as high as it would go and closed his eyes, arms straight out like a wooden cross, mouth half-open to taste the breeze. He was listening. Taking in the smells and sounds. Watching for signs. If these were the men Ramsey called rogue rangers, they looked nothing like the old bearded men Adam imagined.

The light was failing now and a crack of thunder in the distance made him gasp. The first ranger snapped his head to one side, body lit by a flare of lightning. His eyes seemed to dance over the foliage, until they stopped about three feet from where Adam crouched.

He pulled a knife from his belt, squatted suddenly, hand hovering over the grass again and lower still as if tracing a set of footprints.

Adam knew those eyes were searching through the leaves and the ranger would sense any movement, track any scent. There were rifles on their shoulders big enough for mule, deer or elk, only these men were fanned out like they were searching for something smaller. Adam opened his mouth to breathe, looked down at Murphy and shook his head. Hail rattled against the leaves and then the rain came, blotting out any noise they could have made. But the ranger hunkered there as if he knew his quarry would tire of hiding.

Adam slid to a sitting position, thighs trembling from the weight of his pack. He wedged himself in good and hard against that tree, hand patting the air once for Murphy to lie down, one finger raised for combat silence. The dog obeyed.

The ranger stood again, gripping that knife and holding it out in front. He gestured to the others with a nod of his head and they became shadows, slogging down a south facing slope towards a stream and fading into the distance. The first ranger waited in that sea of grass, body lit up with each flash and then he waded forward, just a few steps at a time. He looked big. He looked quick. He didn't make a sound.

Murphy's tongue began darting in and out of his mouth, ears pricked to the threat. His belly wasn't all the way to the ground, front legs at an angle and carrying the brunt of his weight. A shiny black snout twitched in the wind and when another sheer of lightning lit up the sky, the old dog wasted no time. He ducked beneath a canopy of leaves and stalked off, circling the man at a crouch.

Adam was surprised the man couldn't see the dog, one minute a shadow, the next passing slowly between the tree trunks. The ranger turned a half-circle, then he turned back, knife glinting like a silver trout in a dark pool. He knew the dog was there. He just couldn't see him.

Adam could feel his teeth chattering and his body was beginning to shake. His knees squelched through wet mud and he stumbled and fell forward under the weight of his pack. It was heavy, wedged against his spine like a turtle's shell. Turning sideways, he could see Murphy hunkered down on a faint track, tongue pulsing through his teeth and he could see edge of the trees beyond and the silver-gray ruts of a ploughed field. If his gut was right, the hut wasn't more than a mile away.

Murphy lunged forward again and ran a complete circle around the ranger, keeping to a ten foot boundary. He would keep this game up for as long as it took for Adam to break free. Herding, growling, snapping, padding about in the darkness and thwacking the leaves with his tail.

Adam studied the leaning trees and the direction of the wind, and he could hear the beating rain against the canopy. He had two choices. Run for his life or find Ramsey. His feet dug for traction in the mud as he took his cue, racing for a narrow stream at the bottom of the slope, black as tar against the snow. He looked both ways and saw nothing except the beatific face of a big round moon in its reflection; no rangers… nothing.

He scrambled up the bank and veering towards his left, found a gap in the hedge and made a dash for the rutted farm track. All he knew was to get to Ramsey before the rangers did. Warn him so he could make a dash for it. He wouldn't mind sleeping in the leaves with his pack as a pillow. He wouldn't mind because Murphy was there.

Murphy burst through a clump of grass, sneezing and wagging his tail. It was good to have a friend. But it was the name tag that chimed against the red collar that worried Adam, so he unclipped it and stuffed it in his coat pocket.

They hurried along the track, keeping to the ditch beneath the trees. Murphy had mapped it all in his head, found another broken branch and held it in his mouth. He'd even found the hut, tried to nudge his way in with that stick, only he got wedged in the doorway.

Adam expected to find a pile of stinking old rags. Instead, there was Ramsey propped up against the wall, feeding logs through the open door of the pot-belly stove. The gun was on the floor, toothbrush stained with the solvent he'd used. He'd decanted some of the water into two plastic bottles and there were crumbs from a protein bar in his beard. The tear in his jeans was gaping like an open mouth and the wound was soft and yellow and weeping.

"I told you to bring meds not a dog!"

It never occurred to Adam that he would have to tell Ramsey about the dog. "I found him on the road. So… you're not dead then."

Ramsey gave a guttural laugh and shook his head. "It would take a lot to kill me. You should know that by now. And you? You came back. Could have run away. Could have called the cops. Aren't you going to take your coat off?"

Adam stood there breathing out a warm mist between his lips. "The rangers. They're here."

THIRTY-FIVE

Malin pulled into Puerta de Corrales where the boughs of a large cottonwood creaked in the wind. She parked in front of her apartment, a two story building with brown stucco walls and white frame windows, all floodlit by a single halogen lamp. It was the next block to Sergeant and Rae Moran, close enough for company, distant enough for solitude.

Turning off the ignition, she noticed a brown sedan backed into a corner, license plate flush against a low brick wall. A domestic violence situation, she could sniff them out a mile away. If she ordered a registration check it would be in the name of Laura Glass, small, blonde and well into her sixth boyfriend since Malin had moved in. The girl was nice enough; lived downstairs next to Old Man Topper, working as a seamstress during the day and an exotic dancer at night.

Malin gripped the handrail and took the stairs to the second floor, hand resting on the holster at her waist. She wasn't jumpy, just a little wary that's all. It was the wind whistling through the bannisters and playing a mournful strain and she walked to her front door, turning slightly to see if anyone had been following her.

It always smelled of mold, even in the summer, and there was a hint of roast chicken that drifted up the stairwell and she could still smell it in the living room after closing the front door. The kettle was full and slipping a hand behind the lip of the countertop, she flipped the switch.

Unzipping her jacket, she hooked it over a chair and switched on the TV. It was that anchor again, the man with the voice like a game show host.

" . . . Troop 173 has joined the search in the Bosque for Adam Oliver and another search is underway in Gila National Forest. The FBI have sent agents to the scene along with several Shadow Wolf officers from the Navajo nation. Although Mayor Oliver is still in critical condition, his wife and family hold out hope that Adam is still alive and due to regular scouting activities, able to withstand the punishing terrain. The police have not ruled out the possibility of a connection with the Ringmaster murders in 2001 but caution it is too early to draw any conclusions at this time. Anyone with any information can call the number at the bottom of the screen or go to NWAC dot com."

Malin muted the volume and kicked off her shoes, listening to the purr of the kettle. The last thing the family needed was any connection to the Ringmaster murders.

She stared long and hard at that laptop, suddenly afraid of it, suddenly curious. Better get it over with, she told herself.

When she signed in, there were four emails, all junk except for one. Wingman had sent her an invitation to chat.

She began typing a reply to his earlier message and then deleted it. It was hard to relax when you're on a dating site and the man you've been talking to is not who you thought he was.

She felt a nudge of dread, heard the click of the kettle and walked into the bathroom. He knew the case. That made him a cop.

As she showered, she realized how much she hated

this feeling, worrying about what to say. Sending an invitation the minute she signed into Heartfree was overkill. There was a dozen possibilities, of course. Fowler, Jarvis…

She pulled the housecoat off the back of the bathroom door, cinched the belt tightly and walked into the kitchen. The tea was hot against her lips and she sat in front of that computer, staring at the message.

It was longer than she expected.

Wingman: Where have you been, my little dove. Here I was thinking you were lost forever. It wasn't the same without you yesterday. Nobody to talk to. This is our third date. Perhaps you don't want them finding out such a respectable lady like you uses a chat site. Or that you used to be an escort. Do they even know, Malin? No, of course not. But I know everything. What I don't know I find out. And what I find out I barter with.

It was odd that this person, who knew so much about her, should be messaging her in the first place. And equally odd that she had no idea who he was. The feeling of fear was so overwhelming, she caught the taste of bile before that cup of tea almost came up.

Her fingers hovered over the keyboard for a moment and then she typed: Who are you?

Wingman: You said you knew.

She punched her thigh with a tight fist and berated herself for falling for it. Again.

Wingman: I'm a ghost in broad daylight. I don't like spectators, you see. But you need a Wingman, someone to watch your back.

Malin: What do you want?

Wingman: You want to know who took Adam Oliver. I can help you with that. What would be a fitting price?

Malin: Name it.

Wingman: Let's get to know each other first. Feel comfortable. Talk. Go deeper. And then I'll tell you what I want.

His words echoed in her mind and, she suspected, would continue to do so until she was free of it. She wondered what he looked like, whether he pursed his lips, whether he smiled or even laughed at her. She wondered why she was allowing this conversation, this closeness, this stupidity. She wondered if she was safe.

Malin: What are the consequences?

Wingman: Consequences spoil everything don't they? Three strikes and you're out. First, is anyone monitoring your computer?

Malin: No.

Wingman: Why did I think you'd say that?

Malin: I haven't told anyone.

Wingman: And you won't. Not if Adam's life is at stake. I know you better than you think I do. Forgive me if I'm being unkind.

With a strange sense of intuition, it occurred to her then that she didn't know this man at all. His words came back to her with repetitive insistence.

Forgive me if I'm being unkind.

It wasn't Fowler with his obvious charms, it wasn't bumbling Jarvis playing jokes, couldn't have been. This man was stealth reincarnate and he had an eidetic memory.

She typed: You don't know me.

Wingman: I know you prefer Jasmine tea rather than Chai. You don't take sugar. Like everything black. You love Key Lime Pie. You eat at Corrales Café in the late afternoons not because it's close to home, because it's company. You sit on the patio where you can hear the wind in the cottonwoods, see the sunlight through the canvas shades. It makes you feel part of the action like you have a choice. And you always back your car in under that tree.

Malin: You're stalking me.

Wingman: Everyone stalks their favorite heroes and you're mine.

Malin: You're a coward hiding behind a fake name

and a silhouette. Anyone would think you're afraid of me.

Wingman: Perhaps I am. It was so wonderful then, in the old days. I wish you could remember. They were the golden years of which every year since has been only the palest shadow and every year past is wasted. You'll grow to love the silhouette because you can think of me in those precious moments and wonder who I really am. And when you know me better, you'll dream of me.

Malin: You're so full of it.

Wingman: Now, let's get back to business. How does an affair begin? With a glance, a thought. You gape at the sheer beauty and suddenly only that one person stands out to you. For some reason you worship them, as he did. Every day you're standing in the presence of the greatest thing under the sun, catching every word, every nuance. For days, months, it is almost too much to bear and the distance becomes torture. Last night I lay awake thinking about him trying to pinpoint exactly when she betrayed him. When he truly lost her. I tried to reconstruct the scene in my head, the last month together, mad with pain knowing it had to come to an end. Because she did betray him, Malin, when she took another. You have to understand he was obsessed and leaving was the only option. He wasn't good enough for her. He wasn't good enough for the perfect army. And so my question is this. When does a man fully surrender? When does he crash?

Malin remembered something her mother once said, when she begged her to go to church. 'He'll break you, bring you to your knees. And when you're at your lowest, when you can't go any lower… that's when you'll find Him'."

Malin: When he is completely humbled.

Wingman: Excellent. I knew you'd understand. He thought he had her. He thought it was a home run. But he was wrong. Something snapped in him that day, brought him lower than he had ever been. A time to examine himself. A time to fight back. Years later, that's why he took Adam. Pay back.

She had a strange sense—the same one she used to have as a girl when she dared herself to open the cellar door, walk down a few steps only to turn around and run back up again. She had been followed by shadows then.

Malin: Who? Do you know him?

Wingman: Tut, tut, Malin. That's hardly detective work is it? But here's a little taste of what he is.

The ship was cheered, the harbour cleared,
Merrily did we drop
Below the kirk, below the hill,
Below the lighthouse top.

A poem. What's in a poem? She shook her head. The words weren't familiar and what it had to do with this kidnapper she couldn't imagine. The spelling was English and *kirk* was an ancient sounding word. She was about to type when he beat her to it.

Wingman: Btw, Temeke's an excellent detective. He bypassed quite a few big names to get where he is. I have first-hand experience. But he has one flaw, one terrible weakness. Break him and I'll make you the best detective the world has ever seen. That's what I want.

Temeke… he wanted to destroy Temeke. Her mind tried to unravel all the names she could possibly think of. Lawyers, judges, anyone who might have carried a grudge. There were a few.

Wingman: You want to know who I am. You want a face. But it's so much better this way. And one day you'll thank me. One day you may even say those three words I've been longing to hear.

Malin fully expected him to sign off. He'd dangled the first carrot, given her something to chew on. She could almost imagine the magnanimous tilt of his head, an offhand gesture, a sultry look. But the face was always blank.

To her surprise he typed four more lines.

The sun came up upon the left,
Out of the sea came he!
And he shone bright, and on the right
Went down into the sea.

THIRTY-SIX

They scrambled on through the woods that night, Adam in the lead. He felt the weight of Ramsey's hand on his shoulder and he could smell alcohol. The sound of chattering teeth in his left ear made him jumpy. Ramsey must have been sick if he was shivering and cowled in a blanket from his pack.

"What can you see, Night Eyes?"

"Just the path," Adam murmured.

"Look again. Keep looking. And don't stop."

Adam let his eyes flick back and forth, sweeping over the terrain and the path ahead. Sporadic gusts of wind blasted through the trees, branches groaning with the strain.

Ramsey kept muttering and asking Adam if he was sure he could see the path, kept stumbling with the pack on his back. It wasn't like him to make a whole pile of noise and wake up an owl. It scared them both and made Murphy pull at his leash. He didn't bark. Didn't even growl.

"Are you sure those rangers went south?" Ramsey whispered.

"I'm sure."

"Hope they didn't smell the wood smoke and start heading back. They could be anywhere. My gut tells me they're here. Keep listening."

Adam knew at least four were too far away in the

woods, hiking up the slopes and headed south. As for the fifth, he would likely trudge all day in silence, head down and eyes soaking up every footprint they left behind.

"We have to keep moving," Adam whispered, grabbing Ramsey by the arm.

"I'm OK."

"You always say that."

Ramsey straightened then. Like he'd shaken himself out of a drunken blur and decided to wake up.

It was hard going through the leaves and when it wasn't leaves, it was pine needles ankle deep and nipping at your socks. Murphy was so quiet Adam almost forgot he was there, nose twitching and ears flapping in the wind.

Adam didn't know why he wanted to help Ramsey, didn't know what to call him either. Gray Fox… Ramsey. The feeling in his chest was hard to put into words and he let his lips play with each sound in that cold silence. He decided to call him nothing. It was easier that way.

Slabs of snow clung to the branches, some cupped in the leaves like a handful of pure cane sugar. It wasn't as cold as the night before and the rain had washed away all the ice troughs in that narrow wooded path.

Sometimes Ramsey stopped and looked about and sometimes he just stood, ear cocked to the ground. He'd already chewed two of the pills Trader had given him and sucked down the flask of hot buttered rum. Kept complaining about the dark, how he couldn't see beyond the trees.

Adam could see. He didn't know if it was the way the moon fell on the ruts in the track and lit up the silver-gray puddles. He didn't know if it was the pale slatted light that God gave to his nighttime world.

"It's worse than snaps and movers," Ramsey said.

"Know what they are?"

Adam shook his head, took a sip of water from his plastic bottle.

"Targets that suddenly pop up. Anywhere. Anytime. Those are the snaps. Random targets that slide left and right. Those are the movers. They can be fast. Out here, it's different. Those targets are men and you won't know how far away they are. Got to know the wind. Got to keep track of time. Every second."

Snap! Snap, snap!

Murphy snorted and lifted his head. Adam watched his line of focus, saw movement up ahead and he stopped too. Ramsey stooped, breath hot against Adam's cheek, heartbeat thudding against his left shoulder. Time began to crawl over the shifting wind, even the leaves seemed to shudder and become still again.

"What do you see?" Ramsey pushed Adam down to a crouch.

"Something... in the shadows." Adam couldn't see exactly what, but he knew something was there, slender as a man standing against a tree.

"How far?"

Adam calculated about thirty yards. It was the halo round the moon that enabled him to see everything above the brush. "See that tree, the one with the white bark... to the right."

Ramsey whipped a look over his shoulder and listened. Then looked forward and listened again. The wind was playing hide and seek through the aspens, leaves chattering even louder now. "Chances are, he sees us."

To the right of them was the edge of the woodland with a large field beyond. It was too exposed to make a dash for it, every ridge and furrow lit by an eerie glow. They must have been silhouetted against the silvery sky and the ranger could likely see them from the darkness of his roost.

The moon was bright like a frying pan, glowing down on that wintry path. But it couldn't shine behind bushes, nor could it tattle on their position. They were well hidden behind those tall grasses where random shafts of light filtered down between the trees. No one could have seen them.

"What are we going to do?" Adam asked, knees wobbling beneath the weight of his pack.

"We're going to wait until he makes a move."

They didn't have to wait long. The ranger also slipped to a crouch behind that tree, only he couldn't see much more over the tops of the grasses than they could. He stayed that way for a time and then stood slowly and extended an arm.

"He's got a gun. Can't see us." Adam said.

"How do you know?"

"Pointed too far to the right."

Ramsey nodded and squeezed Adam's shoulder. "Moving to the left might be an idea, but we'll wait in case he changes his mind."

The ranger didn't change his mind. He came on with his gun held out in front, moving slowly, eyes trained on a quaking piñon far out in the middle of the field beyond the wood.

"Sure it's not a trick?" Adam whispered.

"Too far in the open for a trick. I could have shot him by now."

Ramsey indicated the need for silence, the ranger was getting too close and the dog was coughing up a growl or two. Adam held Murphy's snout, pulled the dog in closer as they listened to stealthy footsteps crunching on dead pine needles, shoulder snapping off a few twigs.

There was silence then, as if the man was cussing over his mistake and then he lumbered on, no longer listening or looking at the shadows the trees made over the snow. He just trudged towards the field, gun held downwards in both hands. He was all dressed in black, except for that round ashen face.

Ramsey looked up at the sky and then out at the fields. But there was nothing to see. When the man had gone on a distance, they crawled slowly through the grass, hearing their footsteps in the leaves. Adam tried to remember where they had come from, whether they were walking east or west, whether they were walking in circles. Ramsey didn't seem to care. He just sniffed a few times, hiked his chin up and stared at the night sky and then looked back at the field. The man was still walking towards that tree.

Ramsey seemed to know what he was doing. Seemed to know the way. And when he didn't, he just stopped for a while and looked down at Adam, sometimes smiling, sometimes serious. He was brave, walking on that bad leg and not even stopping for a break. His back was straight when he waited for the wind, head aslant as he listened to the rattle of leaves overhead. He said he liked the sound. Reminded him of the rush of seawater on sand.

Adam knew it reminded him of other things too. Of a girl in a black swimsuit with shiny black eyes. Tiny pinched in waist and cream colored skin.

Ramsey stumbled on and then slowed, took one step forward and then another. It was the sound of a truck on a nearby road that seemed to change his mind. Only this wasn't the road Adam heard when he hiked out to Trader's house. This was another road, smaller, snaking up through the aspens and over the brow of a hill.

"This isn't it," Ramsey whispered. He stopped and parted a tall clump of grass with his hands. Looked ahead and behind, especially behind.

A creaking somewhere in the trees above them, the

hoot of an owl. Adam trembled in the cold, watched the gray serpentine of that road and wished a truck would happen by. Clouds threatened to block out that metallic shimmer, the only light they had. There was a lingering odor of damp wood and soil and the occasional rasp of wet grass in the wind.

They heard that sound again, another snap, another groan. Ramsey was focused behind them now, looking out towards that field. He moved his head from side to side, neck outstretched as if he caught something in the shadows. He pulled Adam gently to the ground, made him sit with his legs out in front, back against a tree. The ground they sat on was dry, long grass weaving around them like an old wattle house.

Adam was too tired to look. He'd only slept in fits and starts since Ramsey took him, images of his mother pounding in his head like relentless waves on a pebbly beach. In just over a week he'd had a year's worth of scares and now he was drifting aimlessly in a forever gray world. He hoped they weren't lost.

"Better put a hand over your dog's mouth," Ramsey whispered, patting the air with his hand. "He is your dog, right?" Ramsey must have seen the look on his face and if he couldn't he could sense it. "It says so on the tag. The one in your pocket. Oh, and I took the phone and switched it off. Don't want that giving us away, do we?"

Adam swallowed back some grit in his throat and nearly coughed. He would have taken another drink if that wretched bottle didn't crackle so much every time he unscrewed the lid.

Snap!

"He's come back around," Ramsey murmured. "He tricked us."

THIRTY-SEVEN

Rain crawled down the office window followed by a spatter of sleet. Temeke lit up a cigarette. Didn't care if Hackett could smell it next door. It could have been worse, something slimmer from the evidence locker, only that stuff smelled like burnt sausages and there wasn't a cop in sight who didn't know the difference.

He dialed Serena's number, waited for the sixth ring, resisting that desperate urge to shout when it went to voicemail. Always bloody voicemail.

Taking a long drag and huffing out a large cloud of smoke, he left a message. "It's me, love. Course you know that. But what you don't know is, I'm beginning to wonder if I'm married to the Scarlet Pimpernel. I'm also beginning to wonder if you're too scared to bring me those divorce papers. That's why you called me, wasn't it? And if it wasn't, it must have been on account of the copious quantities of wasp spray in the garage. Two boxes last I counted. You can pick them up any time."

He tapped the END button and slammed the phone down on the filing cabinet. Never mind weeks of silence, he'd rather have a pile of bleeding insults than silence. And the wasp spray? It was her way of warding off Jehovah's Witnesses and any other religious freaks in the neighborhood.

Talking of religious freaks, where the heck was Malin? She was missing all the fun. It was nine o'clock on a Friday morning and the officers were already in the canteen raiding a box of bagels and cream cheese. There'd be none left if she didn't hurry up.

He heard footsteps outside his door, ground that cigarette in the bottom of a china mug and picked up the phone. Just as he expected it went straight through to Mrs. Oliver's voicemail. He left a brief message that he wanted to meet with her and hung up.

A tapping at the door and Fowler popped his head in. "Thought I could hear voices," he said.

"And I thought I could hear an earhole pressed against the door."

"I'd like a couple of words. Preferably not sod off."

"Listen, unless you've got something important to say like Lord Lucan is downstairs and has just given himself up, you're wasting my time. Where's Hackett, by the way."

"He was talking about a cruise."

"On the Marie Celeste? I haven't seen him since yesterday morning."

"You don't miss much, do you?"

Temeke frowned. It was a detective's job to be alert, especially where Hackett was concerned. As for Fowler, he was too cocky for his own good, brass chinking against that starched suit. If he wasn't careful Temeke would find him a cell to kip in with the usual nightly quota of vomiting, screaming drunks.

"Good news," Fowler said, squeaking his way to Malin's chair in a brand new pair of shoes. "Had a Mr. Trader on the phone again this morning. Call box near Glenwood. Said there was something he forgot to mention. Coughing up a storm. Didn't sound too well. Thinks the boy on the news is definitely the one he saw. Said the kid left him a note and a telephone number. It's Mrs. Oliver's number all right. The kid also left him a fifty dollar bill which may have a few familiar serial numbers. Trader said the kid also had a black dog. Now, why would he have a black dog?"

Temeke wondered why Fowler was looking at him all funny and copped a shrug.

"Thing is, the dog had a tag on its collar. 'Murphy' it said."

"Common enough name—"

"Nah, I've never heard that name. Have you?" Fowler turned to Jarvis who was standing in the doorway trying to focus bleary eyes on his wrist watch.

"Sounds Irish," was Jarvis' meager offering.

"Funny thing is, Adam's dog's called Murphy." Fowler pursed his lips for a second. "How the dog managed to make it to Gila National Forest I'll never know. Someone must have given him a ride."

Temeke kept his eyes on Fowler. Never blinked. Never twitched. "Ever seen *The Incredible Journey*?"

"I hope you're not expecting me to believe a trumped up story about a dog traveling two hundred some miles on foot. 'Cause I won't believe a word."

Temeke rubbed his chin. The fact that the same dog had done it in four hours and fifty-two minutes was best kept to himself. "Where does Mr. Trader live?"

"4567 Little Creek Road about seven miles west of the National Monument. I sent Maggie Watts over there. Thought she needed a dose of flu not me."

"It never rains, but it flaming pees. Why send her? I could have gone."

"You're staying right here. Where the action is."

"What action? I've interviewed fifteen bloody people in the past week, three of whom have nothing better to do than listen in to Mrs. Oliver's telephone calls."

"And how is Mrs. Oliver?"

He would bloody well ask. Already got the hots for the poor old bat. "Well, now, there's a conundrum. I've called her a few times and she never picks up. Thank Officer Watts for keeping my seat warm, but I'll take over now."

"You want the even better news?" Fowler said, giving a sly old wink. He waited a few seconds and when Temeke failed to rise to the occasion, he said, "Mayor Oliver's come round. Wants to see you."

That's why Mrs. Oliver hadn't answered her phone, Temeke thought. "Right, I'm on my way. Note to self, get a large box of Darjeeling and two tea cups."

"Before you go," Fowler said, jabbing a finger in Jarvis' arm, "you might want to see this."

Jarvis pulled out a copy of the *Journal* from under his sweaty pit. The front page was full of the usual propaganda; New Mexico's largest semi-conductor manufacturing facility was making investments in six far eastern technology companies. A photo of Hackett opening his front door and waving off the morning crew of the paparazzi. An article by Cyn Wrigley persuading the Chief of Police to get more men on the Oliver case since two thirds of the police department had been assigned to a drug bust in the south valley and the other third were playing silly buggers. It was also noted that Detective Temeke's team were understaffed. All thanks go to Captain Rufus Fowler for issuing prompt press releases and keeping the public notified.

Rufus? Was that a typo? Please tell me that was a typo, Temeke thought. He'd never known Fowler's first name. Never bothered to ask.

Jarvis jabbed a stubby finger in Fowler's arm. "I thought you said your name was Rayford."

Fowler swatted that finger away and dismissed the comment. "They like me," he said. There was a curl to his lips, but the smile was cold. "They trust me. I was born here. You know what they don't like? Foreigners. Because there's no loyalty. No history. My grandfather was Secretary of State to old Governor Mendez. Who are you, Temeke? A nobody. From a nobody part of the world where nobody cares. And furthermore, I don't care..."

Here he was, Fowler the young bastard who was going to the top because of his influential relatives. Temeke stared past the carefully sculptured hair to the clock on the wall. Twenty minutes past nine. If he was lucky, he'd get a few smokes in before lunch. His phone vibrated on the desk; a text from Malin. *The Rime of the Ancient Mariner*, it said. *Sailors lost at sea. Someone shot a bird. Mean anything?*

He tapped out the word *No* and *pick me up at 9:30. Hospital. Mayor.*

Fowler stopped talking then, gave a frown and stared at Temeke through half-closed eyes. "Who is it?"

"Dry cleaners," Temeke said, tilting the phone away from Fowler. "You were saying?"

"I was saying Cyn thinks you should stand down."

If Fowler thought he'd got away with tipping off Cyn at the *Journal* just so he could promote himself, he had another thing coming. "Is your flaming brain on holiday? You think I don't know about your seedy flirtation with Ms. Wrigley, not to mention her assistant? It only takes a phone call to correct her about who's really in charge. I'm sure the people would love that vote of confidence. Women aren't all fools, Fowler. Give them some credit."

Fowler exchanged raised eyebrows and a pulled-down mouth with Jarvis. "You'll never earn any respect, Temeke. Not in this state. It'll take years for you to redeem yourself."

Temeke stood, snapped his top drawer shut and locked it. He slipped the phone in his pocket and shrugged on his jacket. "You'd better watch your step, or you'll be following me out of Albuquerque."

That made Fowler glare and Jarvis wince. It was worth a picture. Temeke was fed up with detectives being at the bottom of the food chain. It was time for a change.

Outside the station a cold wind slashed his cheeks and the smell of ice was everywhere. He walked over to his car and poked a cigarette through the gap in his lips. Smoking did nothing to improve his temper and he filled his lungs with each drag, heart pounding even faster. Fowler had a bloody nerve and if he wasn't careful Temeke would find a way to pay him back.

"Where the hell are you, Marl?" he murmured, seeing a tiny patch of sunlight on the pavement.

At that moment a black Explorer crawled around the corner, driver's window open, ponytail bobbing. "Thought you might need a ride, sir," Malin said.

"Am I glad to see you." He ground the cigarette with the heel of his shoe and slid into the passenger seat. "Fowler's a bit grumpy today," he warned, telling her about the headlines. "Apparently, we're due for a transfer."

"Hopefully, it's Paris." She pulled right onto Ellison and up the hill. "I could do with the culture."

"You're late."

"Had a few calls to make."

"Nothing serious?" he asked, sensing a stab of tension in the air.

She shook her head. Looked like someone had finally told her Santa wasn't real.

"And what's all this guff about the Ancient Mariner?" he said. "Sailors lost at sea and someone shoots a bird?"

"It was an albatross, sir. Very bad luck."

"Maybe they were hungry. Not much to eat at sea."

"There's fish."

Temeke nodded. He hadn't thought of it that way.

"Why are you asking?"

"You're the literary type. You read all kinds of poetry, plays, that kind of thing. Just thought it might mean something to you, that's all."

Temeke held his breath as they drove towards the hospital. He should have been happy. The sun was peeking through a bank of clouds and he was feeling warmer by the minute. It was just the silence he didn't like, didn't like her mood either. "Someone send you a book? A link?"

"A few lines of poetry," she said, turning to look at him briefly. "Thought it was rather nice."

He knew she was smiling to allay his suspicion, but she wasn't doing a very good job. There was something in her tone that made his lips pucker. Something in that tight frown that made her look scared.

THIRTY-EIGHT

Two secret service were standing at the lobby door to the hospital, speaking into their wrists. One stared at Malin as she squealed into a parking space, shooting up a spray of brown water as the front tire ploughed through a puddle. Temeke cringed as he clicked himself out of the seatbelt, glimpsed the dark stain on Agent Anderson's pants. Malin always found a way of soaking important people.

He hated hospitals, especially the clinical smells and gurneys carrying people with faces locked in a grimace of pain. They took the lift to the third floor past the room he had visited every day when Lt. Luis Alvarez was sick. He'd seen Serena, what... twice? What a bloody circus that had been.

Two more secret service ushered them in, eyes scanning the corridor without giving them a second look. Mrs. Oliver waved a trembling hand through the window of the Mayor's room and smiled. Her hair was tied high on her head like a cottage loaf, eyes sultry and lips slightly pursed. Temeke knew they were in for a show.

"Mayor Oliver," he said, extending his hand and looking down at a gaunt husk of a man, well into his sixties, head bald with tufts of white hair visible below the turban of a bandage around his head. There was also an empty carton of ice-cream on the table – bacon and vanilla it said. "I'm glad to see you looking well."

"Much better," Mayor Oliver said with a smile, trying to lift his head from a plump pillow. His voice was gruff and his grip weak. "Weather forecast says no more rain or snow. About time for some sunshine, don't you think?"

"Forecasts have been proved wrong before, Mr. Mayor."

"Not in New Mexico, Detective." He seemed to squint at the badge in Temeke's belt and flicked a sideways look at his wife.

"Good to see you," Mrs. Oliver said, settling in the chair next to the Mayor's bed. There was a large vase of purple roses on the window sill, bathed in a shaft of sunlight.

Impeccably dressed, Temeke thought as he shook her hand. All in beige and black, a dress that screamed several hundred dollars. He held her gaze, forcing her to break away.

His mind began to race. This elderly white-haired man was Mrs. Oliver's husband? He was much older close up, nothing like the round-faced individual he had come to know and admire on the TV. No, the man he saw now, shivered under that thermal blanket, thin tube taped to his cheek and running into his left nostril. Another tube descended from a half empty IV bag, dripping fluids into a vein in his hand.

A nurse technician brought in two extra chairs, briefly checked the patient monitor and tapped an update into the computer. He was gone after that.

"Feeding you all right?" Temeke dared ask.

"I had oatmeal this morning and scrambled eggs." The Mayor shuffled up the bed a little, bracing his arms against the side rail. "Do you think this has anything to do with the Ringmaster murders? Because if it has, this man will get lethal injection. And he better not think Governor Bendish will grant clemency."

"We've no reason to assume it has, sir."

"I expect you want to know what happened on Sunday night." The Mayor's eyes seemed to drift up to the ceiling and there was a crease in that dull gray brow. "I'd been reading a book on the couch… a couple of hours maybe. Adam was late getting back from a scout trip. I was annoyed if you must know. Wanted to go to bed. But he was excited to go. Texted me every hour, said the explosives were the best, real window rattlers. They went to the VLA, saw the antennas up close."

Temeke remembered a time when he was headed east on 60 towards the Very Large Array, how startling those radio telescopes were, rising out of the flat yellow plain.

"I remember hearing the latch on the patio door," the Mayor said. "Saw a man coming toward me with a gun. Funny thing… I wasn't afraid. Thought I knew him from somewhere. Just couldn't place him. He said something about how well I'd done for myself. Asked me if I'd received his letters. I thought he was mistaken. Had the wrong house. I tried to talk to him… asked him to sit down. But he wouldn't. It was the dog, you see. Military trained. Came charging in from the kitchen and nearly bowled the man over. That's when the gun went off. I don't think he meant to shoot me. I think he just wanted to talk."

"About what, sir?"

"He wanted to tell me something…" The Mayor screwed up his face as if shuddering from the memory. "The doctor warned us about memory loss. He said some things never come back. Apparently, the first thing I asked the doctor when I came round was who shot J.R.?"

Mrs. Oliver tucked the blanket tighter around her husband's legs, took a newspaper off the overbed table and began patting it into three neat folds. The Mayor waved a hand, told her to stop fussing, told her to sit down.

She put a glass of water to her mouth, likely to hide a flurry of embarrassment, Temeke thought. He continued to watch her: the downturned head, two hands clutching that glass where only one would do. He suddenly felt a twinge of empathy.

"I think he must have climbed over the wall from the road… from Coors," Mayor Oliver said. "He could have been drunk. Could have been a liberal democrat."

Temeke felt a shudder of disgust at the flippant comment. He decided to plough ahead. "You're the first republican Mayor we've had in over thirty years. Bound to get a few boos now and then. So, someone had a grudge. And that someone's taken your son. When Adam got home that night, did he mention anything about an unfamiliar truck in the neighborhood?"

The Mayor shook his head and took a spoonful of ice cream. "I never got to speak to him. Wish I had. Wish I'd had one last chance—"

"I think that's enough," Mrs. Oliver broke in with a voice that would have sliced through tempered steel. "My husband needs to rest."

"You always say that. Remember, I've been sleeping for an entire week!" Mayor Oliver lifted the carton of ice cream and offered it to Temeke. "Dickies. Homemade."

Temeke declined on account of a piece of bacon which looked like it was doing backstroke in a pool of cream. "Adam got a compass?"

"He always carries one in his backpack. Troop requirements."

"Ever had occasion to beat him?"

"Of course not."

"Ever argued in front of him, shouted—"

"You make it sound like discipline is a capital crime, Detective."

"It depends on the circumstances."

"I've done all the things a father should. Shaped him, rewarded him, encouraged him." The Mayor shared a nod with his wife and blew his nose into a laundered handkerchief. "I want to send out a press release… draft a bill. Where's my notepad?"

"Not now, my love," Mrs. Oliver said. "You don't want your blood pressure going up again."

"A few more questions if I may," Temeke said. "Any strange calls?" He waited. No response. "Blocked numbers, death threats, that kind of thing?"

The Mayor shook his head. "We often get calls from telemarketers. We don't answer them."

Temeke sent a smile from the Mayor to Mrs. Oliver. "Yet, we taped the voicemail the kidnapper left. Monday, I think it was. Mentioned something about midsummer's day and how he should have been there. Any idea what he meant?"

Mrs. Oliver frowned as if she found the question bizarre. "I've no idea."

"Mr. Mayor, the intruder asked you about some letters. What letters was he referring to?"

"We get letters from all kinds of people. I encourage it on my website."

"Any personal letters?" Temeke was hoping to jog the Mayor's memory about that charred letter they had found in the fireplace.

"No one outside the family knows our home address."

"Yet the intruder knew exactly how to find you. No forced entry. Odd, don't you think?"

"You think he was in collusion with someone? A member of staff?"

"If that's the case, it's a question of finding a link between the intruder and this second person. You said you thought you'd seen him before?"

"He looked familiar. A teacher, off duty firefighter,

journalist… No, scruffier than that."

"Hair color?"

"Brown. To here." The Mayor patted his shoulder.

"Eyes?"

"It was too dark. I couldn't possibly see his eyes."

"What was he wearing?"

"A black shirt, khaki pants. No, wait… jeans. Yes, I think they were jeans."

"Well, he certainly covered his tracks, sir. No shell casings. No fingerprints. Not a hair in sight. See, that's what I don't understand. How a casual intruder didn't leave a stitch of DNA, especially with hair as long as it was. Either he was covered from head to foot in cling film, or he knew how to scope a joint. And I'm inclined towards the latter, seeing as you did mention his clothes."

Mayor Oliver grimaced. "Is my wife safe in the house? Should she stay in a hotel?"

"We have around-the-clock surveillance, sir. If Madam Mayor needs someone in the house, detective Santiago here would be glad to oblige."

Malin didn't exactly look pleased. He caught the twitch of a frown and her pulse was likely up about now.

"One last thing," Temeke saw the nod and raced on. "Madam Mayor did mention recently that you rarely speak to your neighbors. In fact, I believe the word she used was *never*. Yet Mr. Eli Sandoval insists you both fish occasionally. I just wanted to be sure I understood that correctly."

"My wife doesn't fish, Detective. Too boring. Rather go shopping with Suzie Bendish." The Mayor looked over at Malin as if she was hard of hearing and said, "Governor's wife."

Temeke couldn't help feeling he was in the middle of an uncomfortable family affair. He cleared his throat and said, "Who would you say you trusted the most?"

"My Press Secretary. Art has been called upon to deal with some very private matters. He's never let me down. We'd be lost without him."

"On a lighter note," Temeke said, turning to leave. "Remember that article in the *Journal*? The one about cutting the size of local government. Had a brief bio at the end. Said something about you being sworn into office on November 1st, 2009. I thought it was October."

A scowling Mayor looked up. "It was December 1st. I called the *Journal*. Gave them a piece of my mind."

"Very good, sir." Temeke bobbed his head, wished them both a good evening.

The corridor was bustling with dark suits, nurses tapping keyboards and staring blankly into their monitors. It wasn't until they were outside and Temeke had struck a match down the side of the wall and lit up a cigarette that Malin spoke.

"That newspaper article was in the Sunday newspaper, wasn't it?" she said, waving a trail of smoke out of her face. "You asked him to see how good his memory was, to see if he was lying."

"If his memory's shot, which I doubt, he wouldn't have remembered detail, wouldn't have remembered dates."

"Like he didn't remember the intruder?"

"Or what the man was wearing." Temeke blew out a small smoke ring, poked his finger through it and watched it wriggle away in the cold air. He could have stayed there all afternoon, anything to delay his return to the flapping of Fowler's mouth. "Interesting how he didn't include his wife in those he trusted."

"You said there was no evidence in the house," Malin said, grabbing his arm. "We haven't even had the report back from Forensics."

"We've got nothing. Not even a sodding life insurance on Adam."

"You think it's her, don't you? You think she's gone and done something."

He looked down at those flashing eyes, chin thrust forward, and couldn't keep it in any longer.

"No, I don't, Marl. I don't think it's her at all."

THIRTY-NINE

Malin yawned at a recent memo Sergeant Moran had sent out. It was headed *Albuquerque West Side Road Traffic Accidents*, including the running totals of car crashes and fatalities as compared to the previous year.

They were no further in their investigation of the Ringmaster murders and it was probably time to pull in a few volunteers. Fresh eyes and all that. Her eyes were heavy and after a while the screen became a blur. If it wasn't for a paper airplane that nosedived with a thud on her desk, she would have been out cold.

Temeke was bored, fingers molding a squadron of them from a note pad. He stood with his back against the filing cabinet, sending one after another towards his new dart board on the wall.

"Go home," he said. "You look bloody awful."

"Thanks a lot."

"Not sleeping?"

Not a wink, Malin wanted to say, but shook her head instead. How to explain an unnatural interest with a chat room stalker was beyond her. And Temeke would only worry and spoil it. She looked at the clock. It was three forty-five in the afternoon. "I need something to eat."

Temeke nodded, finger tapping his lips. "Where would you hide a couple of journals?"

Malin tidied away the files on her desk and grabbed her coat. She knew he was lonely. Trying to keep her there as long as he could. "Garden shed. Floor boards. Burn them. Give them to a friend."

"Give them to a friend…" Temeke repeated. He turned around and began drumming his fingers on the top of the filing cabinet. "But which friend?"

"A close friend, someone you trusted. Someone close enough to visit, but far enough where snoopy detectives wouldn't find it."

"Ah, now that's why they hired you, Marl. 'Cause you're a bleeding marvel."

With a loud sniff, he tapped the spines of several large binders on top of that cabinet, pulled one out labeled Arrest Warrants which concealed a small bottle of Johnnie Walker Double Black and two plastic cups.

Oh, no, not the whisky, Malin thought. She hated the stuff, but didn't dare tell him how much.

"This is what you need," he said, giving the cups a quick blow inside to shift the sand.

He put them on the desk between them, poured a generous measure. "It's Friday and there's luck in a glass of whisky. Course, you don't believe in luck. You don't believe in coincidences either. It's all blessings and miracles to you, isn't it? Bloody miracle Fowler hasn't found it yet."

"What exactly are we celebrating, sir? Let me guess, Fowler's promotion? My promotion. Your promotion."

"Mrs. Oliver doesn't appear to have a best friend. Doesn't use the computer much either. There are a few regular numbers she calls. Suzie Bendish, Alie Meyer, restaurants, boutiques, spas. You've called them all. Then there's Ron King of Ron's Garage. What a name for a bloody hairdresser."

Malin took the tablet from her desk drawer and wiped the screen with her sleeve. "A journal's personal, sir, special. She probably wouldn't leave them with the Governor's wife. Wouldn't want her implicated in any way. She wouldn't leave them with Alie Meyer either, not now the District Attorney has been in the papers for having affairs. It has to be someone you could talk to about anything, but not someone close. Hairdresser's my guess."

"Drink up, Marl. All of a sudden, you need a haircut."

Malin felt the laugh in the back of her throat. She briefly glanced at Temeke's eyes. They were sparkling now as if he'd just seen a vision on Mount Sinai.

Mrs. Oliver had a small circle of friends and large circle of acquaintances; agents, models, actors, hairdressers, photographers. It kept her up with the in-crowd, kept her fashionably elite. If Malin was jealous of anyone, Raine Oliver would be it.

Better get the whisky over with, she thought, swishing it around the cup before swallowing the lot. It crawled down her throat like syrup and then came the explosion, the stomach punch, the stars. Made her face red, made her cough, and made Temeke laugh.

"Blimey, Marl, it's not bleeding tequila. Hope nobody breathalyzes you on the road."

"I'll blame you if they do." She covered the cup before he could pour a second shot. "You know I don't drink."

Then she stood up, giving the room a chance to steady itself. A warm wind was waiting for her outside as she edged the car out of the parking lot. She called Ron's Garage and got an appointment for tomorrow at nine o'clock.

She was becoming a little light-headed, even on a few sips of whisky, and took Alameda all the way to Corrales Café. Hooking that small tablet under one arm, she ordered a plate of fish and a cup of coffee from the bar. Went outside to the patio because nobody else would be mad enough to sit in the freezing cold. It was warm beneath a canvas shade where slits of sunlight shone through onto the flagstones below, melting the last of the snow. Her body was stiff and a pain shot through her shoulders. Rolling her neck from side to side, she listened to the breeze in the cottonwoods before studying the tiny buffering circle on the screen as she logged into Heartfree.

Wingman was on line. It suddenly occurred to her that he had a routine. Every afternoon between four and four-thirty, he was in the chat room. It was a small window of time, but time he clearly found important. Then again from eleven-thirty at night to one o'clock in the morning. It was possible he worked shifts, she thought, probably the hotel industry where people slept in the afternoons and checked email before the evening shift. It wasn't like she stumbled on that idea. It was something he'd said, something he'd intimated.

She watched that screen, watched the clock. Four-fifteen. Nothing. And then…

Wingman: Well, well, little bird. Fancy seeing you here. It's our fourth date, isn't it? Only one more. That's all you get.

Malin began to prepare a speech, started typing accusatory sentences which she hastily deleted. It wouldn't do to make him angry. Whoever he was. She wanted information not a relationship.

The waiter brought her order, apologized for the lateness. She took a sip of coffee and then typed: What do you want?

It must have been nerves or lack of sleep, but the curtness of the words even surprised her.

He was self-assured, calm in his response.

Wingman: I want a lot of things, don't you? The warmth of a body next to mine. A heartbeat. Love.

Two words rolled out of her vocabulary. So what.

Wingman: It's no good pretending you don't care, Malin. I know you want to hear what I have to say.

Malin: I prefer not to.

Wingman: You've been an excellent friend. My senses tell me you will be a friend forever. Perhaps you think I'm a little forward. I don't like to waste time. After all, there's so little of it. Now, where were we?

She kept thinking of the poem, wondered what it had to do with anything. The Ancient Mariner. The poem.

Wingman: Day after day, day after day,
We stuck, nor breath nor motion;
As idle as a painted ship
Upon a painted ocean.

Ships, no wind… what was he trying to tell her? Before she could ask, he had already typed three more sentences.

Wingman: And a dead bird. Don't forget the bird. Lovely word picture, don't you think?

Malin: Do you know the perp personally?

Images began to appear in Malin's head as she waited for a response. A man in an out-of-the-way gas station with oil-stained fingers. A man in a lab coat with latex covered hands. A self-satisfied businessman, a sure winner of a stalker. A man in a black hoodie who tugged at his belt as if a gun hung there.

Wingman was off again. With a paragraph this time. It's amazing how word gets out. Could have done with a Budweiser. What a victory that would have been. He didn't have the stamina or the commitment. So he made a stand. Chose to fail. The girl was his undoing. He could have been great. Instead, he was mediocre. He paid the price. And so did she.

Her back went rigid, pulse rising with each word. She was trying to have an intelligent conversation with him and all he wanted was a beer. It was the same feeling she'd had out jogging one night. When she heard the crunch of gravel behind her, saw a man in a black hoodie and sweat pants cruising along at an unnaturally slow pace. It made her muscles ache, brain battling fear before she turned. Saw him breeze past without a word.

Nothing to be afraid of. Not really, not now she was in the gardens of a local café, tables inside filling with the dinner crowd. Life in process. It was both comforting and strange at the same time. As if the man in the tablet was no threat at all.

Are you there? he said.

Malin: Yes, I'm here.

Wingman: I know you think of death sometimes. All good detectives do. They see it firsthand. I've seen it firsthand.   Remember the Bassinger case? Yes, I thought you did.

How did he know? She tried to spear a bite of fish on the end of her fork and felt suddenly sick. There was a heaviness in her chest, as if she was trying hard not to breathe in a room full of gas in a confined space. Like her grandmother once had as a child. In the concentration camps.

Malin clutched the edge of the table and thought, this is how it is to be stalked, to be observed through a cage as if you were a lab rat. Something stirred in her subconscious. A young man's face behind a windshield, wipers swishing away the evening rain. He was pale. Dead. Now came a distant memory. A suicide in Camden, a seventeen-year-old whose life came to an end when he found out his father was having an affair. Took the jag for a joyride. Drove it into a river. When they pulled the car out they found a bloated body and fingernails torn down to the quick.

It was the doctor's voice wheezing between clenched teeth that had haunted her for years. *He must have panicked in those last moments. Tried to get out. It was all a mistake.*

Wingman: You're crying now, aren't you?

Yes, she typed, seeing darkness now as if a cloud has just passed before the sun. Bassinger was her monument of grief.

Wingman: No hit of cocaine could ever blot out that

memory. Isn't it true detectives get sick to the stomach from the horror? The type of sick when you get home and realize you forgot to lock the gun safe. It leaves you feeling empty, fixated on the moment as if time had suddenly stood still. You can't tell anyone, can you? Because they'd never understand. Never see it through your eyes.

Malin winced at that, felt like she'd already been slipped a drug without knowing. Worst of all, she had no idea what all this had to do with the case. With an even stranger suspicion, she knew he was procrastinating, drawing the fantasy out as long as he could. She was fed up with the hints, the never ending barrage of games.

Malin: How about just telling me who this man is?

Wingman: You're obsessed with names, Malin, you know that? And here I was thinking you wanted mine.

She tried to think of some witty comeback, something to confuse him. But her patience was wearing thin.

Malin: So what's the connection to the Oliver case?

Wingman: Now you're fishing and that doesn't serve any purpose.

Malin: Your purpose or mine? She was beginning to feel the icy claws of panic. It was four twenty-seven.

Wingman: There was a 19th Century landowner who died in 1854. Something to do with trains. Close to your heart. Last name only.

He logged off then. Left her to the wind in the cottonwoods.

FORTY

They had slept and woken in the darkness, huddled beneath the trees. It had been a whole day since the ranger stalked past them, headed in a northerly direction, rifle muzzle balanced against his shoulder. He was smart and he was quick, and Ramsey said if they didn't keep moving, they'd be skinned like two ground squirrels before the night was out.

Adam lifted his head from Ramsey's shoulder, opened his eyes to another gray world. It had been tough going through the hills, up and down, up and down. It was the down that had made his calves sore and the lack of food that made him weary.

"Are there bears out here?" he asked.

"A few."

"Will they come out and get us."

"Not if we make a noise."

"You said not to make a noise because of the rangers."

"I said that?"

"Yes."

"Then don't make a noise."

They waded through pine needles and slippery roots by day and aired blistered feet at night. And sometimes when they staggered downhill they could see the bleak sky through the trees and wonder how much further.

Ramsey said the ranger was about three hundred

yards ahead. Said he was hiding out near a stream, waiting for them to fill up their bottles. Said he could hear his feet stirring the water with a gentle slosh. Said it was good to keep the enemy in your sights.

"What if there isn't a stream?" Adam asked, shading his face from a sudden burst of sunlight. "What if we run out of iodine tablets?"

"We'll suck leaves and strain rainwater through a sock." Ramsey sounded impatient, had a slight snigger to his voice like he thought it was funny. He also had a yellow-white tinge to his cheeks like one of those perfumed candles Adam's mom liked to burn. Here they were like two hunted animals that didn't know which way to go.

"You do know which way, don't you?" Adam said, watching the light bouncing off the compass in his hand.

"West. That way."

"Are you sure?"

"Quite sure."

His eyes were heavy and he seemed to be looking for somewhere to sleep. Sometimes he frowned and stared off into the distance, sometimes he winced and rubbed the side of his leg. Adam knew he was in pain, couldn't hide the sudden suck of air between those teeth.

Murphy sprang into the slough at the base of a piñon tree and chased a squirrel. Caught it too before bounding towards a shallow recess of rock further down the slope, a weather-beaten niche nestled in a bay of cliffs overlooking a valley of trees to the south. It was the perfect place to sleep and Ramsey said it was about six feet deep and ten feet long. He coaxed that squirrel right out of Murphy's mouth and let it go. It looked too gnarly to eat.

They lay against the warm rock and talked about guns and squirrels and campfires until their bellies began to rumble. Murphy lay down beside Adam, taking short, quick breaths and drooling out of the side of his mouth.

"Can't make a fire," Ramsey said, fumbling for the painkillers. He threw a few down his neck and snapped the lid shut. "The light will carry those rangers to us. Men like that can smell smoke for miles."

It was the first time Ramsey had said the word *men* and it struck Adam as different. He had thought rangers patrolled parks, sat in wooden lodges and took your money when you drove in. But not how Ramsey explained it. Not with that hard-eyed look.

"What are we going to eat?" Adam asked.

"Baked beans."

"We don't have baked beans."

"We do."

"Where?"

"Found five cans in the cabin."

Adam opened the backpack, rummaged around a pile of clothing and pulled out the cans and the opener too. He scooped the beans into his mouth with two fingers, swallowed so fast he coughed up a few. Found a small piece of bread, hard as a dog biscuit, and ate that too.

Ramsey said nothing, even when Adam fed the dog with the second can, he just lay there with his lips slightly parted and a soft rumble in the back of his throat. There was a sheen to his forehead Adam hadn't seen before, tiny glistening drops that trickled down into his beard.

Adam sat staring over the tree tops at the blue beyond and for a moment everything was peaceful. A brisk wind crept through his coat and sweater, and he was glad he was layered up to the neck. It wasn't long before the day turned to dusk and up in that sky were a million pinhead stars.

He slept well into the following morning, one of those dream-filled sleeps that leaves a dry taste in your mouth. The slack drip of rain and bloated clouds overhead made him sad, as did the gray wilderness he would now call home. It was Sunday or Monday, he didn't know which, but he found himself wrapped in a blanket with a sweater for a pillow, snug and warm like his mom used to do. He tried to swallow a lump of grief then, tried not to cry.

Ramsey handed him a bottle of water and a few dried crackers. He opened the map and laid it out on his knee. "We'll go west first," he said, tracing a finger along a deep crease and staring out at the horizon. "And then north."

"Isn't that where the ranger went?"

"He went south."

Sometime after they had packed, a helicopter blew through the valley. Adam heard the thud of the rotors echoing against the cliffs

"Someone must have broken out of jail," he said. "A serial killer. Maybe it's the same one that murdered that nasty old man."

"I murdered that nasty old man," Ramsey said. "It was either him or me. Or it could have been you."

Adam felt a tremor in his belly, felt a gasp in his throat. "They'll put you in jail… send you to the electric chair."

"It's lethal injection, son."

"Will it hurt?"

"Most likely."

Adam wondered why Ramsey was being so brave about it all, why he was so calm. All he did was squint off in the distance, eyes fixed on that helicopter as the thudding grew louder.

"It's search and rescue!" Adam screamed.

Standing on the lip of that small recess, Adam was engulfed in a whirlwind of leaves before he ran up the slope, arms waving. He could hear Ramsey's shouts to stay down but he didn't care. The pilot must have seen him because that big machine turned towards him, nose down and powering over the land. Adam began to scream now, voice drowned over the steady *thud, thud, thud*, his body consumed by a cloud of dust. His voice was nearly at a squeak; arms flailing, neck craning at a dark underbelly as it headed north.

The trees bowed overhead, leaves rustling in the slipstream and Adam ran after it until it was a black speck in a many colored sunrise. Losing it was like a fist to the stomach and he leaned against a boulder to keep from throwing up. He began to rock back and forth, sobbing and groaning and clawing the air.

Then he felt strong arms around him, heard that gravelly voice. "It'll be OK." And then softer this time. "I'm sorry. I'm so sorry."

"He saw me. I know he did!"

"It's all right," Ramsey whispered.

"I'm scared."

"Only a mile left."

"They'll put you in jail?"

"Yeah. Leave me there to rot."

"But you did it because you had to."

"Nobody's going to believe that."

"They will if I tell them."

For the next few moments Adam lay against that warm chest seeing nothing but a blur of greens and browns fading into black. A wet tongue grazed his hand, nose nudging his thigh. Murphy was there beside them, ears pricked to a rustle and slide of rocks. It must have been a skunk tripping down the hill, tail sweeping the ground. Raccoons, chipmunks and squirrels skulked in roving bands and rattlers hardly made a noise. This was a continual rush of rocks as if something much larger slalomed down the slope. Adam stiffened just as Ramsey did and they lowered to a crouch.

Another wave of nausea washed over him and he gripped the dog by the collar, leaning forward to listen. He could smell the earth and the last of the rain on the leaves, and he could hear birds and the heavy thudding of his chest. The afternoon was mild and had a strange silence to it and beyond the trees, the northern horizon was a sullen haze that threatened to darken the sky. That helicopter was long gone.

God? Are you up there?

God didn't bellow through the clouds nor did he whisper in your ear. Adam knew it was the Bible that spoke. His words, not yours. He wished he'd read it more often just to hear what God had to say, what he might do in a lonely wilderness, where he might go.

Ramsey pointed to a narrow track leading up through the trees to the left, not manmade, but a dried up streambed where water flowed down into the valley after a flash flood.

Adam trembled against Ramsey's arm. He couldn't think, couldn't move. Saw the backpack and the duffel on the ground, knew they had to get out of there and now was their only chance. They stumbled along that wooded track, dog tugging and wheezing and pulling him onwards. Adam prayed for a clear view of a village on the other side. But when they reached the summit there was nothing but rolling hills of brush and boulders and big thorny trees.

He just stared at it all, mouth open, eyes flicking from left to right. No wind. No rain. No sound. He wished he had Ramsey's binoculars to glass the countryside for signs of smoke, just a simple trail rising into the sky from a log cabin. It was all he needed.

Standing on the edge of that barren outcrop, something caught his eye. To the right was a slope that led back down to that shallow cave and between the trees, about halfway up, he saw a man. He must have been fifty yards away all rigid and black against the hoary shingle, hand resting on the trunk of a fir tree.

He wasn't one of those demons Adam had read about, ones that belched out from a pit in the ground and swarmed the earth for a time. No, this one didn't have wings or a curly tail. This one had mud smeared on his face, a black jacket and gloved fingers he wriggled now and then. He pushed the butt of the gun on his back to one side as he crouched, eyes trained on the southern horizon.

The only way out was the narrow track which snaked around to the south and away from the crouching man. Adam took a step and felt the anchoring hand against his left shoulder.

"Don't move," mouthed Ramsey, other hand around Murphy's mouth. "Not a twitch."

FORTY-ONE

Hackett was taking sadistic pleasure in making her wait, slouched in that big leather chair and wearing the rare disguise of a smile. Without lifting his eyes from the file he was reading, he flicked a wrist at the chair opposite his desk, pen crawling over the correspondence as if intensifying the suspense.

"You wanted to see me?" Malin asked, sitting. She hoped it was quick. She had a hair appointment in half an hour.

"I wanted to see you yesterday. Left a message. Several, actually."

A theatrical rummaging brought the offending phone from Malin's pocket and she turned it over in her hand a few times. Screen was blacker than Hackett's temper and the battery was flat. "I'm sorry, sir—"

"I would have thought your Unit Commander's name on the caller ID took priority. Neither of you were at the briefing meeting. It's not a trivial matter. It's not just this kidnap case we're handling. There's stolen cars at the mall and another break-in at the Norcross Bank. Correct me if I'm wrong, but it would be the fifth break-in we've had in six weeks."

"I haven't been keeping count, sir, but you're probably right."

"I'm exactly right as it happens. Five break-ins on the north side, same window smashed, and customers robbed of their life savings. What are you doing about it?"

What the hell could she do about it? "He doesn't leave any forensic, sir, and no one's ever seen him without a mask. It wouldn't be so bad if he was spending some of that cash. We might have got a whisper."

"What about the white van?"

"One customer said it was a small white van, the other said it was a big brown Fed Ex truck."

"Well, it's a lead, Santiago, which presumably you're following up."

"Do you know how many white vans there are on the west side alone, sir?"

"It doesn't matter how many. We've a computer that churns out license plates in seconds. And there's video."

"That computer might be smart, sir, but it still hasn't come up with a name… an address. That takes time and time comes out of our budget. I thought the Oliver case took priority?"

She heard a loud exhalation of breath and a tutting.

"I was ashamed to get Fowler's email," Hackett continued. "Fortunately, he didn't copy it to the Chief of Police. But your performance is below standard." Hackett put down that file and made a steeple with his hands. "There have been complaints. First off, Fowler reported the smell of alcohol in your office."

Malin tensed. She had the sense not to ask if Fowler had found any. "Alcohol, sir? Are you sure it wasn't mouthwash?"

"As it happens, he did find some mouthwash in your drawers."

"What was Captain Fowler doing in my drawers? Oh, don't tell me. Same as he does in every woman's drawers."

"He's also concerned he hasn't had all the witness reports," Hackett muttered, eyes still running along a series of words he clearly wasn't reading. "The housekeeper. What's her name?"

Malin waited for Hackett to read it out aloud. It wasn't like this was a game of Trivial Pursuit and besides she had a sneaky feeling Temeke left that particular witness report in the car. "I'll get it to you first thing tomorrow, sir."

"See that you do. Two things. Tell Temeke, no more sleeping in the cells. Hotel's full tonight. Oh, a small bit of news. Officer Running Hawk's air team got a sighting on a man and a young boy in the mountains, headed towards Pleasanton. Can't confirm its Adam Oliver."

"That's good news, sir."

"It could be a false alarm." Hackett stared over those half-moon glasses and took a deep breath. "I also had a call from Mrs. Oliver this morning. Said you upset her husband in hospital. Can't have detectives upsetting victims. He could die, you know."

Malin had hardly said a word in the hospital and now here she was fighting Temeke's wars. Her blood was almost at boiling point. As for the Mayor, the only thing that might kill him was the bacon and vanilla ice cream."

"This case isn't going anywhere. I want cold, hard facts!"

"Give me three hours, sir, and I'll bring you a cold, hard fact."

It was early afternoon when Malin left the office. About the only thing she had learned was there was something about Mrs. Oliver that had her radar humming. She was in her frame for better or worse. And as for Ron King of Ron's Garage, it was a freaking hairdresser dressed up to look like an auto store.

Malin sat outside the small adobe house on Driftwood. Couldn't see much through the drawn blinds, but the window was open and the soft murmur of voices wafted over a nicely clipped hedge. It was a private house. Private business. But not so private once you'd climbed over the wall and edged your way along the sidewalk and pressed an ear against the stucco. A man and a woman talking about planets, blood moons and what would happen during a zombie apocalypse.

The last thing Malin needed was a herd of zombies raiding the pharmacy up the road. In light of how much medicine cost these days, she began to wonder if it was a bit inconsiderate.

She noticed a lizard as it scuttled beneath a bunch of cactus as she opened the front door. There was nothing glittery about this particular salon. In fact, it had the oily rag, coveralls feel to it and there was a sign in the shape of a hub cap above the front door. She would have felt right at home if the décor hadn't been so damn masculine. She was going to stick out like a hen in a hog house.

The reception area was small, gray painted walls and a large steering wheel for a clock. Ron gave a throaty welcome, beckoned her over to the chair just as an elderly lady with blue rinse left a tip and waved goodbye.

He was in his forties, gray hair slicked back and a manner Malin rather liked. He didn't mess around. Covered her in a black plastic gown and studied the style like a pro. They agreed on a dry trim.

"Where are you from?" Ron asked.

"Originally?" Malin saw the nod through a mist of water. "New Mexico. My father was Hispanic, my mother was Norwegian. You?"

"Farmington," he said, separating her hair into three sections, scissors snapping as if they had a life of their own. "So what do you do?"

There was no point in tarting up a profession like hers. "Homicide."

Then came the raised eyebrows, the straight back, the how-do-you-do-it talk and how much the public appreciate all the police do. Ron rattled off a few names of cops he knew. Malin hardly paid any attention. It was the square footage of that tiny salon she was interested in and the room just inside the front door. "Like the garage theme."

"Thought it worked better with my image," Ron said and grinned. "I wondered if it would put off the ladies after I repainted the place. Never been busier."

The room was basic, a sink in one corner and a small chair in the other, and that empty room on the right-hand side of the front door was narrow and dark.

"May I ask how you heard of me?" Ron said.

"Raine Oliver." There. The name in the papers. The name everyone was talking about. The name Ron should have mentioned when Malin told him she was in Homicide.

She watched that face, saw a smear of pink that started beneath the eyes and seeped down toward the neckline. He seemed to take a couple of breaths as he ran a comb though the final section of hair.

"Very nice lady. Thank her for me, will you?"

"My pleasure."

"Awful what happened." Ron bit his bottom lip. "I hope the police find the boy. You working on that case?"

"As a matter of fact, I am. How many times do children turn up dead after a week? Imagine, twelve years old, lost in a wood with a madman. Poor kid must be terrified, hoping the police will come. But they won't. I shouldn't be telling you this, so keep it between ourselves." Malin saw Ron nod and drop the scissors in his apron pocket. "There's some valuable information that went missing last week. A couple of journals from Mrs. Oliver's bookcase. Probably the cleaner."

She noticed Ron wipe a glaze of sweat from his

forehead and blink, and she carried on. "There's something she wrote, something important. Something that would help us find poor little Adam."

Ron put both hands against Malin's chair and swung his head towards the door. He was itching to get out, wanted to get it over with.

"That's what I like to see – empathy," Malin said, pointing at the mirror where Ron's cheeks had turned a rich shade of puce. "There's so little of it about. You'd care if it was your son. Got any kids, Ron? Two. How nice. I hope they don't ever go missing."

"Would you like some bottled water?" Ron said. "I've got some in the house."

He left then, walked right out of the salon and into his front yard. Malin ripped off that plastic cape and slipped into the dark room, flipping through as many books and magazines as she could find. The sixty watt bulb was barely an apricot glaze over a wrap-around desk and three shelves full of magazines. The only drawer had the remnants of old bills, a calculator and a box of ultra-grip gloves. She began to panic.

Peering through the glass door at the front yard and the courtyard beyond, she could see no sign of Ron. That's when she remembered the water fountain by the sink, full by the look of it. Ron had only gone and done a runner because those journals were here. Somewhere.

Malin rummaged through the product cupboard, reaching behind bottles of shampoo and conditioner and boxes of aluminum foil. And there, balanced on a large tub of pomade were two leather-bound books.

"Let the fireworks begin," she said, feeling the stirrings of light-headedness. She also felt an unnatural desire to laugh.

FORTY-TWO

Temeke tossed away his cigarette, watched it arc over the front steps and bounce on the hood of Hackett's car. He was proud of Malin. She had the journals and without a bleeding warrant from the judge.

He flung open the front door, feeling a sudden downdraft of hot air from the ceiling. Swept the waiting area from the corner of his eye, couldn't see Fowler but he could hear him. The terrible sounds of cussing and a few whiny responses from Sergeant Moran seem to rise up from behind the duty desk.

Temeke crossed the lobby in four long strides and he leaned over the desk see what all the commotion was about. Crouched, with their backs towards him, were two tightly trousered rears. Sarge and Fowler were picking broken glass off the floor and blaming the stout wind every time someone opened the front door.

"Someone have a Greek wedding?" Temeke asked.

Fowler swung around, face red and glaring. "We don't need a useless detective to tell us what's happened. Dropped a glass that's all."

"Doesn't look like a glass. Looks like Hackett's plaque."

"It's a glass!" Fowler's voice was loud and brash, body trying its best to cover up the accident.

Temeke squeezed his way around the desk just as Fowler was sweeping up a few shards and tipping them into the trash can. "Move that belly out of the way and let me have a look."

Temeke picked up the wooden base and read the words on the brass plate. "Northwest Area Command – lowest crime rate in 2012. That's something to be proud of. Who broke it?"

A consultation, a pointed finger and a swift nod. "It was him if you must know," Sarge said, sounding sure this time.

Temeke shook his head. "Trust a bloody useless detective to get the truth out of a crook."

"Crook?" Fowler hovered over Temeke like he was about to gouge out chunks of flesh. "You've got a nerve walking in here and calling me a crook. If Hackett found out about your stash of African Black, he'd ring your neck."

"Been in my office? Thought so. That's a bag of loose leaf Lapsang tea if you must know. You've got a thing about drawers. If your hand isn't in one, it's up one."

"That's your province, not mine."

"Province? Oh, big words, now. Who's Northwest Area Command's super stud? Red hot is what I heard. Must have a bloody blow torch between your legs."

Fowler's mouth dropped open and there were two deep lines etched into his forehead. The sound of Sarge's sniggers were still with Temeke when he reached the top floor, knuckle wrapping on Hackett's door.

"Slight accident downstairs, sir," he said, voice lowered. "Looks like your pride and joy took a nasty fall."

Hackett flew down those stairs like Fred Astaire, shouting words a pastor would blanch at. It was the fist pounding against polished mahogany that shook the windows and made Temeke close his office door. He would have locked it too if he'd had a key.

There was Malin sitting at her desk, hair loose to her shoulders, hands resting on two leather bound books.

"Where did you find them?" Temeke asked, feeling a surprising desire to kiss her.

She tapped her nose and slid them towards him, tucking her face back behind the computer.

Temeke stuck his nose in the coffee pot. It was well stewed, half an inch of sediment rolling along the bottom like a clump of brown algae. He put his feet up and marveled at the last rays of sunshine. It was going to be a long night.

He flipped open the first journal, found Malin had already tagged the relevant pages with a yellow arrow. There appeared to be nothing remarkable about the entries after December 1999. Except for one in 2004.

June 21, 2004: I saw you in the park this afternoon, heard you call my name. And then you were gone. I dream of you.

Temeke screwed the sleep from his eyes and squinted at his watch. Six-thirty in the evening. Bang went his usual shift of three o'clock in the afternoon until eleven. It had been teeth-gritting hard work ever since the start of this case and it was downhill all the way until they got results.

He glanced out of the window at a dark world, wind howling through the trees and leaves drifting across the parking lot. Raine Oliver was beginning to burrow under his skin, almost as much as that bottle of whisky as it whispered his name over the wailing wind. True, there were cracks in her perfect world; a relationship that somehow went south and a diary to talk to. She had married a father figure to fill that void and she'd been playing the grieving widow ever since.

Temeke cast his mind back to Art's conversation,

heard that voice go from flashy to sober.

I think she's a doll. She's been through a lot. Not so as you would know. Hides it all behind a brave smile. But you can sense it, feel it.

There was no reason for Cesar or Megan to pry into her private affairs unless they had witnessed something they weren't telling him. And as far as he could make out, there was no new slander about the Olivers in the newspapers, unless...

He struck a match on the side of the desk and took a few drags of his cigarette. "Jennifer Danes... you crafty little cow."

He saw Malin look up as he dialed Jennifer's number at the *Journal*, put the phone on loud speaker. The light, squeaky voice was as greasy as ever and Jennifer was appalled he hadn't called, felt slighted and somewhat offended. He scoffed it off. Told her to put on a pair of big-girl knickers and stop playing games.

"You can play with me any day of the week, Detective."

"And this day of the week you can tell me what you have on Raine Oliver."

She repeated the name like it was something far back in her memory. "I'll let you know if I do."

Bloody liar, he mouthed at Malin. "How are things in your neck of the woods? You know, the love triangle."

"The what?"

"Captain Fowler. He's been dressing different. Got a new do. And he's been sobbing in his office ever since the breakup. You can hear his pathetic whine through the wall."

"You mean... him and me?"

"Yes, him and you. Who did you think I was talking about? Cyn? She's too old, love." He lowered his voice just a little. "By all accounts, poor old Fowler had to use a strap-on. Cucumber and duct tape."

He could hear the giggle on the other end of the phone and then a sigh of relief. She was probably sitting back in that white plastic chair, staring at the ceiling all teary-eyed and excited.

"You know," she whispered, tapping the keys of her computer. "I do have something. It's not much. An article in a San Diego newspaper dated June 15, 2001. It says, 'A U.S. Navy SEAL was badly injured in an accident during a training exercise, the Navy said. BUD/S Instructor William Oliver stated that a trainee whose name has not been identified, was shut in an overflow drain at 2:30 p.m. on Friday. The cause of the accident is under investigation.' BUD/S stands for Basic Underwater Demolition training."

Temeke had already read the Mayor's résumé and an impressive list of SEAL acronyms. It was the expression BUD/S that began boring into his mind.

"And that shows up when you do a search for Bill Oliver?"

"Yes," Jennifer confirmed. "When I do a search for SEAL articles around that time, they mentioned two recruits who were injured badly during training. It looks like only one didn't go back to complete the other stages. There's no name, but it says he failed to complete Stage 1. He was removed from training due to an accident in a flooded drain where he lost partial sight of his left eye'."

"Was he reclassified?"

"Doesn't say."

"Instructor's name?"

"William Stanton Oliver."

"Very good, Jen. I'll be in touch later. Oh, and you might want to call Rufus before he keels over from all that pining. Hasn't had a good meal in days."

"BUD/S," he said, as he ended the call. "Why does

that ring a bell?"

He took one last deep drag from that cigarette before it dropped out of his hands and landed on the carpet. He ground his dirty boot in to stop the smell of burning wool.

"Megan…" Malin said. "It was Megan. When she overheard Raine talking on the phone, she referred to something about PST and LSD. Thought it was drugs. And then she said something about goals and buds."

"In Navy SEAL terms," Temeke said, "PST is an abbreviation for Physical Screening Test. LSD… Long Slow Distance. It's a term used in one of three types of training… swimming speed and distance, I think."

Malin displayed a row of shiny teeth behind that grin. "Here's a few more interesting entries," she said, grabbing one of the journals and reading them aloud.

June 18, 2010: Questions, so many questions. He says I talk in my sleep. Even asked if I was having a nightmare? Living with him is a nightmare. I don't know why I did it.

June 19, 2010: I almost left today. But he was waiting for me downstairs. I don't know how long I can stand it.

Temeke couldn't help feeling a familiar tightening in his throat. Raine was being monitored, even then. Malin read on.

June 20, 2010: Isn't it foolish how we always wish we could turn back time, to stop ourselves from doing the stupid things we did. I'm sure you ask yourself, why me? Was it fair?

June 21, 2010: There is one thing I wish and that is to say I'm sorry for the terrible things I did. I should have waited.

June 22, 2010: I learned two things today. Never tell him what I'm thinking and never tell him where I'm going. Easy to fool a pursuer if they're driving in front. Harder to do it if they're following from behind. He hit me again. Always in the stomach so no one can see the bruises.

There was something different about her emotions then, something fiercer, like a loaded gun waiting to fire. Temeke could only stare at Malin and wonder how, for all these years, Raine was able to hide such a terrible secret. Now they were more like letters she was too afraid to send, letters that intimated a phone call, a chance meeting that would have put an end to all the what-ifs.

"Bill Oliver was following her all right, through Andrew Blaine Investigative Services," Temeke said. "The bastard was trying to exhume the part of Raine's past he dreaded the most."

"There's two empty years with a few general appointments." Malin shot him a squinty-eyed look. "There's a paragraph at Christmas. I'll read it to you."

December 20, 2012: He was supposed to leave for DC tonight with Art but they're still here. I can hear them whispering. He's sending Adam on a scout trip next weekend. I think they're watching me.

Bill Oliver found out Raine had a lover and he never intended to let her leave, Temeke thought. Probably hated her because she'd betrayed him. Wasn't going to let the wound heal without grinding a fistful of rough salt into it. Of course, he'd followed her, watched her. Hired a PI to reel her in just tight enough to drive that knife in a little deeper and give it a sodding good twist.

FORTY-THREE

There was a 19th Century landowner who died in 1854. Something to do with trains. Close to your heart. Last name only.

Malin scrolled through three listings on the internet. 1854 Broad Street cholera outbreak, a British landowner named Ramsey who was a philanthropist and High Sheriff of Berkshire. Then there was Ramsey, a borough in New Jersey, named after a Peter J. Ramsey. And lastly, the New Jersey Transit rail station serving Bergen County Line, Main Line and Port Jervis line. Better known as the Ramsey Route.

She scrolled through eighty-one listings on the database. Nothing. Called that hokey number Temeke had tried for Andrew Blaine and got him on the first ring.

"Andrew?" she said.

"Yes."

"This is Detective Santiago. We've been trying to reach you—"

"Yes… yes, I know. Well, you've got me now."

"Ramsey," she said. "How well do you know him?" She heard the sharp intake of breath, the loud sigh.

"Miss… What did you say your name was?"

"Santiago. Detective Santiago."

"Berkeley Police?"

She grunted a yes, let him believe she was.

"Couldn't tell me where I could find him?"

"You talk to Bill Oliver yet?"

"I'm with him right now. Thought you might want to fill me in with the rest."

"You can't blame him for looking, watching, all that stuff. It's what any man would have done. Ramsey? No, he's all brawn and brains and full of spite. I got a ticket and flew to Albuquerque a couple of weeks ago. Followed him to Motel 6 on Alameda and I-25. He wasn't there for long. Three nights. Ate well."

He gave her the dates Ramsey had stayed in that hotel and a running commentary of where he bought vegetables and meat, times he came and went, and how often he drove that nice black truck. Blaine emailed a report to Bill Oliver and flew home after that.

"Retaliation?" She could only guess.

"Oliver had to fail him because of the accident. Took his life away. His pride. Took the two things Ramsey wanted the most. His Trident and Raine Leveque. Listen, don't call again, OK? You damn people have already taken everything."

Malin listened to the dialing tone for nearly minute. Rubbed her brow and sat thinking for a while. The laptop was on the kitchen counter, open when she thought she had closed it.

You're hallucinating. Probably left it open because you're always in such a rush.

Heartfree. Forty-five people in the chat room. Including Wingman.

Wingman: This is our last date, Malin. Make it count.

She blew out a hefty sigh and began typing. Tell me about yourself. Tell me who you are.

Three little dancing dots and he was off.

Wingman: People on the outside don't know what evil is.

Malin: Are you evil? She hoped he wasn't.

Wingman: Somewhat. Evil knows evil. Did you know

that strangulation only takes about four minutes? Sometimes less.

Malin had to ask. Ever strangled anyone?

Wingman: I knew a man once. Had strong hands. Killed his girlfriend. Crime of passion.

Malin: Who?

Wingman: Not going into details. He had a lot of women then. I guess you could say he was enjoying himself.

Malin: Why did he kill her?

Wingman: She started seeing someone else.

Malin: Does infidelity warrant killing someone?

Wingman: He thought so.

Malin listened to her strained breathing, thought for a few seconds before typing. What did he look like?

Wingman: I can't tell you that. But I can tell you this. He went back to see the body. To clean up.

Malin: Where did he leave the body?

Wingman: Bodies. He drove this one under a bridge, opened the door and kicked her out. Watched her roll into the arroyo. The police found her body frozen in the ice. He didn't kill again for two years after that.

Malin: Why?

Wingman: The FBI profilers had highlighted his pattern and decided to follow his tracks.

Malin waited for a moment, not sure if she should push him too far. She grabbed a pad, drew a few small circles to wake the pen up.

Malin: You like helping the police?

Wingman: I get a kick out of it. Killers don't have control over what they see. Mental seizures, bright lights, bodies, lots of them. In offender rehab they call it a toxic combination of psychological and physical damage. I call it life. But your man's different.

Malin stared wide-eyed at the screen and continued taking notes: Was he abused in some way?

Wingman: No. He was loved.

Malin: So what changed?

Wingman: She made it change.

Malin gave him a few seconds, screwed her eyes shut, forced her pulse to slow down. His name's Ramsey, isn't it?

Wingman: Clever girl.

Malin: How is he able to go unnoticed?

Wingman: Because he's a regular guy doing a regular job. But then he's smart. Had all the training. If a man sits down beside him in a restaurant, says all the stupid things police decoys say, he'll know. Go carefully. Otherwise you'll never see him again.

Malin: What's his first name?

Wingman: You tell me.

She pressed her hands to her cheeks, felt them tremble. He was making her angry now. If you really want to help, you'll give me a place, an address.

Wingman: Helping doesn't mean telling. But I'll give you a place. He could be headed for Apache land. Or he could be headed for the hatchery.

Malin: Why the hatchery?

Wingman: That I can't tell you.

Malin: Meaning?

Wingman: Too many questions, Malin. Remember, two strikes and you're out.

Malin peered out of the window at a faint horizon, snowflakes drifting towards the cottonwood. He had to know. The bastard knew everything.

Malin: You don't know, do you?

Wingman: I know this. You'll go for a drive tonight like you always do. To Temeke's house. Watch him through the window, wonder what it would be like. Remember, you're Top Cat. Gonna get that raise, Malin. Gonna go higher and higher. We will meet again someday. Because you owe me. Big time.

FORTY-FOUR

It was seven minutes to eight on a cloudy, dark Tuesday morning when Temeke switched on his computer. He could hear Hackett smacking his desk next door, accompanied by a snort or two. Fowler's coarse, hearty laughter was at the expense of ridiculing Brits and a vulgar joke he was sharing, and that made Temeke's heart rate gallop.

These were the corridors of command, where the mighty rule. And God help the people of Albuquerque if they knew how quickly things could change, how many good cops had been destroyed in a matter of seconds.

His cell phone gave a piercing ring. It was the debonair doc. Old Ginger's teeth and blood samples had finally found a match, Red Shearer, a former ranger at Gila National Forest. He hadn't visited a dentist in years and the unusual occurrence of an engraved silver amalgam was traced back to a doctor in Ohio. The engraving was an eternity symbol, like the one on his right wrist.

Shearer was fired in June 2000 for assaulting a young boy and never showed up for his court date. Spatters of his blood were found on the tree Evan Trader was tied to and ballistics verified the helicopter was brought down by bullets from Ginger's Enfield. By all accounts, he had quite an armory in that tent of his and he clearly didn't want police sniffing around his turf.

Temeke wanted peace, only it had been too damn quiet in his house last night. Too damn cold too. He'd turned down the thermostat when he started sleeping in the cells and forgot to turn it back up again. All he did was pace from room to room, smoke a packet of cigarettes and carve a path in the living room carpet. His mind was wired from midnight to two o'clock, thinking of a woman's belly blotched in blue and yellow from an old man's fist. What had Adam seen? What had he heard in those last days?

Temeke saw his father hit his mother all those years ago. Heard him shout at her, wrench the rent money right out of her hands and come home drunk from the pub. What had he left her with before dying at the end of a rope? Misery and broken bones, and a generous helping of insecurity.

The door clicked open and in rushed Malin with a half-eaten donut in one hand and a file in the other. Apart from a thin film of sugar on her upper lip, there was something different about her. "I've got it," she said, handing him the file.

"Got what?"

"The name."

She put the donut on the desk and patted her chest as if that would stop the panting. "Ramsey. Christopher Ramsey."

Temeke's mouth dropped, saw the tilt of her head and the raised eyebrows.

"They're headed for Glenwood. I'm not kidding. There's a trout hatchery there. That's where they are."

"Fish? Blimey, Marl." Temeke watched that face, the sucked in bottom lip and the hint of a frown. "Did you get a phone call from the Almighty and forget to tell me about it?"

He was exhausted. Had to sleep soon, find his rhythm, take a sodding long vacation. "You carry on eating that big-ass breakfast and don't get an ulcer. So who told you about the fish farm?"

"Listen, I called Andrew Blaine. We talked. He thought I was Berkeley Police." She grinned then, gave a small chuckle. "Said he was working for Mayor Oliver to find a Christopher Ramsey. Ramsey was the SEAL Jennifer was talking about, the one who had the accident in the storm drain. Blaine followed Ramsey to Albuquerque to the Motel 6 on Alameda. He was there for three nights, rented a black truck, made several calls to Raine Oliver. Threatened to come to the house."

"What did he want?"

"Ramsey failed BUDS because of the accident, couldn't see too well after that. Mayor Oliver... instructor Oliver, whatever he was then, took away Ramsey's chance of getting his Trident. Raine Oliver was Ramsey's girlfriend. It's all there," she said, pointing to the file.

It still wasn't enough. Temeke wasn't buying it. "And he told you they were headed for Glenwood?"

It was the raised chin and the staring eyes which quickly dissolved into a nodding head. She was keeping something from him.

"Remember the sweet old lady in the cells at Christmas?" he said. "The one with the whitest buttocks you ever saw. She held those goods in tight and proper until we bent her over. Must have been such a relief when we took them out."

"Nice try, sir."

The phone gave a shriek on his desk, followed by Sarge shouting from downstairs. "Forensics!"

Temeke snatched the phone. It had to be something, anything...

"Detective Temeke? This is Matt Black. We found a match for the blood samples on the Buck 110. Christopher A. Ramsey. Last known address, 4565

Lakewood Road, San Diego, California. Adam Oliver's blood was found on a length of twine Officer Running Hawk found at the site. But here's the clincher. Ramsey shares fifty percent of genetic markers with Adam."

It was the loud knock on the door that threw Temeke out of his trance. Jarvis with a worried frown. "Mrs. Oliver... she wants to see you right away."

They drove to the Mayor's mansion in silence, with the ring of Matt Black's words in the air. Temeke sat in the passenger seat and read the short report in the file.

Malin bit her lip more times than he could count, stiff as a ramrod behind that wheel. She turned to look at him briefly after braking for a red light. Turning left by a small branch of the Norcross bank, she took a deep breath and held it for a moment.

"The Ancient Mariner was a sailor... a tortured sailor. I should have made the connection," she murmured. "Couldn't sleep last night. So I went for a drive. Parked outside your house. Saw you walking from room to room. Head up one minute, down the next. Memories, isn't it? That's what happens when you're on your own. Start thinking things. Taking a few steps backwards. I didn't realize you were so lonely. But I'm glad you know how it feels because a third of the population in New Mexico live alone. Elderly, singles. You could spare them a prayer or two."

Temeke swallowed a dried lump of spit in his mouth, tasted the sour upsurge from his belly. Should have drawn the sodding blinds. It was lucky he couldn't speak because his voice was about to disintegrate into a blubber of tears. He thought of his mother then. How she died. Alone. In that redbrick apartment with the pale green door.

They stood in front of another door now, doorbell chiming in the innards of the house. No sign of cracks between the frame and the flashing, just smooth and glossy like the day it was built.

Raine Oliver stood on the threshold, gave a sharp nod and led them into the library. There were three newspapers on the couch showing pictures of the crime scene and the Chief of Police, and an article on the Mayor who was determined to spend more time with his son when they found him. Megan left a tray of tea in front of them and scuttled off to the kitchen.

Raine poured three cups without speaking and then sat with her hands in her lap, fingers smoothing a red painted nail.

"Bill was watching me for years. Had me followed," she said. "I didn't believe it at first, not until I saw the invoices from Blaine Investigative Services. He didn't want me to leave him. Not because he loved me, because I was the only one who knew about the accident."

"The accident?" Temeke said, downing a cup of surprisingly unpleasant tea while looking at the bookshelves. The gap between *Huckleberry Finn* and *The Last of the Mohicans* had been filled with a plump Bible.

"When he found out I had once been involved with Christopher Ramsey he wanted to kill him." She looked around then. Seemed like good old fashioned paranoia. "He was one of Bill's students. Training to be a SEAL."

"Christopher Ramsey was your ex?"

"My first love. Talking intimately has never been my strong suit. Even my parents never discussed how they fell in love. Ever loved anyone, Detective?"

She must have seen the slight indentation on the fourth finger of his left hand. The ring was no longer there. "Was it your father who never liked him? Or your mother?"

"Dad. He wanted me to marry an ambassador and Bill's father was the closest to a diplomat they had ever met. They figured Bill would go the same way."

The Olivers were a well-known New Mexican family, but Temeke had never heard the name Leveque. He asked her, of course. She said they were Belgium socialites who immigrated to California in the seventies.

"If Christopher Ramsey was training to be a SEAL that takes some bad-ass courage and determination," he said. "What's not to like?"

"Dad met him once, said that was enough. He found out Christopher smoked weed now and then. Sold it too. He told me to promise I wouldn't see him again. But I couldn't." She waved a hand as if her mind played back girlhood memories in an arbitrary manner. "I never met anyone so kind, so wild. I don't think he cared if he lived or died."

"But he cared about you."

"He said not seeing me was like being under fire. You never really knew if you'd come out of it alive. We used to meet at the end of the road when mom and dad were asleep. It was exciting and dangerous because somewhere in the back of my mind I knew it would all end. But I wanted to soak up every minute with him, to experience the ache, the fever of it all. And then there was good old dependable Bill."

"You never loved him?"

"Not like that. Dad said Bill was good for marrying and Christopher was good for nothing. Said I'd thank him one day. I know what he means… in here," she said, patting her chest. "Dad wasn't all words. He was heart too. I think he felt sorry for me. Thought I'd be in the right place if I married Bill. Never have to want for anything, you know."

"And you and Christopher Ramsey wrote letters?"

"Yes." Raine looked out of the window. Temeke followed her gaze and saw fluttering birds scattering seed on a small bird table. "We'd leave letters under a tree in the park. That's how we knew when to meet. It was one of those letters… a stupid letter. It tore Bill up."

"A love letter?"

"Christopher always carried them between his body armor and his uniform. Only he must have dropped one on the beach during an exercise. Bill found it… showed it to me one night. Said he'd forgiven me. But I knew he'd never forgive Christopher."

"And Bill Oliver was Christopher Ramsey's UDT/SEAL instructor?" A man, Temeke thought, with a couple of deployments under his belt; a man who ran PT; a man who had access to the men, and got close to them.

Raine ran a finger under one eye, catching a large tear before it ran down her cheek. "A few of them decided to go to the beach after dark. It was Bill's idea. He wanted to see who'd man up to the challenge. They were told to swim out… I don't know how far, but it was far. And then they were told to ride the waves all the way back. They lost sight of Christopher. It was too dark to see. They found him three hours later in a storm drain. Unconscious. The medical report said he had a heart murmur. There was no proof Bill did anything. But I think he knew Christopher had a weak heart."

Raine's body just flinched as if hit by an ice cold blast of wind. She rolled up her sweater to reveal a vicious map of blues and yellows on her stomach. "He did this," she said. "He would never have let me take Adam. That's why I stayed."

Temeke had sat in that room for less than thirty minutes and already felt the desperate urge to run. He heard Malin say how sorry she was as he skimmed through his notes, brain slowly slipping into autopilot.

"Tell me," he said, suddenly aware of the monotonous ticking of the library clock. "The letter we found in the fireplace was thought to be an eighteen page report. The last few words would have said *respectfully submitted,* and *signature of the petitioner.* A petition for what, Mrs. Oliver?"

Raine looked out at the birds, eyes glossy as she disappeared into the past. "Paternity."

"Christopher A. Ramsey… what's his full name?"

Tears ran down Raine's face. No sobbing or any movement. "Christopher Adam Ramsey. He's Adam's biological father."

FORTY-FIVE

Above them the sky was dark blue and the mountain ridges were wreathed in a snake-like mist. It was early in the twilight before they came to a stream and a log cabin.

"They're not far behind us," Ramsey kept whispering, eyes wide so you could see the whites in them. He was breathless too. Like he'd been running for miles. "Don't drop anything. Don't even spit."

He staggered for the nearest tree, bent and vomited. Bang went the 'Don't drop anything. Don't even spit'. His skin was slick with sweat and there was a deathly pallor to him, a gray rubbery look as if his smile no longer worked. Adam rubbed Ramsey's back, offered him water, and told him to lie down in the cabin.

"We're not going in," Ramsey said, covering what he'd done with a thick layer of pine needles. He washed his beard with a few squirts of water and drank the rest. "We'll find a place and watch."

"It's getting cold."

"We've got the blankets, the dog. Put your hood up."

"I need to pee."

"You always need to pee."

Ramsey found a tree, moved the topsoil with the toe

of his boot. The dog did the rest, digging with those claws until it was about a foot deep. They both relieved themselves, teeth chattering as they filled in the hole.

Behind a stand of aspens was a broad-skirted fir tree thick enough to hide under and far enough from the cabin to risk being seen. Ramsey pushed Adam to the leeward side and they sat on their packs and stared through the leaves. Adam wondered if they were the only ones who had ever sat under that tree, whether other children had once played in the same forest, listened to the same sounds. Murphy scooted close to Adam's side like he sensed something.

"You're getting sicker, aren't you?" Adam said.

"I'm fine."

"You just threw up."

"Everyone throws up now and then. Can you see anything?"

"No."

"Can you hear anything?"

"No."

"You're just saying that because you're mad."

"Not."

"Are."

Adam peered into the darkness allowing his eyes to sweep one way and then the other, and he saw the path curving away to the north. As far as he could see, there were paths everywhere if you zigzagged around the trees, only this one was wider as if it was manmade.

Adam followed the line of that path, saw the bone-white branches of a dying tree in the distance. Just as his eyes began to tire and wander back to the ground, something moved. He thought he could see a man in the shadows about thirty feet away, gun aimed in a gloved hand. But he knew he was seeing things. Too many ghosts in one day.

"Better start praying to the big guy those rangers don't find us," Adam whispered.

"He doesn't know who I am."

"Of course he does. He made you. He made me."

"What with?

"Dirt and breath."

The moon was overhead now, shedding its nightly beam into that small clearing and turning the leaves a bluish-gray. There was light enough to see. Adam heard the distant trickle of a stream, heard Ramsey crunching something in his mouth. It was those painkillers again. He must have eaten eight since noon and he was looking stranger by the minute. "You OK?"

"We're out of food."

"We are?"

Ramsey rubbed that leg again, face all winced up like a twisted rag. "It's not that far now. If it comes to it I'll give you the gun and the money. You'll go on ahead. Get help."

Adam didn't want the gun. Never had occasion to shoot it. Wasn't trained like a real man. There was something deep down in his gut that bothered him, a whisper of sadness that wouldn't go away. His chest hurt and so did his throat and he wanted to sob. "They'll catch me."

"Nah, you're too quick for that." Ramsey must have heard the hitch in his voice because he pulled Adam closer. "You know a thing or two. Got the dog and all."

Adam began to sob. Couldn't help himself. Laid his head on Ramsey's shoulder, heard him say *shhh* like a dad. When the sob was all run out, he wiped his nose on the back of his sleeve and said, "You won't die, will you?"

"Of course I won't die. What do you take me for?"

It was one thing to be with someone else. It was

quite another to be in a cold, dark world all alone. They hadn't been able to have a campfire, watch the flames twist and curl and then die to a pile of ash. Hadn't smelled a good roasted meal that stubbornly played hide-and-go-seek with his senses. And they hadn't laughed much or told any jokes in these last few hours. Something had changed.

The heat from Ramsey's body would need a fire hydrant to put out and the smell of him was woody and stale. Those pills weren't helping. Maybe they were making him sick.

In less than a minute they heard the snapping of a twig, a droning sound like a dragonfly and a dull thud. Another low hum about ten feet to the right of them, nasal like a druid's chant.

"Slings," Ramsey whispered. "Over there."

Face covered in a mask and one hand resting on the log siding, a man swung around the front deck. Each leg crossing in front of the other as he moved sideways, gun leveled at the cabin door. Adam couldn't hear much over the shrieking wind and that infernal hissing the grasses made. All he wanted to do was run.

"Riflescope," Ramsey murmured, looking out at the man. "Probably see a hundred yards or more."

Adam felt the back of his throat go dry. He had no idea what Ramsey meant but he knew it was bad. If that scope could see that far, it could probably find them under the trees and then they'd be dragged out, stripped naked and tied to the front of the house. Left for the animals. Chewed right down to the bone.

Two other rangers broke out of the trees behind the first, one dangling a sling from his hand and a dead rabbit he'd shot. The other had a wooden frame on his back, the type hunters carry to transport game. They wore masks with slits for eyes, drifting like ghosts through the brush.

The first man crouched, eyes level with the bottom of the first window. He laid the rifle down on the deck, unsheathed a knife and played it between his fingers. He must have stayed there for over a minute and all the while the men behind stood like statues, breath misting through their lips.

The leader made a gesture to move forward. He made his way into the house, two others following close behind.

Adam began to shiver as Ramsey crawled out from under the tree, clutching the backpack and urging Adam on with a flapping hand.

It was twenty minutes of stalking on the balls of their feet, twenty long calf-aching minutes before they stopped beneath a stand of pines to catch their breath. Branches groaned overhead and leaves scampered along the path in front of them, drowning out any sound they could have made. Ramsey said there was a mood in the air like they were two souls adrift under a cold moon.

"What do you mean?" Adam said.

"Feels like we're the only ones out here, running like prisoners of war." He blew on his hands, trembled a little and coughed. "Feels all empty and dark."

Adam knew when Ramsey got all sad he was missing his special smokes and the black stuff. He'd get all moody, start quoting poetry before he fell asleep. Or he'd get plain mean.

Sometimes he'd tell stories of a girl he once loved. The one with the nut brown hair. Then he'd pause every now and then beside a tree trunk, push the hood off his head and wait one full minute like he always did. He was sweating and he could hardly breathe. Ramsey was losing it and that's what made Adam scared.

And then he started singing something about spades

and swords of a soldier and clubs are weapons of war. It was a sad song that made your heart feel all twisty and sore and Adam half-wished Ramsey would stop it.

Murphy padded out in front like a scout, sniffing scents in the wind. Every so often, he stopped and waited for them to catch up, mouth open one minute and closed the next.

Ramsey stopped and looked around. He cupped his ear to a rumble in the distance and pointed at a gray procession of boulders. You could see them between the trees. "Nearly there," he said.

"Nearly where?"

"Where we need to be."

Where the trees ended, there was a rocky ledge with nothing beyond it but a dark gray sky and a mountain range in the distance. They sat on a boulder with their backs to the forest staring into the valley below. It was a town all right; a haze of car lights like a string of red and white beads. Adam wiped the wet hair from his brow and smiled. It was beautiful to see.

A few spits of rain, a boom of thunder and light shuddered on the horizon. They watched that too for a time until Adam twisted his head to the trees, ear bent to the wind. "Can you hear that?"

Ramsey was too far gone to notice, leaning against Adam, eyes twisted and wet. "Take this," he said, laying the gun on Adam's knee. "Keep it for me."

Adam took the gun and put it in the backpack. He didn't want to hold it, didn't want it going off in his hand.

He turned his back to the lights and looked into the forest where a white mist hovered above the ground as if there were hot springs deep in the earth. Six black flames trembled behind it, getting bigger and bigger as their guns ripped through the hoary shroud.

"Get down!" It was Ramsey's voice, deep and rasping.

Adam felt a tug on his sleeve as he was pushed behind the boulder, heard the shouts, heard the command to come out and raise his hands.

"Ramsey..." Adam tugged at Ramsey's jacket.

Ramsey wiped the sweat from his face and shook his head. "They won't hurt you, son. But they'll hurt me."

"Why?"

"Because I killed a man."

Adam felt the finger against his lips, felt that tight warm hug. Ramsey's eyes were wet and he was trying to smile. He was trying to stand too, bracing himself against that boulder.

He turned his head towards the men, put his shaking hands inside his jacket like he was cold or embarrassed or something. "You're a great kid, son. I couldn't have done it without you... without your eyes. I'll always carry a piece of you in me. And a piece of the big guy."

Ramsey stood there shaking like he'd fall over. He stumbled forward three steps towards the men and then he stood still. Lifted his head, straightened his back and slowly took his hands out of his pockets.

It was the loud bangs that made Adam scream and the smell of firecrackers in the air. He covered his ears, closed his eyes and swore he'd never open them again.

FORTY-SIX

The helicopter landed in Glenwood at eleven forty-five on Tuesday night. No sign of the Shadow Wolf officers and no sign of an ambulance. But there was a coroner's van in the parking lot and a hunter's frame smeared with blood. It all confirmed the radio report they had just heard.

The gravel driveway of the Santo Nino church wasn't exactly a helipad, but it was brightly lit and the closest thing in a town where the population was less than two hundred. Temeke climbed out on shaky feet, clutched his stomach and wanted to throw up. Not a park bench in sight.

Christopher Ramsey was dead, zipped up in a body bag they were now loading into the van. The report said the Shadow Wolf officers knew he had a gun in his jacket, they tried to detain and arrest him and decided as a last resort to open fire. He would have shot them, they said. He posed a serious threat to Adam. And to themselves.

Temeke wound a scarf tightly around his neck as he made his way to the church steps; three simple concrete slabs leading to nothing more than a portable cabin. He struck a match and drew smoke and fresh air into his lungs. He wasn't fond of heights and flying around in a thunderstorm only added to the thrill.

Malin wasn't happy either. You could tell by the

look on her face. The coldness was gone and a white rage shone in her eyes. And then she tried to squint it away by looking up at the sky like she could see a face up there. There was something on her mind no matter how hard she tried to pretend otherwise. "Where is everyone?"

"Buggered if I know." Temeke flicked some ash on his shoe. "Too damn quiet out here."

"How long have you known?" she said, one foot on the step he was sitting on.

"Mrs. Oliver never asked the kidnapper if Adam was still alive. If you were his mother, you'd be begging with all you'd got. Begging to hold the son you've given birth to… for his body… something to bury. They all beg. And where was the bloody dog bowl, the dog bed? All gone, like she'd closed the chapter on something. Do you know what I hate?" Temeke watched the coroner's van as it pulled out into the road. "Not knowing Christopher Ramsey. I might have actually liked him."

"He killed a man and kidnapped a child."

"He killed a serial killer. One the police couldn't track. Did us a favor. Did himself one too."

"You know what I mean," she said, rocking back and forth slightly.

"I wish I could have talked to the Mayor. But she was there… struggling with her ghosts."

"What ghosts?"

"Her past, her parents. What they'd done."

"It's not their fault she got pregnant."

"It was their fault she married the wrong man."

"Chris Ramsey was threatening her. Doesn't sound like love. Sounds like a lost cause. An old fling gone bad."

"Who told you that?"

"*I'm* telling you."

"Those aren't your words. Too insightful. Deep."

"Oh, you think I don't go deep?"

"Not that deep."

"You can be such a pig sometimes."

"If I was anything less, you wouldn't recognize me."

"I won't be intimidated."

"Not by me, that's for sure."

"What's up with you?"

"All this talk of intimidation makes me wonder if your confidence has taken a beating. You talking to a psychic?"

"Easy, Tonto," she said, smile lurking behind those eyes. "A man of your age could end up in hospital. That could be lonely without family."

"You'd come and visit me."

She started laughing then. Turned a full circle, swinging one of her gloves with one hand.

"Chris Ramsey knew he was dying," Temeke said. "Wanted to see his son. It was his last chance."

"And Raine?"

"She was expecting Ramsey to call. So she could take Adam to the park, let him meet his dad. Then she got cold feet. Knew she was being followed and didn't want Ramsey hurt. But he came anyway because he had an old score to settle. It must have been a shock for her to come home and find Bill on the floor and Adam gone. That wasn't part of the plan." Temeke took another drag of his cigarette and felt that unmistakable sense of relief. "When I showed her the burnt letter we found in the grate, she knew what it was. I could see it in her eyes. Bill Oliver never knew. But I wonder if he ever suspected."

"You're a genius, sir."

"And you've got a generous heart, Marl. Got a good head. With any luck you'll have Raine packed in a U-Haul to San Diego before the Mayor's discharged from hospital. Course it'll be in the bloody papers. *Mayor on fundraising trail to get wife back.*"

"It's better this way, sir. Better Raine gets out before those bruises start migrating to her face. You know what they say? Hate can easily turn to love."

"Then hate's a good starting point."

Temeke felt a presence behind him and saw a swarthy man in a black hat, hand clutching a Browning rifle sling embroidered with a southwestern weave. Temeke hadn't heard him coming, hadn't heard his footsteps over the gravel. It was Running Hawk.

Temeke introduced Malin, noticed a smile that played on Running Hawk's lips when he took her hand.

"Where's Adam," he asked.

"In the trees." Running Hawk jutted his chin towards a porta-potty which appeared to be surrounded with sandbags.

"What's he doing in the bloody trees?"

"Reading a book."

Temeke was astounded. The poor kid had been left all on his own and given a book to read.

"Wanted to be alone," Running Hawk said in that slow drawl of his.

Temeke had no idea what Running Hawk was blabbering on about, but it sounded deeply spiritual. He flicked the last of his cigarette in a nearby puddle and stood to shake his hand.

"Better take this. Fell out of the deceased's jacket pocket." Running Hawk handed Temeke the photograph of a young woman in a swimsuit. "Boy was scared of us. We could have found him sooner if they hadn't kept running. Thought we were rogue rangers. We carried his pa down the mountain. Most of the money was there. Just finished counting it in the church. Had a knife wound in his thigh. Septic by the look of it. He was alive most of the way."

"And Adam?"

"He held his pa's hand. Watched him die. He's a man now."

Temeke didn't doubt it. He had a vision of a boy clutching a dead man's hand and what that must have felt like. "So Ramsey didn't hurt the boy?"

Running Hawk just shook his head. "Boy's good. Cried when they took his pa away. Told me he taught him to shoot. Hunt rabbit. Told me he could survive in the wilderness on his own if he had to. He's waiting for you."

It was dark in the woods, the type of dark where you couldn't see a bear in the shadows and the scenery all looked the same. A boy could get disoriented out here. And so could a detective.

Temeke went alone into the trees behind the church, listening to the hiss of a cold biting breeze. It was Murphy that bounded towards him, tail wagging, foam dripping off black lips. He led the way, eyes expectant and urging Temeke onward with a snort.

A thick layer of gray clouds gathered overhead and Temeke's head was beginning to throb with all that fresh air. He walked on with Murphy at his side, stopping every now and then to listen. A gash of lightning lit up the sky behind the mountains and he was aware of the sweet scent of rain. Crossing a small stream, the surface of the water was suddenly dimpled with the first drops and then a deluge that rattled along the surface of the leaves.

Snapping twigs alerted him to movement in a thicket. It was a large elk walking silently between the trees, nostrils sniffing the wind, ears twitching on the side of its head. A few seconds and the great bull detected Temeke's scent and flew through the underbrush, hurdling over a log with the grace of a horse. Murphy took chase as far as the log and then thought better of it. He stood in a clearing, ears pricked and panting. He was tracking a scent with that twitching nose of his.

Temeke hunched along a narrow path to the clearing some twenty feet to his left. It was the flashlight he saw, diffracting through a gap in the trees. It was a good cover from the rain and he allowed himself to listen to the constant patter. If he wasn't mistaken, he could hear a boy sobbing.

Adam was wrapped in a large black ski jacket, wooly hat drawn over his ears. A few strands of brown hair fluttered over his collar, cheeks red and glistening.

"You OK, son?" Temeke showed Adam his badge.

"I'm OK." Adam wiped his eyes on his wrist, breaths hitching as he spoke. He hugged a book and the flashlight to his chest. "Have they taken him away?"

"Yes." Temeke heard a wail of sirens and sat down beside Adam on the log. He handed him the photograph. "Might want to ask your mom about that."

Adam gave the photo a cursory glance and slipped it inside the book. He didn't say anything. Just stared at the ground.

"I don't know if the police told you," Temeke said, "but your dad's much better now. Sitting up in hospital eating ice cream. He asked us to come and find you. So here we are."

"Thank you."

Temeke heard the relief in Adam's voice, saw him flinch and blink at a sudden downpour of sleet.

"Tell me what happened." Temeke shouldered the backpack and hooked his arm through Adam's. "So I can understand."

"They shouted at him… he was going to put his hands up… but they shot him. All of them."

"He could have shot them, son. He had a gun."

"No, Ramsey gave me the gun. It's in the backpack."

Temeke felt that unmistakable churning in his

stomach, felt the back of his throat go dry. It would have been dark on that ridge, too dark to take any risks. And the very men Adam was afraid of were the very men who could have saved him.

"I'm sorry," was all he said.

"I called my mom. She said I had to wait for you." Adam just stared ahead and after a minute or two, he said, "His heart was cracked down the middle. He said it hurt sometimes... I didn't understand what he meant. But I do now."

FORTY-SEVEN

The book felt good in his hands. A wedge of pages all tart from wood smoke and still carrying a fresh memory. Wrapped in Ramsey's coat, Adam could still feel those big arms around him, still hear those throaty mutterings. It was like Ramsey had just walked into the next room. Except Adam had seen him fall asleep, sensed he was gone.

The detective handed him a steaming cup of hot chocolate. It didn't have a marshmallow bobbing on the surface, didn't taste of chocolate much either.

The walls were gray and so was the trim around the door. It made Adam feel like he was in a dream, made him feel in the halfway place between happy and sad. Sometimes his eyes just timed out and they just stared at a sheet of glass. Even the dog was somewhere else.

"Now, I can leave you alone if you want, or I can sit here quietly," the detective said.

"I'll be OK on my own, thank you."

That way he would hear Ramsey's voice and it would make it all better. Like he was sitting right there beside him telling the same old stories he always did.

"One more thing," the detective said, handing him a flip phone with a blue screen. "Officer Running Hawk found it. I think you'll find it still works."

"Thank you." Adam felt a surge of pride. Of course it still worked. It was brand new, wasn't it?

"Mr. Ramsey was a bit off his chump, son. Most of his brain was missing and what was left of it rattled around in that head. So I doubt this book will make much sense."

"It'll make sense."

"I'm glad you said that, 'cause I almost called in an interpreter."

Adam half smiled, even as his eyes watered. "He couldn't stand being away from us. Said it was unnatural. Like putting a pig in a sty and taking away the mud. Anyway, if you don't mind."

"I don't mind at all." The detective stood up and smiled. He left after that.

When Adam thought of Ramsey he wasn't a monster. He was a man who taught him to hunt, a man who made him laugh. It had been an adventure.

He opened the book.

I don't remember when it all began, but I do know this. You were always part of it. A bright spark in a dark world. You were the last thought in my head when I went to sleep and the first when I woke up.

Now don't get blubbery, cause I need to tell you how it all started.

The weather was unusually cold that night and there was a ring around the moon. I walked to the beach with six other men, hearing only the sound of my footsteps. Your father was standing there, arms by his sides. I couldn't be sure, but he was laughing. Raised his gun in the air, held it there for the count of three.

I had time. A second or two. Waded into the shallows until my feet were well covered. Until I could feel how cold it was. I could almost touch that trident, smell it against my collar.

Unless my heart missed a beat. There was always that. Tricky things hearts. They can switch off without you knowing.

I heard a click and a laugh. Nothing new. It's what he always did to see if we'd take off. But we stayed right there until we heard the crack, the echo, and then shouts as if the beach was alive with voices. I could hear the men behind me, feel hot sticky breath against my neck.

I was first when we plunged into the breakers. First when we got to the red buoy. Then it happened. I couldn't breathe, couldn't move. Swallowed a wash of salty water.

There was a bright light streaking to one side, a tunnel tracking down into the earth. I thought I was seeing things.

Adam remembered a time when he was afraid of the tube slide in the playground at school. How he heard the pounding of his footfalls on the platform and the occasional drip of water from the trees above. And then he was sliding, tumbling, arms bracing as he broke out into the sunlight. There was snow on the ground, spread out like a bright shimmering mirror. He would have slid all the way to the parking lot if his mom hadn't stopped him.

I woke up in hospital. There was no going back. No trident. There's a hole in my heart now where the pain comes in. And when it does, I see dead leaves all spiny and withered. I'm reminded of the things I left behind. You. Her. Family.

Adam could see Ramsey in his mind's eye, hair matted across his face, teeth clenched in a moue of pain. One hand clasping his chest, blood oozing between his fingers.

You probably want to ask me what I loved the most. Your mom. She wouldn't approve of me now. It wouldn't have been fair to expect her to suffer my appalling relapses. That's memory to you. My tattered clothes, a body that could have done with a shower. If she had seen me in the street, she would have made appropriate noises of sympathy, dropped a nickel in my hat and passed me by.

Didn't stop me loving her though.

Adam took his mind back to that night in the tent. The words were right there. In the book. How Ramsey brushed her hair, how it turned red in the sun. Adam remembered how the lantern swung in the wind and he could still smell the camp fire. He was afraid then. But not now.

That Spitfire's just the small piece. Maybe you'll have a good laugh at some of the things we did. Maybe you'll find it in your heart to forgive me. And maybe you'll marry Runa and tell your kids about me. I'd like that."

Adam made the sound with his lips, strange at first. It was the second time he'd said the word and it would be the last.

"Dad."

You probably want to ask me what I hated the most. Silence. You have to fill it with something. A good laugh, a good story. Like the time when I met your mom's dad and how he used to say, 'it must be March when the mad hares breed.' He was probably hoping for a personal tragedy, hoping I'd disappear down a manhole so he could wake up from that particular nightmare and chalk it down to experience. He even told me I was a crook. But crooks aren't that stupid.

I went away for a while. But don't think for one moment, I forgot. 'Cause I stalked the crap out of you, followed you to New Mexico. I saw you in the park. Yes, that was me. Watched you grow up.

I know your dad's strict. I know you sometimes don't get along. But you're a great kid. He saw to that.

I had a strict dad once. Used to hide behind the tub panel when I'd done something wrong. Strange, because it was a screamingly obvious hiding place, I'm surprised he missed it.

I flushed four small dinosaurs down the toilet once. Velociraptors I think they were. They did a number on the honey dipper, sewage everywhere. Amazing those raptors got past the U-bend. Don't try a T-Rex. Too big.

Adam chuckled. He felt very lucky. Because some kids only have one dad. He had two. Three actually, if you counted the big guy in the sky.

You probably want to ask me what I regret most. I should have fought for you. Because in two short weeks we went everywhere together. Did things other people never get to do. I learned a few things too. Doesn't matter where we come from. It's the people we meet, the trials we face.

I met you. That makes me a man.

Now don't go tearing up when I tell you you'll see me in the thunder and the lightning. Means I'm up there somewhere having a party. Probably drinking a few beers and hurling them against a tree. Might not have my trident, but I have a son.

And don't get too excited either because I'm not about to go down on my knees. But you're right. Truth is the only father. I can see him clear as I can see you. Got my ticket. So I'll wait for you at the entrance... save you a seat.

But while you're still there, it's very important you follow instructions. Paper's for sissies. So just use grass.

Adam felt the sweat popping on his forehead and the shudder in his legs, and he felt the soft brush of fur against his arm. He heard a laugh that never broke for breath and somewhere in the pit of his mind, he realized it was his.

ABOUT THE AUTHOR

Claire Stibbe is a graduate of the Albuquerque 50th Citizens' Police Academy, Citizen Police Academy Alumni Association and a volunteer for Stand True 4 Blue. She is also a graduate of the Bernalillo County Sheriff's Office Citizens' Academy.

Claire writes crime fiction books set in New Mexico, USA. She has written three books in the Detective Temeke Crime series. The 9th Hour, published in 2015, was a finalist in the New Mexico/Arizona 2016 Book Awards for Fiction - Mystery/Suspense. The second in the series, Night Eyes was published in 2016 and the third, Past Rites was also published in 2016 (excerpt attached). She is now working on the fourth.

Claire has written short stories for Breakwater Harbor Books, a publisher of anthologies. The collection won Best Anthology of 2014 in the Independent Book Awards hosted by eFestival of Words.

For news and updates, why not sign up for her newsletter here. Claire blogs at **Wordpress** and loves meeting new people on **Twitter** (@CMTStibbe) and **Facebook**. You can also follower her on **Google**.

www.cmtstibbe.com

Also by Claire Stibbe

THE 9TH HOUR

When the ninth young girl falls into the clutches of a serial killer, maverick detective David Temeke, faces a race against time to save her life.

The Duke City Police Department in Albuquerque, New Mexico is no stranger to gruesome murders, but this new serial killer on their block keeps the body parts of his eight young victims as trophies and has a worrying obsession with the number 9. The suspect is incarcerated in the state's high security penitentiary but Unit Commander Hackett is faced with a dilemma when another teenage girl goes missing.

Detective Temeke and his new partner, Malin Santiago, are sent to solve a baffling crime in the dense forests of New Mexico's Cimarron State Park. But time is running out. Can they unravel the mysteries of Norse legends and thwart the 9th Hour killer before he dismembers his next victim?

This is the *first* in the Detective Temeke mystery series.

"An intense, superbly crafted reading experience.
I guarantee you'll go on reading well past the ninth hour."
~ *Jim Pingelly, Kingdom Writing Solutions*

"Gripping, innovative, brutal and yet redemptive.
This is crime fiction with a serrated edge
and a brilliant sheen."
~ *Marco Storey, author and speaker*

An Excerpt from PAST RITES.
The third in the Detective Temeke series.

PAST RITES

Claire Stibbe

United States of America

ONE

Gabriel dropped the poker and reached for the camera. He had planned this night for a long time. It might seem a despicable act to some but what others thought didn't bother him in the least. He had been hounded for the greater part of his teenage years but now he was deaf to every insult, every condemnation, every dismissal of his right even to exist.

At high school there had always been whispers in the darkness, boys in the gym or on the soccer field, and girls in the corridors. They had said things, wanted things, demanded things.

Then Demon whispered to him. "You don't have to suffer this. There are things you can do. Permanent things. I'll help you."

It was a harmless comment on the face of it, but there was something in the tone that let Gabriel know nothing would ever be the same. Demon was wild, exciting, insane. Right from those very first words, the life Gabriel once knew was forever gone.

They say patience is a virtue so Gabriel waited until after high school graduation. He knew the girls and boys would all go to the same college because they were the very best of the gene pool. He bided his time, watching for that special moment when the mind conjures up the worst of those memories and the body breaks loose in a perfect gush of hatred. That exquisite moment when there's no turning back.

Catching sight of the poker on the carpet and his pale reflection in the full-length mirror made him flinch. He looked like a man who had a skin disease and who never saw the sun, chest speckled crimson, even down to the gloves and military boots.

He lifted the camera. Gabriel relished the sound of the motor drive; it reminded him of a howitzer. Fast, heart-pumping, like a model working it to the last drop. He photographed the girl on the floor, the living room, the view of the park from the window and a dangle of dead mistletoe inside the front door. The things Asha once saw, things she once felt. Precious things locked up in another head now, a head that yearned to be part of her.

There… captured and sealed.

Haunting his prey had been the fun part, until Gabriel was so pumped up with anticipation he couldn't hold it in any longer. He sent Asha five Calla lilies in a black vase with a typewritten card that said, *You light the lives of those you touch. But none as much as mine.* It was funny now he thought of it, especially the quick scrawl on the back. *Saturday. Eight o'clock. Your place. P.*

The flowers were on the mantel with a note propped up against the vase. Asha was expecting a visit from a law student she had the hots for. Dark hair, blue eyes, everyone's crush. Even at school.

It explained the stylish sheath dress she wore. The pearls and the burgundy lipstick. It also explained why Asha hadn't gone out with her friends to an all-night frat party with two hundred dancing drunks, a freshman's idea of a hot Saturday night.

Gabriel couldn't remember how it happened, how he tore the life out of another human being or how he severed two of her fingers with a knife he'd found in the kitchen. It was the release before the blackout that worried him. He had no idea how long he had been there.

All he did remember was taking the key and letting himself in. A typical south side house, two bedrooms and a large open hall that led to a kitchen. Asha had been playing the piece she always played on a small Steinway grand. Chopin's Prelude in E minor, fittingly depressing and suited Gabriel's black mood.

She never heard the soft clang of the iron poker, nor did she feel the heavy thump against her skull. She may have heard a voice, excited and loud that made no sense. She may have heard nothing at all.

Blood pooled out from under her head, a dark stain on a Persian rug. Gabriel now couldn't stand the sight of her. Those singular eyes mirroring a full image of him.

It was the Smarts that made all the difference. Tiny little pills that made him happy. Made him float on thin air. They awakened him to the book he had come to find.

Only it wasn't there.

There was a blue shower curtain in the bathroom. Rolling one hundred and twenty some pounds of dead flesh in the vinyl wrap wasn't a problem. Dragging it out to the van was exhausting.

He went back inside, took the poker and wrapped it in a towel, wiped the piano, walls and furniture with a damp cloth. The blood had soaked into the deep pile carpet, camouflaged within a red medallion design, and as for her fingers, they were safely hidden where no one could find them.

With the knife, he carved a name on the kitchen door frame, one inch beneath the first hinge. *Mahtab*. It would mean nothing to the finder. But it meant everything to him.

Taking the typewritten note from the mantel, he replaced it with another. *Come away, come away with William Tell, stick an arrow up his ass and run like hell.*

Asha's mentally incompetent roommate would think she had gone on a long vacation and would likely celebrate her absence with a round of applause.

She would hear from Asha of course, because Gabriel took that smart-looking Mac from Asha's bedroom and made it his own. He would pretend to be Asha, out-of-town Asha, party-animal Asha, Paddy-mad Asha.

Gabriel was good at manipulating the system. It was probably why he had so many enemies. If he hadn't been a scholarly stick insect, he might have been popular at school.

No, he would never be one of the elite. They made that plain enough. It wasn't about what he'd done or what he hadn't done. It was about luck, about uncertainty, about the cards a person was dealt.

Gabriel would do whatever possible to prolong the fantasy. Because luck, uncertainty and cards were not enough.